# NOTHING BUT LIES

*Recent Titles by Lyndon Stacey*

CUT THROAT
BLINDFOLD
DEADFALL
OUTSIDE CHANCE
SIX TO ONE AGAINST
MURDER IN MIND

*The Daniel Whelan Mysteries*

NO GOING BACK *
NO HOLDS BARRED *
NOTHING BUT LIES *

* *available from Severn House*

# NOTHING BUT LIES

A Daniel Whelan Mystery

## Lyndon Stacey

This first world edition published 2014
in Great Britain and the USA by
SEVERN HOUSE PUBLISHERS LTD of
19 Cedar Road, Sutton, Surrey, England, SM2 5DA.
Trade paperback edition published
in Great Britain and the USA 2015 by
SEVERN HOUSE PUBLISHERS LTD.

British Library Cataloguing in Publication Data

Stacey, Lyndon author.
 Nothing but lies.
 1. Whelan, Daniel (Fictitious character)–Fiction.
 2. Ex-police officers–Fiction. 3. Undercover operations–
 Fiction. 4. Ex-convicts–Fiction. 5. Detective and mystery
 stories.
 I. Title
 823.9'2-dc23

ISBN-13: 978-07278-8400-8 (cased)
ISBN-13: 978-1-84751-538-4 (trade paper)
ISBN-13: 978-1-78010-583-3 (e-book)

*All Severn House titles are printed on acid-free paper.*

Severn House Publishers support the Forest Stewardship Council™ [FSC™],
the leading international forest certification organisation. All our titles that
are printed on FSC certified paper carry the FSC logo.

Typeset by Palimpsest Book Production Ltd.,
Falkirk, Stirlingshire, Scotland.
Printed and bound in Great Britain by
TJ International, Padstow, Cornwall.

This book is dedicated with great fondness, to the memory of my agent, Dorothy Lumley, who sadly passed away last year. Kind and endlessly encouraging, we became friends and I shall miss her greatly.

# ACKNOWLEDGMENTS

Thanks go to my good friend 'Cloudy' Clare Kirk, who was endlessly patient and helpful while I struggled out loud with the plot details. As ever, huge thanks are due to Mark Randle for police-related queries. Also, to Chris Fenton for advice on family law and a suggestion that changed the course of the story; and Teruko Chagrin for help with all things Japanese.

# PROLOGUE

It was a warm night. The waxing moon tipped the waves with silver and cast a halo on the thin high mantle of cloud that every now and then hid it from view.

The man on the cliff top walked slowly, listening to the soft sighing of the waves on the beach and the intermittent barking of a fox in the river valley he had just left. He was in no hurry. Dawn was a way off yet and he had plenty of time to set up his camera at the seabird colony. He had come out earlier than he needed to, wakeful and unable to resist the lure of the lonely coastal path at night. A remote, rocky stretch of shoreline, beyond the looping reach of even the tiniest rural lanes; by day it was visited only by hardier walkers passing along the way-marked coast path, and at night belonged solely to the wildlife.

The walker paused, glancing out to sea, enjoying the exhilaration of altitude and the cool breeze that ruffled his hair and rippled through his thin cotton sweatshirt.

Then his gaze sharpened.

Something was out there, bobbing in the waves. Two small, rounded shapes. Seals? He'd not heard of them being seen this far south but he knew that occasionally vagrant seals were seen in the most unusual of places.

Keeping his eye on the dark blobs, he sat down on the short turf and lifted his binoculars. Even brought nearer, they remained tantalisingly indistinct. Now he wished the dawn were closer.

Clouds passed across the moon, spoiling his view, and he lowered the glasses, muttering his frustration. Minutes ticked by and then the light shone through again, lifting the landscape to a mottled tapestry of greys. But the man had no time to appreciate the beauty of the land, his eyes were fixed on the waves below.

There they were. Much closer now, still side-by-side, forging quite quickly through the surf, and something about the way they moved made him frown. Approaching the rock-strewn beach the dark heads surged upwards, revealing their true shape. Not seals at all, but two human figures wading through the shallows with the soft moonlight gleaming on facemasks, now pushed onto the tops of their heads. By their silhouettes they were both male. One stumbled and the other steadied him, before they made it onto the thin strip of gritty sand the tide had uncovered. Here, the one who had tripped found a shelving rock and sat on it, taking off flippers. The other one removed his and, standing, looked up and down the beach and then, suddenly, up at the cliff top, catching the watcher by surprise.

Without knowing why he did so, he drew back from the edge, out of sight. There was no law against swimming at night, and in the middle of August, the sea was certainly pleasantly warm, he'd waded in the shallows himself, the previous day; so why should he be so loath to be caught watching? Drawing further back from the edge, he got to his feet and continued on his way.

'There's someone up there,' the man on the beach told his seated friend. 'On the cliff top with binoculars.'

The second man turned and looked up. They both had snorkels and wore shorty wetsuits, with waterproof duffel bags strapped to their backs.

'I can't see anyone.'

'No, he's gone now. Disappeared when I caught him looking.'

'Doesn't matter. Nothing to say we can't go swimming.'

The first man grunted. The moonlight gleamed on a small, gold earring.

'Don't like being watched.'

'You've spent too long in the wrong company,' his companion said. 'OK. Let's go. I'm fine now.'

In the shadow of the looming cliff, they changed in silence, peeling off wetsuits and stowing them in the duffel bags, replacing them with combat trousers and dark-coloured T-shirts. In deck trainers they walked along the pebbly sand for a short way and then turned between the rocks at the point where a stream tumbled down through a tree-lined gully worn away by centuries of rushing water.

The climb was more of a scramble but none the less, both men were breathing heavily by the time they reached the top of the gully and they sat on rocks in the shadows cast by the trees.

One man sat with his head down, rubbing his eyes, while the other again spent his time scanning as much as could be seen of their surroundings in the light of the moon.

'Stay there,' he said softly to his companion, who looked up.

'Where are you going?'

'To get the lie of the land. Won't be long.'

Leaving his duffel bag, he moved away, keeping to the shadows, his rubber-soled shoes making no noise on the turf. Within seconds he had disappeared.

He was gone for several minutes, and his companion had started to glance uneasily into the surrounding gloom but then suddenly he was back, as silently as he had left. After a short, murmured conversation, the two men picked up their packs and started to walk, heading inland, keeping to the shadows, with only a hunting fox to see them pass.

# ONE

'So what's on your mind?' Fred Bowden placed his beer on the table and sat down. A stocky, well muscled man in his mid-fifties, with a shadow of grey hair, he looked what he was – a no-nonsense, ex-army sergeant, but there was a redeeming glint of humour alongside the toughness.

'What makes you think anything is?' Daniel Whelan slid into the bench seat with his back to the wall, and glanced briefly round, watchful by habit. It was mid week and the pub was quiet. He relaxed and Taz, his black and tan German shepherd, settled at his feet with a sigh.

'Because you've been distracted ever since you got that call earlier.'

Daniel took a sip of his own brew and shook his head ruefully. 'Am I that easy to read? I must be losing my touch.'

Bowden shrugged. 'I guess I've known you a while now. So what is it?'

'I'm going to need some more time off.'

Since leaving the army, Fred Bowden had built up a moderately successful retail haulage business, supplying the farms and riding stables of Devon. Daniel had been working for him for a little over a year, now.

'I see.' Bowden raised an eyebrow and contemplated his beer. 'It may be my memory playing tricks, but haven't you just got back from nearly five weeks leave?'

'And whose idea was that?' Daniel enquired mildly. 'And you say "leave" like it was some kind of holiday!' He'd spent a month helping out an old friend of Fred's who'd been in trouble, and restful was not the word he'd have used to describe those weeks away.

Bowden's steel-grey eyes regarded Daniel shrewdly over the rim of his beer glass as he took a long, appreciative swallow.

'You must be on edge,' he observed, when he finally put the glass down. 'You'd never normally rise to the bait like that. What's up? I'm guessing it's not a holiday you're after.'

'A mate needs a favour.'

'You have a friend? I thought you were Billy-no-mates.'

'Yeah, well to be honest, I don't really know him that well. He's a colleague from the old days. He was on the dog squad, like me, but with shifts. I didn't see that much of him, though he did give a couple of us a few martial arts lessons.'

'So, is this the guy that's got info for you in the past?'

'Yep. Jo-Ji Matsuki – known to all as Joey Suzuki. He took on my drugs dog when I – er, left the force. He's a nice guy and a pretty neat martial artist as well. He taught me a few useful moves. The thing is; he's worried about his fiancée – thinks she might be in danger. Wants me to keep an eye on her. He helped me out, now it's my turn.'

Fred Bowden pursed his lips. 'OK. But what is there in that to make you edgy? You're not exactly the nervous sort.'

Daniel shrugged. 'I don't know. Maybe it's a bit too close to my old life for comfort – Joey being a cop still.'

'Well, I can understand why you feel you have to go, but you could have timed it better. With Colin off sick and Whitey leaving at the end of the month, we're a bit short of cover already. I've advertised but you wouldn't believe the dross that turn up expecting to be put behind the wheel of a twenty-five ton lorry.'

'I can imagine. I'm sorry to leave you in the lurch.'

'So why can't this Joey's colleagues look out for his fiancée?'

'Oh, come on! Your son's a copper. You know as well as I do that staffing levels dictate their every move. Joey says they've promised to swing by every now and then when he's on duty and there's a patrol in the area, but what use is that? From what I can gather, they live out in the sticks, pretty much; not an area they'd be patrolling very often.'

Bowden grunted and shook his head. 'So who does she need protection from, does he know? An ex-con with a grudge?'

'That's what he thinks.'

'And you're just going to rack up with "Bodyguard" on your T-shirt?'

'Not exactly. Apparently she also needs someone to drive her horsebox to shows, so that's my cover. He's telling her that I'm down on my luck at the moment and need a place to stay.'

'Horses and a horsebox, on a copper's pay?'

'She works too, and anyway, I don't think it's actually her lorry. It belongs to a friend who's out of action. Look, I'm sorry, Fred. I know you're pushed at the moment, but I owe this guy.'

'Yeah, well, we'll get by. I can always draft Meg in to drive one of the lorries, if we get really stuck.'

'Thanks. I appreciate it.'

'It's only because I know you'd go anyway,' his boss said, draining his beer and standing up. 'I'd better get back, it's my turn to cook. You gonna come by for a bite after you've walked that hound of yours?'

'Don't mind if I do,' Daniel said. 'If Meg's not getting fed up with me dropping in.'

'She seems to like having you. Women! There's no understanding them,' he added, and dodged as a beer mat whistled past his ear.

Maiden Ashton, the village where Jo-Ji Matsuki and his partner, Tamiko, lived, was on the south-western outskirts of Bristol and was surprisingly rural, given its proximity to the city. The couple lived in an end-of-terrace Victorian cottage, in a lane leading off the main street. Much of the space in front of the green-painted front door had been gravelled over for parking, and on this Thursday afternoon, as Daniel drove slowly up to check the house number, one half of it was occupied by a blue hatchback. A ceramic plaque adorned with a horse's head confirmed that this was indeed No 5, Tannery Lane and, swinging his ageing Mercedes estate into the free space, Daniel switched the engine off, stretching his arms and back to ease the stiffness of the journey from his muscles. In the rear of the car, Taz stood up and whined, recognising journey's end and hoping for action.

The cottage was built of faded red brick with a slate roof, its paintwork white and in need of attention. Through the shrubs to the right of the main body of the cottage, Daniel could just see a ground floor extension, finished in cream render and so new it still had tape on the French windows.

On the phone, the previous evening, Jo-Ji had told Daniel that he would be working when he arrived and that Tamiko, who worked from home as a massage therapist, might be busy with clients, but as he approached the front door it opened and a face with elfin features peered out.

'Daniel?'

'That's right. You must be Tamiko.'

'Please – call me Tami.' She pronounced her name with more emphasis on the second syllable. 'Come in.'

She opened the door further and stood back, revealing a petite figure in denim jeans and a black T-shirt with a dragon on it. Her thick black hair was cut into a jaw-length bob and framed an attractive heart-shaped face that currently wore a slightly anxious expression.

As Daniel stepped forward, Taz barked sharply, twice, in the car behind him.

Tamiko glanced at the car.

'Ah. Your dog. Do you want to bring him in?'

'No. He can stay there for a moment. He's just being a diva.'

'Oh, OK.' Tamiko looked a little doubtfully towards the car again, then smiled at Daniel as he passed her in the doorway. 'Jo-Ji say he's sorry he not here to meet you. He's on late shift.'

'That's OK.'

The cottage was small, the front door opening into a narrow hallway, with an even narrower flight of stairs leading steeply upwards. Tamiko gestured to a closed door on Daniel's left, saying that it was Jo-Ji's den, before leading the way through an opposing door into a tiny sitting room, at the far end of which a full-width archway led through to a kitchen diner beyond.

The room was furnished with simple style, having a two-seat, leather sofa and a large beanbag for comfort, and a tiny pot-bellied wood burning stove for warmth. On the entertainment front, a small TV stood on a cabinet with all the usual hi-tech gadgetry underneath, and well-stocked bookshelves lined one wall, from the top of which a Siamese cat regarded the visitor with a basilisk stare, sitting so still that Daniel had to do a double-take to convince himself that the animal was indeed real.

'That is Shinju,' Tamiko told him with a shy smile. 'She disapproves. She is not fond of strangers.'

'Shinju. What does that mean?'

'It means pearl.'

'Pole?' he repeated. Tamiko's accent made the word difficult.

She frowned and tried again, holding up finger and thumb to indicate something small. 'Pearl.'

'Oh, pearl!' Daniel said, understanding, and Tamiko smiled sunnily, nodding her head.

'I also have her brother. His name is Yasu. That means peaceful,' she added anticipating the question.

'And is he?'

'Unless you are unlucky to be a mouse,' she said laughing. 'What is your dog's name?'

'Taz. And no – before you ask – I have no idea what it means. He was called that when he was assigned to me. If I had to hazard a guess, I'd say Pain in the Arse!'

Tamiko laughed. 'But you love him, right? Jo-Ji is always calling his dogs names, but sometimes I think he love them before me.'

'I'm sure that's not true.'

She shrugged with an impish smile. 'I don't know, but he often say he thinks he comes second after my horses, so all is fair. Come, I show you where you can sleep,' she said, leading the way back into the hall and up the steep flight of stairs. 'It is very small here, I'm afraid. Did Jo-Ji warn you? You'll have to be in my treatment room. I hope you will be OK.'

'No problem. As long as there's room for a bed.'

At the top of the stairs, the double bed in the first room they passed was presently occupied by another Siamese cat, curled into a ball in the centre of the duvet.

'Yasu,' Tamiko said, seeing Daniel's glance. 'He is always sleeping. He's a lazy cat.'

On the opposite side of the narrow landing, she opened a door to show Daniel a rather dated bathroom, and pointed to a second door. 'That's a tiny room that Karen is use for treatments, but she's not here now. She only works in the morning.'

'And Karen is . . .?'

'Oh, sorry. Karen is a beauty therapist. She lives in the village and rents this room from us. She is a friend. She rides, too. That room isn't big enough for a bed,' she added, quickly, as if expecting Daniel to suggest it. 'In here is my treatment room.'

She opened the door into a light and airy room with a window looking out over the back garden. In the centre was an adjustable and rather firm-looking couch on which Tamiko presumably carried out her massage treatments. The air in the room carried a slight but pleasant fragrance, which Daniel attributed to a number of small candles positioned about the room, unlit at present. There was a small hand basin, a shelf that held several books on therapies he'd never heard of, piles of towels, neatly folded, and a CD player.

He became aware that Tamiko was watching him, anxiously.

'It's fine,' he told her with a smile.

'It's very quiet. No noise from the road. It has to be quiet for my clients. I have mattress topper to make the couch softer.' She hesitated. 'The only thing is – I have to keep it very clean. No fur. The cats aren't allowed in here.'

'You're thinking of Taz? No problem. He can sleep downstairs or outside the door. You definitely wouldn't want that great hairy goofer in here; he's constantly moulting. It's the breed. Some people call them German shedders!'

Wandering over to the window, he looked out over an area of grass and mature shrubs to where, behind a large apple tree, a row of three stables stood against the far hedge. There was also a smaller wooden structure with a wire netting run. Most probably a kennel, Daniel decided. To the left of this, he could see a gate leading into a turnout paddock of perhaps half an acre that presently played host to two horses.

'They yours?'

Tamiko joined him at the window.

'Yes. The bay with the white face is Babs, she I have had the longest time; the chestnut is Rolo – he's still quite young. He belongs half to me and half to another lady who doesn't ride anymore. She likes just to watch him jump at shows.'

'He's very handsome,' Daniel said, responding to the pride in her voice. 'They both are.'

'Thank you. Do you ride? Jo-Ji says he thinks you do.'

'A little. I can usually stay on and in some sort of control but I'm no great horseman.'

'Maybe you can help me exercise them,' Tamiko suggested. 'Many days I have to ride one and lead one, because there is no time. I think you have no trouble to ride Babs. She is very easy. Now sometimes I ride Natalie's horses, too. Natalie

Redfern; she's the lady who owns the horsebox you're going to drive.'

'So what happened to her? Jo-Ji said she was laid up with a broken leg.'

'Yes, she have a riding accident. Her young horse was behaving badly on the road and slipped. Her leg is trapped underneath. It happen right in the middle of the jumping season; she's really fed up.'

'I bet she is.'

Tamiko glanced up at him a little shyly.

'I hope you won't be bored.'

'I'm sure I won't. I'm rarely bored. Anyway, I needed a place to stay so we're helping each other out.' He didn't like lying to her but Jo-Ji hadn't wanted to scare her by revealing Daniel's real purpose, if he didn't have to.

They went back downstairs and out to Daniel's car, where Tamiko was introduced to Taz, who favoured her with a polite sniff and gentle wag of his tail.

'You're honoured – he's not a tail-wagger, generally,' Daniel told her.

'Will he be all right with the cats?'

'He'll ignore them, unless they attack me, of course!'

'I don't think that's very likely,' she said with a flash of her attractive smile.

Having discovered that although Daniel had plentiful experience of driving lorries, he'd never actually hauled livestock before, Tamiko suggested that he accompany her to Natalie's yard later that day and take the box out for a trial run.

'I have to go over there, anyway, to feed her horses,' she said.

'How on earth do you find time to look after her horses as well as your own?'

'Oh no, I don't have to. Not all the time. Natalie has a groom but today she has afternoon off.'

Daniel offered to drive, and as they pulled out of Tannery Lane onto the main road through Maiden Ashton, he noticed Tamiko casting several looks over her shoulder. He made no comment until it happened again at the next junction.

'Is there a problem?'

Tamiko straightened up immediately.

'Oh, no! It's OK.'

In spite of her denial, there was something in the air between them, and after a moment, Daniel said gently, 'But . . .?'

Tamiko stared straight ahead, biting her lip.

'It's OK. You don't have to tell me,' Daniel said, and the release of pressure brought the confidence he'd hoped for.

'No, I'd like to. I don't suppose Jo-Ji have say anything to you because I don't think he thought it was anything to worry about, but a couple of times lately I have the feeling that someone watches me – follows me, even. It's horrible. I find I always look, now, to see if he's there.'

'I can imagine. When did you first notice it?'

'Three, maybe four weeks ago. I'm not exactly sure. It wasn't until it happen a few times that I really begin to notice, if that makes any sense?'

'So you've actually seen someone?'

'Well, not exactly – I know, that sounds silly. At first it was more of a feeling, and when I turn round, no one is there. Then, a couple of times, I see a man in a hoodie at the end of the lane as I drove by. The second time, Jo-Ji was at home, and when I tell him he goes up there to look, but the man is gone, so maybe it is nothing after all. You need to turn right, just before that white house,' she added, pointing. 'Then it's about half a mile, on the left side. It's called Ashleigh Grange.'

'Was he there just now?' Daniel asked as he slowed and made the turn. 'When we left the cottage – was that what you were looking at?'

'Yes, I look but he wasn't there. It was somebody else.'

'How do you know? If he wasn't wearing the hoodie, would you know him?'

Tamiko looked at him, eyes wide beneath the black fringe. 'I don't know. No, I suppose not. I didn't think of that. You don't think I'm being silly, then?'

'Of course not, and I'm sure Jo-Ji didn't either.'

'No. He said to take care who I opened the door to, and to try not to be alone, but it's difficult. I mean, I have to take the horses out, and there isn't always someone to come with me.'

'Well, perhaps it's a good thing I'm here, then,' Daniel said as though the thought had just occurred to him. 'I can keep an eye out for Mr Hoodie, too.'

Although built in the local Bath stone and a period style, Natalie's house and yard had clearly not graced the landscape for very many years. The cut edges of the stone mullions on the house were sharp and clean, and the slate tiles on the roof were immaculate. Pale green paintwork adorned both human and animal housing and the weed-free, golden pea-shingle drive that swept up to the house also formed the central area of the stableyard, which was built on a quadrangle.

Sleek heads appeared enquiringly over several of the stable doors as the car drew to a halt in the yard, and one of the horses neighed and began banging on his door even before Daniel and Tamiko had a chance to get out.

'Samson is always hungry,' Tamiko said with a smile. 'I'd better feed them before we take the lorry out.'

The feed store and tack room were accessed by way of entering a code on a keypad next to the door, and following in Tamiko's wake, Daniel found the interior to be as clean and tidy as the yard, with racks holding gleaming leatherwork, folded rugs and shining bits and stirrups. Impressed, Daniel commented on it.

'That's Natalie's groom, Inga. She is amazing. If it was left to Natalie, the place would be not so tidy!'

'How many horses does she have?'

'Too many,' Tamiko said frankly. 'There are three that she is competing at the moment, and five or six youngsters. She keeps buying more. The trouble is, most times it's left to Inga to look after them.'

'Why does she want so many?'

'She wants a Grade A horse to take her to Olympia – that is what she dreams – and she thinks the more horses she has, the better is her chance of finding one.'

'That sounds logical,' Daniel commented.

'In a way, it is. But only if you will do the hard work and the many hours. Natalie is a social . . . What is the word?'

'Socialite?'

'A socialite,' Tamiko repeated, struggling with the consonants.

'Yes. She is good rider, but for this sport you have also to be dedicated.'

'For most sports,' Daniel agreed. 'But you can't live someone else's life for them.'

'No. And she is a nice girl.'

'And she lets you borrow her horsebox.'

Tamiko opened her eyes very wide. 'That is not why I say it!'

He laughed. 'It's all right. I'm teasing you.'

In the feed store, Daniel watched while Tamiko measured out fodder for the horses, consulting a chart on the wall, and then under her direction, helped to distribute it to the eager occupants of the yard, taking heed of such comments as: 'Don't let Magpie bully you, she will try to, but just push her out of the way,' and 'Raffa's bucket you will need to empty and fill again, he always drops hay in his water.'

The stables all bore brass nameplates above the doors, so Daniel was able to identify the potential troublemakers. After all the horses had been fed and watered and their droppings skipped out, he and Tamiko were able to turn their attention to the horsebox, which stood in navy and gold majesty in the custom-made, open-fronted barn that formed the fourth side of the quadrangle.

'It has all the mod-cons,' Tamiko told him as they walked towards it. 'And Natalie puts you on her insurance.'

'That's very trusting of her,' Daniel joked. 'She doesn't know me from Adam.'

'Adam . . .?'

'Adam and Eve, Adam. I mean – I'm a stranger to her.'

'Oh.' Her face cleared. 'Jo-Ji, he vouches for you. And you were a policeman.'

Daniel reflected that he knew many coppers he wouldn't lend a pen to, let alone quarter of a million quid's worth of horsebox, but he held his tongue.

'Well, let's give it a go then, shall we? Do you have the key or is it so high-tech it doesn't need one?'

Tamiko held out a small bunch of keys with a shiny brass fob and moments later they were in the cab, Taz settling on a blanket behind the seats, where a door led through to a compact living area.

Daniel shook his head in wonder as he took in the opulence

and sophistication of the vehicle, which compared to Fred Bowden's workaday fleet in much the same way as a Monte Carlo yacht might to a fishing smack. The seats were the last word in comfort and amongst other things, he noted a small TV monitor positioned in one corner of the windscreen.

'So we can keep our eyes on the horses,' Tamiko said, seeing his interest.

The lorry had a powerful engine, and once Daniel was on the open road and had learned where everything was, he began to enjoy himself.

'You will have to drive a lot slower when you have horses in the back,' Tamiko observed presently. 'Particularly for the speeding up and slowing down. Natalie say the man who teach her to drive her first box tell her to imagine she have a grandfather clock standing in the back. Horses can't hold on; they rely always on balance, and if they ever have a bad experience, they will refuse to go in the next time.'

Daniel accepted the mild rebuke with an apology and moderated his speed.

After a short while, Tamiko expressed satisfaction. 'That is good. You learn quickly.'

'Thanks. So when's your next show?'

'On Saturday in Devon. Will that be OK?'

'Of course. That's what I'm here for.'

Back in Maiden Ashton, Tamiko had her own horses to see to. Again, Daniel did what he could to help and after they were settled, Tamiko announced that it was time she prepared the evening meal. Daniel left her busy in the kitchen, locked the door behind him and set off to give Taz the run that he was eager for, using it as an opportunity to see a little more of the village and the surrounding area.

He knew from the map that the village consisted of a main street, which was basically a section of the B road that ran through it, roughly north to south, and three narrow side roads; two on the west side of the main street and one on the east. Tannery Lane was one of the western ones. Flanked by cottages for half a mile or so, it then ran on between fields for several more miles, dotted by one or two further cottages and farms. A footpath ran through the farmyard of one of these, which must have been a source of constant annoyance to the farmer – a burly individual who came out of a doorway as Daniel crossed the uneven concrete towards a field gate. Two border collies ran to the end of their chains and barked furiously at the interloper until a shout from the farmer sent them sulkily back into their kennels.

'Mind you keep that dog under control on my land,' he growled. 'Had a ewe with her back end bit half off last week by a dog like that.'

'Taz won't touch your sheep,' Daniel assured him.

The man grunted.

'That's what they all say.'

Following the way-markers, Daniel found his way across the farmer's land without any damage to his sheep, which Taz regarded, as always, with supreme indifference. Nonetheless, Daniel kept him close, knowing that the farmer had cause to regard dog walkers with disfavour, even if it was only the stupidity of a few that spoiled it for the rest.

Emerging onto a single track lane, he walked along it for a short while, back in the direction of the main road and then followed a footpath into a deciduous wood, where Taz was able to run free to his heart's content and just be, as Daniel liked to think of it, a dog.

Reaching the other side in due course, they found themselves crossing another field, where a few cows regarded them lazily from their position around the water trough, and then a kissing gate led to an alleyway between houses and out to the main street.

The street was pretty much deserted. Daniel exchanged greetings with another dog walker and a middle-aged man who was lovingly washing his BMW saloon, but there was no sign of any suspicious-looking characters, hoodie-wearing or otherwise.

Back at the cottage, he let himself in with the key Tamiko had given him, and found her in the kitchen stirring something fragrant. The two cats, Shinju and Yasu, were by the back door eating from bowls on the doormat, their tails curled neatly around their rumps, but upon hearing Taz's nails on the tiled floor, Shinju stood up and arched her back, swearing at him with teeth bared.

Daniel sent the dog to lie down in the sitting room.

'She will get used to him. She take no notice of Bella and Dexter.' Tamiko wrapped her hand in a tea towel and took two plates from the oven. 'We will eat now, yes? Jo-Ji not back until later.'

'Whenever suits you. That smells wonderful,' he said and was rewarded by a flashing smile.

'It is Thai.'

They ate at the small table in the kitchen and during the meal, with gentle probing, Daniel learned something of Tamiko's background. Born in Japan on the island of Honshu, she had, at an early age, developed a passion for horses and riding, unfortunate in a country where usable land is at a premium, and such pastimes are as a consequence very expensive.

'Have you ever been to Japan?' she asked Daniel, and when he shook his head, she explained, 'Much of it – about seventy-five percent – is mountainous. Almost everybody live around the coast, which you can imagine is very crowded. I don't know from where comes my love of horses, but I have always had it. When my uncle die, he leave us some money and my father pay for me to come to English university. He thinks it will improve my chance of good employment, but for me it is the chance to study in a land where there are lots of horses and many chances to ride.'

'Is that where you met Joey – I mean, Jo-Ji? At university?'

'I was at university; he was working. He is older than me. I was sharing a flat with another student but then my sister arrives.'

'Did she come to study, as well?'

Tamiko shook her head.

'She is not interested in study. She came to get away from home. We are a big family. I have three other sisters and two brothers. It was very crowded. When she came, Hana said she would look for work and help pay for rent, but she didn't. She was looking for – what do you say – a good time.'

'So you were supporting her.'

'I tried to but I didn't have much money myself. I had just met Jo-Ji and he told me I should be more hard with her but what am I to do? She's my younger sister – there is only a year but because I am the oldest, I have always take care of her. I couldn't just throw her out.'

'It's difficult,' Daniel agreed.

'But then Hana met this man, Samir, and he started staying over. Within a few weeks it seems he is always there. It is only a two-bedroom flat and I already share, so they sleep on the couch. Before long my flatmate has moved out, and I am left with all the bills to pay because Samir never seems to have any money, either. Hana and I argue all the time and my study is not so good. Then Jo-Ji suggested I move in with *him*, and I did. We have see each other for over a year and we know we want to be together.'

'So what happened to your sister?'

'We have very big row when I tell her. Three weeks after I move out, the landlady throws Hana and Samir out. I think they don't pay the rent at all. My sister was keep phoning me, wanting me to lend her some money but I didn't have any. I say I will help her if she leaves Samir but she say I am being unfair, she loves him and is going to have his baby. I tell her *he* should look after her, then. She hung up on me. Then, after I get my degree, Jo-Ji is offered a placement in Bristol and we move down here. Since then, I hear nothing from her . . .' Tamiko paused, the memory obviously painful. Then she looked at Daniel. 'I don't know why I'm telling you this . . .'

'Because I asked,' he said. 'Sorry. I'm just naturally nosey – goes with the territory.'

'Being a policeman, you mean?'

'Yeah.'

'But you're not a policeman now,' she said, getting to her feet and gathering their empty plates.

'No.' The word sounded abrupt in the silence that followed. The premature end of his career wasn't a time he cared to revisit but, perversely, when Tamiko didn't pursue it, he felt he owed her some explanation at least, after her frank confidences.

'Would you like cup of tea?' she asked in her slightly stilted way. 'Or coffee? We have a machine. I can do cappuccino but I only have soya milk.'

'Coffee would be great.'

'It's OK you don't want to talk about it,' Tamiko said as she busied herself. 'What happened, I mean. Jo-Ji tell me you make some powerful enemies and they force you to leave police. You must have been sad. You enjoyed your job, no?'

'I loved it,' Daniel said with a depth of feeling that surprised even himself. 'But I couldn't ignore what was going on. And afterwards, I became a pariah – an outcast. It started to affect my work because no one wanted to work with me. When a girl got hurt because of me, I knew my career was over. It wouldn't have been so bad if my whistle-blowing had achieved something worthwhile, but it didn't. The main players got off Scot-free.'

For a few moments the noise of the coffee machine doing its stuff ruled out any chance of conversation, but when Tamiko returned to the table carrying two brimming mugs of frothy coffee, she said, 'I still think you were right to do what you did. In my country I think it would have been ignored totally. Most people don't like to step out of the line. They do as they're told and don't ask questions. I think you were very brave and I know so does Jo-Ji.'

'Brave or stupid. And look where it got me.'

'You have your honour,' she stated simply.

Daniel nodded. 'True,' he said. Tamiko had a way of cutting things back to the bare bones that was refreshing.

'Anyway,' Tamiko said with a mischievous smile. 'Jo-Ji says what's bad for you is good for him, because if you were still in police, he wouldn't have Bella.'

Daniel was just formulating a suitable reply when he saw Taz, who was lying under the archway, become suddenly alert.

'What have you heard, fella?' he asked, and the dog got swiftly to his feet and ran to the front of the sitting room, where he stood listening with his head tilted, before uttering a series of short, sharp barks.

Daniel looked at Tamiko who widened her eyes and shook her head.

'It's too early for Jo-Ji,' she said.

Daniel got to his feet and followed Taz, giving the command for silence, but had to repeat it more sternly after a long, shrill ring on the doorbell sent the dog into a frenzy of barking.

'Do you want me to answer it?' Daniel offered.

Tamiko, standing in the archway, shook her head and came forward.

'I will, but you come too?'

The bell rang again, the note sustained for even longer, and with an anxious glance at Daniel, Tamiko unlocked and opened the door.

With a hand in Taz's collar, Daniel stepped up to Tamiko's shoulder in order to observe the visitor.

On the doorstep stood another young woman of oriental origin holding the hand of a small boy. She had black hair cut in a spiky crop and was somewhat taller, but even though her expression was deeply troubled, the woman bore a strong enough resemblance to Tamiko to leave Daniel in little doubt as to her identity, and Tamiko's breathless exclamation confirmed it.

'Hana!' she said.

# TWO

'Tami.' As the newcomer stood looking at her sister, her eyes filled with tears and her lower lip began to quiver. 'I had nowhere else to go,' she said and began to sob. The little boy looked up at her with worried eyes, then turned to cling to her leg and started to cry in sympathy.

Tamiko seemed rooted to the spot. She made no move to go to her sister who, after weeping for a moment or two, sniffed hard, swallowed and said in a small voice, 'Please, Tami. Can we come in?'

Beyond the visitors, Daniel could see the dark outline of a car standing in the lane with its engine running. Its lights illuminated the front hedges of the neighbouring cottages and a sign on its roof labelled it a taxi.

'Can we come in?' Hana repeated, her eyes beseeching. 'Jahan is so tired.'

Tamiko glanced over her sister's shoulder at the waiting car. 'Samir?'

She shook her head. 'No. He's not here. I've left him. You were right – I'm so sorry.'

The driver of the car was clearly becoming impatient. He opened the door and stepped out, looking up at the cottage.

'Oi, lady! Sometime tonight would be good. I've got other fares to pick up.'

Hana looked at Tamiko with a measure of desperation.

'I'm sorry. I told him you'd pay. I haven't got any money.'

'I'll get it.' Daniel spoke up, and with Taz at his heels, went past the girls and strode down the path, fishing his wallet out of the back pocket of his jeans. The fare made his eyebrows rise.

'Where did you pick her up?' he queried.

'North of Cheltenham,' the driver said. 'Out of my range, this, but she said she was desperate.'

Resignedly, Daniel settled with the man and returned to the house, where he found Tamiko and the two visitors in the kitchen. Hana had picked the child up and he was nestling into her shoulder, his eyes closed. The atmosphere had not noticeably thawed, although Tamiko was refilling the kettle from a filter jug in the fridge. Their own unfinished coffees stood on the table.

'Sit down,' he told Hana. 'You look fit to drop. When did you last eat?'

'Yesterday,' she said, gratefully making use of the chair he had pulled out and repositioning the boy so that he sat on her lap, eyes half open and sucking his thumb. 'Jahan had a sandwich at lunchtime but I had no more money.' Suddenly her face crumpled and she began to cry again. 'I've been so scared, Tami, and all I could think about was getting to you.'

Finally, at the sight of her genuine distress, the familiar role of older sister kicked in like muscle memory and Tamiko left the tea-making, put her arm round Hana's shoulders and bent to kiss the cropped black hair.

'*Hana-chan, daijobu dakara, mou nakanai de,*' she said, slipping back into her mother tongue as she hugged her. 'It's all right, you're here now. We'll sort something out. Shush, don't cry.'

With their heads close together the family resemblance was striking, although if he hadn't known better, Daniel would have guessed at Hana being the older; her features were drawn and her skin lacked the smooth freshness of Tamiko's. The hairstyle was youthful and she wore a small crystal nose stud but dark circles under her eyes added to the ageing effect, a legacy, perhaps, of the stress she was quite clearly under. Even had his name not pointed to it, the boy's darker skin and more aquiline features told of a mixed-race ancestry.

'Your lovely hair,' Tami said softly, after a moment or two. 'It's so short now.'

Hana sat up a little and her sister passed her a handkerchief. 'Samir cut it,' she said, after mopping her eyes and blowing her nose.

'*Samir* did?'

She nodded. 'A friend of his came to the flat when he was out and he came back and caught us talking. That's all it was, Tami, I promise you, but Samir thinks I am flirting. That's when he cut my hair.'

'That's awful!' Tami was clearly shocked.

'It's because he loves me very much that he is sometimes jealous,' Hana explained.

Tami snorted. 'That sounds like his words. You don't do that to someone you love!'

'I was upset at first,' Hana admitted. 'It was very short. But Samir gives me some money to get it cut properly and now I like it. Tami, can I stay? I have nowhere else to go.'

'For tonight, at least,' Tamiko told her. 'I'll make up a bed on the sofa. We'll talk more tomorrow.'

'She can have my room,' Daniel suggested, from where he had taken over the tea making. 'Be better for the boy.'

'Thank you,' Hana said. 'You are kind. Are you sure? I'm sorry if I make trouble . . .' She looked across at Daniel, as if seeing him properly for the first time, and then back at Tamiko, questioning. 'Where is Jo-Ji? You haven't . . .?'

'Jo-Ji's at work. He'll be home soon. This is Daniel, he's a friend of Jo-Ji. He stays for a while.' Tamiko left her sister and went to the cupboard, where she took out two plates and divided the remainder of the curry and rice between them. The little boy brightened visibly at the sight and smell of the hot food.

'This was for Jo-Ji, no?' Hana asked, hesitating. At her side Jahan tucked in hungrily, not troubled by any such scruples.

'It's OK. He'll understand.'

Jo-Ji, when he arrived home a couple of hours later, took the news that his supper was no more in surprisingly good part, although Daniel thought that he looked less than overjoyed to learn who had eaten it. By this time, Hana and Jahan had retired to the room upstairs and the bed that had been intended for Daniel, so his demands to know what Tamiko's sister wanted and how long she was likely to stay could be made without her hearing.

'I don't think she has made any plans,' Tamiko replied handing him a mug of tea. 'She had to get away from Samir, and she didn't know where else to go. It was natural that she should come here.'

'So what made her finally see sense?'

'She doesn't say, and I don't want to ask in front of the boy, but it's obvious he has been abusive. I tell her we'll talk about it more in the morning, when she has rested. Now I find you something else to eat.'

'Thanks,' Jo-Ji dropped a kiss on Tamiko's hair and moved to join Daniel at the table. 'So, Daniel. How are you? Quite a welcome for you – I'm sorry.' A scant five feet eight and slim, he was nevertheless whipcord strong and, as some of those who had crossed his path could testify, a martial artist of considerable skill. Although Japanese on his father's side, Jo-Ji had lived in England for much of his life, attended a top school and spoke English with only a trace of an accent. Good-looking, with a fringe that flopped into his eyes, he had engaging manners and an open, friendly face that could, when trouble flared, become basilisk cold.

'I'm good, thanks,' Daniel replied. 'Did you have a busy day?'

'No. Pretty quiet, actually, but yesterday Bella and I were working the airport. That was great fun. She made several finds. One guy had half a kilo of cannabis stashed inside a guitar – she was onto that in a flash. She's a good girl, my Bella.'

'That's it – rub it in,' Daniel complained. 'Anyway, where is she now?'

'Out in her kennel, having her tea. Dexter, my young Lab is out there too. I'll bring them in later, if Taz is cool with it.'

'Taz'll be fine. Interesting to see whether he remembers her.'

It turned out that he did, and while he wasn't overly demonstrative, a waving tail showed his pleasure.

Bella had burst into the house, a tornado of black, working cocker spaniel, wriggling in ecstasy to find, not only visitors, but visitors she knew. On Daniel she lavished a huge welcome, plainly showing that even though she now worked with Jo-Ji, she hadn't forgotten the one who had trained her. The young, black Labrador who followed her in was scarcely less effusive in his welcome, even though he had never met Daniel before, but that's the nature of the breed.

'Dexter is a firearms dog,' his handler said. 'Only a rookie, but showing good promise.'

'He's a nice dog.'

'Do you miss it?' Jo-Ji asked.

'I miss the work and the lads – and ladesses; I don't miss the politics.'

'Ropey sends his love.'

'Yeah, right! I bet those weren't his words.' Ropey was the nickname of the senior trainer at Dog Central or the headquarters of the police dog unit, where all the dogs and handlers were trained, spent much of their down time, and where they returned at regular intervals for refresher courses and assessments. Daniel had indeed been on good terms with the huge bear of a man that oversaw the kennels, but his terminology had always been inclined more toward that of a squaddie than a poet.

'Well, no,' Jo-Ji admitted with a smile. 'Not his exact words. But I won't repeat what he actually said in front of Tami. Anyway, he's always banging on about you. Holds you and Taz up as examples.'

'Good or bad?' Daniel asked quizzically, but he was pleased, nevertheless. As rookies in the dog unit, he and the others on his intake had looked up to Ropey with great respect; a respect which hadn't diminished with the passing of time.

'Oh, you could do no wrong! Bloody angels, the pair of you!' His eyes twinkled to rob the words of their bite but then he became more serious. 'You've still got friends, you know, and Ropey is one of them. He said to tell you, if you ever need anything . . . Well, you know.'

'He's a good bloke. If he hadn't been on holiday when it all kicked off, things might have been a whole lot different.'

'The benefit of hindsight,' Jo-Ji said. 'It may not have seemed like it at the time but I know a few of the lads were on your side – it just wasn't seen to be a good idea to shout about it. It's old hat, now. You were talk of the locker room for a while and there were some worried faces amongst the middle ranks but you know how it is, life goes on and new dramas come and go. That whole business has been neatly filed away and I'd say there are one or two who are very happy about that.'

'I can imagine,' Daniel said with feeling. When he had decided to come forward with the allegations of corruption that had eventually ended his career, he had inadvertently taken his suspicions to a senior officer who was a party to the whole set-up. Having thus made an enemy of a fairly high-ranking officer, he found the tables turned against him. His own integrity had been called into question and his position within the force had quickly become untenable. Pulled from dog unit and put back on basic duties, Daniel had found no one prepared to endanger their own prospects by backing him up.

Another controversial incident on duty left an innocent girl dead and Daniel assigned to what was not much more than a desk job, and with his career prospects bleak to non-existent, he had resigned. Shortly after that, his marriage fell apart under the strain, with his young son suffering the inevitable consequences. The only silver lining to the stormy cloud that hung over him at the time was the continued partnership of Taz, who had been forced into retirement through injury, shortly before – as Fred Bowden would have termed it – the manure hit the cooling device.

Daniel awoke early after a somewhat restless night on the sofa to find Tamiko tiptoeing past him to the kitchen. Taz was awake and watchful.

'Oh, I'm sorry. I hope I not wake you,' she said, seeing Daniel sit up.

'Not really.'

'Did you sleep OK?'

'Yeah, not too bad at all,' he said brightly.

'I think you're lying,' she told him. 'I have sleep once on sofa when friends are here. It was very bad.'

Daniel laughed. 'OK. It wasn't great, but I've had worse. You're up early.'

'I have to see to the horses before my clients come. Can I make you a cup of tea?'

'If you're having one.'

'Yes. I take with me,' she said, pointing in the direction of the stables.

'I'll come and help,' he offered.

She shook her head with that wide-eyed look he was coming to know.

'No. You don't have to, really.'

'Might as well make myself useful.'

By the time the horses had been fed, turned out in the paddock and their stables mucked out, they found Jo-Ji in the kitchen making breakfast. Of their visitors there was as yet no sign and it was agreed that they should be allowed to sleep for as long as they wished.

Shortly after nine, Karen, the beautician arrived and hot on her heels, Tamiko's first client. The little cottage felt full to bursting and with Tamiko safely chaperoned, Daniel took the opportunity of taking Taz out for a run.

When he returned, Hana and Jahan were sat at the kitchen table with Jo-Ji drinking tea. Tamiko's sister looked tense and unhappy, but Daniel could detect no hostility in Jo-Ji's manner.

As if Daniel's appearance gave her a chance to escape, Hana muttered something about Jahan needing the bathroom and took the child upstairs.

'Sorry, Joey. Did I interrupt something?' Daniel helped himself to tea from the still-warm pot, but wrinkled his nose slightly when it came out green.

'No, I don't think there was much more to be said,' Jo-Ji said with a sigh. 'She says she left Jafari over a month ago and has been staying with a friend until earlier this week. Then, apparently, the friend had family coming to stay and she had to move out.'

'Jafari?'

'Samir Jafari. The loser she's been living with for the last four years.'

'Presumably the child's his?'

'She says so. Apparently Jafari is Iranian and the boy definitely looks to have mixed blood.'

'So why did Hana choose to leave him now?' Daniel asked,

bringing his cup of unappetising tea to the table and sitting opposite Jo-Ji.

'She says he beat her up. It wasn't the first time, I gather – she says he drinks – but apparently this time he hit the kid, too. I think if it weren't for that, she'd have still gone back to him. It never fails to amaze me how much some women will forgive.'

'Mm. The devil you know. Did she report him, do you know?'

'Once, she said, but I gather the bastard sweet-talked her into not taking it further.'

Daniel sighed. 'So what now?'

'In the long term, I'm really not sure. In the short term I suppose she'll have to stay here. Sorry mate, that sofa's a killer, I know. We'll try and sort out something better for you. Maybe chuck a bed in the new extension. I know it's not finished yet but I could run a cable out there for light, and it's not too cold at nights at the moment.'

'A bit detached though, isn't it,' Daniel said. 'OK at the moment, but maybe not so good when you're on nights . . .'

Jo-Ji's eyes narrowed.

'Has something happened? Have you seen someone?'

'No. Just being careful. After all, that's what I'm here for, right?'

'Yeah. Thanks mate. Well, hopefully she won't be here too long. We'll have to get social services involved. Single woman with a young child – abusive partner. Maybe we can find her a place in a refuge.'

'Look, about Tami . . .' Daniel said. 'She told me about her feeling of being watched – I didn't ask her, she just seemed to want to confide – but you mentioned an ex-con you were worried about; someone who might have a grudge?'

'Yeah. Roy Bartlett, a crack dealer I helped put away. Not so much of the *ex*-con, though. He's done his time – or at least, all the time the judge saw fit to give him, minus a couple of years for being a good boy – but if he's a reformed character, then I'm Pope Francis. He's a serial perp, and he went down swearing to get even. They let him out a couple of months ago – a week or two before Tami first mentioned this man in the hoodie.'

'You still think it's him?'

'Not in person, no. I called in a favour and asked a mate in

Bartlett's neighbourhood to keep an eye, and I'm pretty sure he
hasn't been far from home since his release, but that's not to say
he doesn't have friends who'd do his dirty work. He had quite
a little network before he went down.' Jo-Ji drained his mug.
'Look, can I ask another favour? Hana needs to get some clothes
and stuff for her and the boy, too. She says she walked out with
just a shoulder bag. Said she was taking the boy to the park. The
thing is, by the time Tami's free to go with her, I shall have to
be off to work. I don't suppose you could take them and keep
an eye . . .?'

'Sure. No problem.'

In the event, it was mid-afternoon before they set out on their
shopping expedition, as with her eye on an unpromising weather
forecast, Tamiko decided to exercise her horses when she had
finished treating her clients. Hana had made friends with Karen
during a chance meeting earlier in the day, and when Tamiko
and Daniel left the house, the two women were chatting compan-
ionably over coffee in the kitchen.

The ride went without incident, the big, bay mare, Babette,
being as Tamiko had promised, a steady animal, whose only vice
was a tendency to take a strong 'hold' in the faster paces.

'You said you were no horseman but I think you are perfectly
good,' Tamiko observed as they clattered back down the lane
towards the stables. 'It is nice to have company. Jo-Ji, he doesn't
like riding. Says he prefers something with an on and off button!'

'What? Like dogs?' Daniel had quizzed. 'That excuse won't
work!'

The shopping centre that Tamiko presently directed him to
drive to was a modern arcade built chiefly of concrete and glass
which spread over three levels, and they had only been there
twenty minutes or so before Daniel began to suspect they were
being watched.

Whoever it was kept a very low profile and Tamiko, who was
engrossed in helping Hana choose clothes and necessary toiletries
for herself and Jahan, did not appear to have noticed. Unable to
enter many of the shops by virtue of having Taz at his heels,
Daniel was at liberty to scan the surrounding walkways and a
couple of times saw a tallish figure in a grey hooded sweatshirt

either looking in a shop window or moving quickly out of sight as he turned.

It was difficult to be sure that the man was actually watching them, or even to say for certain whether it was the same person each time, and as he thought it unlikely that the man would approach while he was so obviously chaperoning the girls, Daniel decided to say nothing for the time being.

It took the best part of two hours to complete the shopping, by which time they were all ready for coffee and cake in the central foyer café, with ice cream for Jahan.

Daniel chose a seat with a good view of the surrounding area and while listening with half an ear to the girls' conversation, kept an eye on the likely vantage points for a watcher. They had been sat there for little more than five minutes when his vigilance was rewarded. The retail outlets were arranged around the central atrium on avenues that ran outwards like the spokes of a wheel, and at the entrance to one of those avenues on the top floor he saw the man in the grey hoody leaning against the glass shopfront, apparently talking on his mobile phone. As Daniel's gaze swept across him, he took a smooth step backwards out of sight, but Daniel had a feeling he wouldn't have gone far.

'Stay here!' he said sharply to Tamiko and Hana, cutting through the flow of their talk. 'I'll be back in a moment. Taz, on guard!'

'But what . . .?' Tamiko looked bewildered.

Daniel was already out of his seat. 'Tell you in a minute. Just don't move.'

In a flash he had gained the cover of the lowest covered walkway and, shunning the central escalator, ran through the thinning crowds to the lifts, praying for there not to be a queue.

His luck was in. Not only was there no queue but one of the lifts had just opened to let out its two teenage passengers and he was able to step straight in. A woman and a man made to follow him but he shook his head.

'Sorry. This one doesn't work,' he said, closing the doors on their bewildered faces. He pressed the button for the top floor, keeping his finger on it to avoid anyone stopping it at the first floor, a trick he had learned from a busy maintenance man at a hospital.

Leaving the lift, he made his way swiftly towards the circular, central walkway and was rewarded by the sight of the man in the hoody, who had moved forward once more and appeared to be looking intently downwards, quite possibly wondering what had become of Daniel.

Daniel's plan was to come up behind the man and catch him by surprise, but this was thwarted by a couple of teenage lads just ahead of him, who caught sight of someone they knew on the other side of the atrium and shouted out something that sounded remarkably like 'Oi! Scabby!'

Instantly, the man in the hoodie turned his head, saw Daniel behind the boys and took to his heels without hesitation, sprinting round the walkway to the head of the escalator and charging down it, knocking several people aside in the process.

Cursing his luck, Daniel ran in pursuit, trying to avoid further collisions but still catching the verbal flak from those who'd been manhandled by the man in front.

Racing round the walkway and on down the second escalator to the ground floor, the man ahead of him ignored the two girls sitting open-mouthed in the foyer café and ran instead down the avenue marked Exit & Car Park.

Out of the corner of his eye as he followed, Daniel saw Taz get to his feet, his eyes alight with excitement.

'Stay there!' he shouted at the dog, and all those who hadn't so far stopped to gape at the real-life pursuit, did so at the sound of his imperative command.

The man in the hoodie pushed through the heavy swing doors to the car park and, meeting them on the rebound a second or two later, Daniel turned to hit them with his shoulder. The impact broke his stride for a moment and when he pushed through, he had to pause to determine which way his quarry had run. Then he saw him, weaving between the thinning ranks of parked cars to his left.

He darted forward but was hindered by two cars coming down the bay on their way out. Narrowly avoiding a collision, he was forced to wait while they passed, and when the way was clear, he heard the slamming of a car door and an engine starting. As he began to run, further down the bay a white van reversed out of its space into the path of the two vehicles, causing them to brake hard, and in the next moment, the van accelerated away up the ramp to the exit, paused briefly to open the barrier and then disappeared out into the brightness of the street.

Daniel jogged to a halt.

'Hell and damnation!' he swore, turning to thump the nearest concrete pillar in his frustration. With the two cars in the way, he had only been able to get a partial plate, but nevertheless, he took his phone from his pocket and keyed in Jo-Ji's mobile number as he began to retrace his steps.

In the foyer café, Taz was still on guard and Daniel released him with a word of praise that set his tail wagging. The aftermath of the disturbance was still rippling through the shopping centre and he was just attempting to explain to the girls what had happened, when a shrill voice called out, 'That's him! He's one of them! Nearly knocked me flying!'

Daniel looked up and into the face of an oncoming uniformed security officer, who was being almost propelled forwards by a lady of ample proportions in black leggings and an over-tight cerise pink T-shirt. She had a rose tattoo growing from the top of her impressive cleavage and black-rooted blonde hair scraped back into a ponytail. She was dragging a mini version of herself along by one hand and an assorted bunch of varyingly disgruntled shoppers were trailing along in their wake. Sighing, Daniel waited for the storm to break over him.

The security man, a none too athletic individual whose profession was proclaimed by the fluorescent tabard he wore, halted a few feet away, a decision probably precipitated by Taz, who had taken the shrill-voiced woman in strong dislike and was rumbling under his breath, his whiskers bristling.

'These – ah, people say that you barged into them on the escalator,' the man began, after clearing his throat. He looked out of his depth, as though shoplifters were his thing and anything else beyond his comfort zone.

'He did,' the woman averred. 'Pushed me into the side. I'll be bruised all over and it could easily have been much worse!'

She pointed an accusing finger as she spoke and Taz upped the decibels until Daniel had to silence him.

'Did you push this woman, as she says?'

'Callin' me a liar?' the woman exclaimed, before Daniel had a chance to answer.

'No, no. Not at all,' the security man said hastily. 'But we should hear what he has to say. It's only fair.'

'I don't think I pushed anyone,' Daniel stated. 'But if I did, I apologise.'

'It wasn't him. It was the other bloke,' a man piped up from behind Daniel's accuser.

Silently, Daniel blessed him.

'It's true. It's the other guy you want,' he agreed. 'Tried to nick my wallet. That's why I was chasing him.'

'You got it back?' The security man looked happier now that the situation appeared to be resolving itself without any need for decision-making on his part.

'Yeah. He dropped it.'

'Did he get away?'

Daniel checked an instinctive sarcastic response, saying simply that he'd lost him in the car park.

'Well, it looks like that's it, then,' the uniformed one stated.

'You can't say that!' the woman screeched. 'What about my injuries? And who's going to pay for another packet of fags? Mine got all chewed up by the escalator.'

'Best place for 'em,' a voice suggested.

Daniel's mouth twitched but he took his wallet out and proffered a ten-pound note, which the security man stretched out his hand to take, with a wary eye on the dog, and passed back to the woman. She glared at Daniel but took the money quickly enough and, still grumbling, turned and led the tubby child away.

'OK. There's nothing more to see here,' the portly one said then, with more authority than he had thus far shown. He turned away from Daniel, waving his arms at the gathering of interested people rather as one might shoo a herd of inquisitive cows, and obediently, they began to disperse.

Looking pleased with himself, he came back to Daniel.

'Do you want to make a complaint? Call the police?'

Daniel shook his head. 'No point. He's long gone. I've got my wallet. Case closed.'

The security guard nodded, looking patently relieved, and moved away. Turning, Daniel found Tamiko standing close behind him. Hana was still at the table with Jahan, wiping ice cream off the boy's face.

'Did he really try to steal your wallet?' Tamiko asked, frowning.
'I saw him. He was wearing a hoodie, wasn't he?'

'I'll tell you in the car. Are we ready to roll?' he enquired,
aware that there could still be interested ears listening and keen
to get away from the arcade in case some over-zealous shop worker
had indeed called the police during the initial disturbance.

Jo-Ji rang back as they made their way towards the exit, giving
Daniel a name to go with the partial registration plate he'd
reported and when they were settled in the car, Daniel repeated
it to Tamiko and Hana.

'Does the name Assim Kahn mean anything to either of
you?'

Tamiko instantly pursed her lips and shook her head, and a
moment later Hana did the same.

'The van the man got away in was registered to an Assim
Kahn. It's a Manchester plate,' he added.

'Oh my God! You think someone has come after my sister?'
Tamiko said.

'It's possible.' Daniel looked at Hana, who had turned pale,
clearly alarmed at the idea.

'Samir has a lot of friends but he never introduces them to
me,' she said. 'It's so far, I thought I would be safe here. How
has he found me? Why won't he leave me alone?'

'You have his son and it would be easy enough to find out
where Tamiko lives. He might guess you'd run to her.'

A distressed sound from Jahan interrupted them.

'Daddy not coming?'

'No, my little one. Daniel won't let him,' Hana responded,
and Daniel realised with resignation that his brief had just
expanded to include bodyguarding the entire UK branch of
Tamiko's family.

'Do you have any other relatives in England?' he asked Tamiko
whimsically, as he steered the Mercedes for home.

She frowned.

'No. Why do you ask?'

Daniel shook his head.

'Ignore me, I'm being silly.'

Although he remained vigilant on the return journey, the
Mercedes' mirrors showed nothing to cause him alarm. He wasn't

sure that was significant, however, because he was beginning to think that if Tamiko's 'stalker' and the man at the shopping arcade were one and the same, he well knew where she lived and would have had no need to follow them home.

# THREE

A second night on the sofa hadn't attracted Daniel overmuch but a moment of inspiration whilst waiting outside Argos had resulted in him purchasing an inflatable mattress, which could be stored upright against the wall in Jo-Ji's den when not in use. It was a huge improvement, and when Tamiko awakened him at five thirty the next morning, he felt a lot more rested.

As Jo-Ji would be leaving the house around midday for his shift, it had been decided that Hana and Jahan would accompany Tamiko and Daniel to the show and accordingly, by the time the horses had been hastily mucked out and groomed, the two of them were in the kitchen having breakfast. Grabbing a slice of toast, Daniel left the house and drove the five miles or so to Ashleigh Grange to pick up the horsebox and one of Natalie Redfern's horses that Tamiko was going to ride that day.

Although Tamiko had furnished him with the code for the gates, he found them standing open and was met in the yard by a slight, thirty-something, blonde female who introduced herself as Inga.

The lorry had been driven into the centre of the yard and stood waiting with its ramp down.

'Samson is all ready,' Inga informed him. She had a slight Scandinavian accent but her English was impeccable. 'He's a perfect gentleman and shouldn't give you any trouble. Normally I would come but I promised to go shopping for wedding stuff with a friend. Will you manage?'

'I'm sure we'll be fine.'

Samson was a big, dark chestnut gelding with a white blaze. He was led from his stable clad in a rug and leg protectors of navy and gold to match the horsebox. Evidently Ms Redfern would spare no expense to create an impression. With Inga's help, he was quickly loaded and the ramp lifted and secured behind him. His tack and two haynets were stowed in the forward compartment and Daniel was ready for the off.

'Look after my boy,' Inga said as he climbed into the cab.

'I will.' Daniel switched on the video link and could instantly see a black and white image of the horse pulling contentedly at his hay. Bearing in mind Tamiko's advice, he eased the lorry out of the yard and down the drive to the road, waving goodbye to the groom. Samson calmly adjusted his balance as the vehicle began to move and went on with his hay.

By the time Daniel stopped the lorry in the lane beside Tamiko's stables, he was feeling quite at home with his precious cargo, and once they had loaded Rolo and Babs and all their gear, they were ready to go.

The cab was fairly crowded, with Daniel, Tamiko, Hana and Jahan all sharing the bench seat and Taz on a blanket behind it. Jo-Ji waved them off and they made good time in the light, early-morning traffic, heading for Taunton and the southwest.

Hana had shed the haunted look she had worn on arrival and began to relax, the family likeness between her and her sister becoming more marked than ever. Even Jahan had become more talkative but remained markedly shy when Daniel addressed him. Daniel supposed that if his main experience of men had been that of living with his abusive father, it was hardly surprising that he viewed all men with a certain amount of trepidation.

The show was near Barnstaple and the route straightforward. With no major traffic issues they reached the showground a full half hour ahead of their ETA, by which time Daniel felt completely confident in his new role as horse transport driver.

A steward waved them into position, Daniel gently applied the brakes and the powerful engine finally shuddered into silence.

'Thank you,' Tamiko said. 'You drive it very well now.'

'Thanks.' Daniel stretched his cramped muscles and glanced at the monitor. Two of the horses were still pulling wisps of hay from their nets but Rolo, the youngster, held his head high, ears flicking back and forth as he tried to make out the sounds from beyond the box walls.

Jahan was fidgeting and when Tamiko announced her intention of getting the lie of the land before unloading any of the horses, Hana said she'd come too, as she thought it would be a good idea to find a toilet for the boy.

'That's right. You just go. I'll look after everything here,' Daniel said, but the girls just laughed and went on their way.

Jumping down from the cab, he let Taz out, who – being no respecter of other people's property – immediately lifted a hind leg against the wheel of Natalie's horsebox.

'For goodness sake! You'll get me into trouble!' Daniel exclaimed, but Taz merely ran up to him with flattened ears and a waving tail, pleased with the attention after the boring drive.

'Is that Natalie Redfern's box? She's not here is she?' A voice called from behind Daniel.

He turned to see a slim and attractive woman of perhaps forty or forty-five, with dark auburn hair and frank, brown eyes. She wore jeans and a T-shirt, with a Puffa jacket to ward off the morning chill. Standing just behind her and to one side was a stocky, fair-haired man of about Daniel's age, engaged in lighting a cigarette. He had a close-cut beard and the clothes he wore were casual but Daniel didn't need to check the labels to see that they hadn't been bought from any budget high-street store.

'No, she's not,' Daniel replied. 'But you're right, it *is* her box. Tamiko's borrowed it for the day.'

'Oh, OK. Yes, I know Tamiko. Sorry, I'm Boo. Boo Travers. And this is my son, Harrison.'

'Hi. Daniel Whelan. I'm a friend of Tami's. I'm driving the lorry for her. She's gone to have a look at the ring layout, I think, and I'm hoping she's bringing some coffee, too.'

Boo smiled.

'Yes, that's where we're going. I might see her. See you later.'

It was fifteen minutes or so before Tamiko and her sister returned to the lorry park, during which time one of the occupants of the horsebox had started to get restless and was making his feelings known by banging on the side of the lorry. Daniel opened the side door and went in, taking a handful of chopped carrots from a bucket, which he distributed between the three waiting horses. It was the novice, Rolo, who was becoming agitated, the other two apparently inured to the periods of inactivity that were part of every show day.

'Rolo has been complaining,' he told Tamiko when she reappeared bearing a cardboard tray of Costa coffees and a bag containing muffins.

'He always does. I'm sorry we were so long. I meet someone I know and she asks about Natalie.'

'Someone called Boo?' Daniel asked. 'She came over to see me, too.'

'Oh, you see her? Yes, her name is really Belinda, but everyone calls her Boo. I don't know her very well but Natalie introduces us one day and now she often stops to talk. Actually, I was surprised to see her here. It's her daughters who usually compete these days but she tells me they are gone to a summer camp.'

'Probably enjoying taking time for herself,' Daniel suggested, taking the lid off his coffee and having a sip.

'Yes, I think so. From what Natalie has tell me, she has a lot of bad luck in her life.' Tamiko offered chocolate and fruit muffins from the paper bag. 'First her husband dies and now her son is very ill.'

'He didn't look particularly ill.' Daniel helped himself to a chocolate muffin.

'No, because that is Harrison, who is older. It is the younger one who is sick. Natalie says the doctors don't think he will get better. It's leukaemia, I think.' She struggled with the word. 'It must be very hard for Boo – for all of them.'

'Yeah, that's tough, poor woman,' Daniel agreed. 'So, when's your first class? What's the order of the day?'

Balancing her coffee and muffin in one hand, Tamiko took a crumpled show schedule from her pocket and shook it out.

'First class is Rolo in ring three, then Samson in ring one. Babs is in that class, too, so it may be a bit tight. Do you mind being my groom for the day? I usually share Inga with Natalie – she's brilliant. Here, you can look at the ring plan.'

Once the coffee and muffins were consumed, the business of the day got underway. Hana cleaned the surplus chocolate off Jahan's face and then led him off to see the show's attractions, while under Tamiko's instruction, Daniel helped unload Rolo, hanging on to him for her as she flicked a brush over him, tacked him up and screwed studs into his shoes for grip. The horse fidgeted and threw his head up and down, trying to barge into Daniel and loosen his hold on the bridle. Getting him to stand still long enough to fix the studs was a battle, but at last it was done.

Tamiko disappeared into the lorry and re-emerged in clean, cream-coloured jodhpurs and a white shirt and stock under a quilted coat. Beneath a navy crash cap, her black hair was confined in a net.

'I'll take him to warm up and try to get him to settle, then come back for my jacket,' she said, taking the reins from Daniel. 'Oh no! I've forgotten his martingale.'

'OK. What does it look like? Can I get it?'

She frowned. 'I think it easier if I do. Too hard to explain. But it should have been hanging with his bridle, that's why I worry.'

Daniel had his work cut out trying to hold on to the tall chestnut gelding, who was becoming increasingly keen to be off, and to that end, started to walk round Daniel in tight circles, throwing his head up and down to try and loosen his hold. It had been said, in the past, that he had a calming influence on horses, but it didn't seem to be working with this one.

When Tamiko reappeared it was with empty hands and anxiety writ large.

'I look everywhere but I don't find it. I don't know what I should do. I can't ride him without it because if he puts his head too high, he can't see where he goes and he almost hits me in the face.'

'Could you borrow one, perhaps?' Daniel said, unsure if it was a viable suggestion or not. 'What about that Boo person?'

Tamiko looked at him.

'I suppose she might. I'll go and ask. Are you OK there?'

'Fine,' Daniel replied, leaning into the horse's shoulder and whisking his foot out of the way an instant before it would have been trampled by the metal stud-wearing Rolo. 'Just don't be too long.'

Thankfully, for the continuing health of Daniel's feet, Tami returned in a very short time, triumphantly bearing a handful of leather straps and rings, which she proceeded to buckle onto the restless horse with deft fingers, adjusting to fit. She then fastened the strap on her crash cap and Daniel boosted her into the saddle with one hand, whilst restraining Rolo with the other. She was thistledown-light and he found it hard to believe that she had a hope of controlling the big sport horse, but at her nod, he let go of the rein and she was on her own.

Rolo made a spirited attempt to take off; leaping forward and then crabbing sideways, but Tamiko was ready for him. With a smile and a thank you for Daniel, she sent the horse on into a trot and was quickly lost to view between the other lorries.

Left behind, Daniel tidied around the box, checked on the two remaining occupants and then sat on the ramp with Taz, waiting for Tamiko to return. He found himself thinking of his son, Drew, who had recently begun to show a great enthusiasm for all things equine. How he would have enjoyed this day. He wondered if there would be an opportunity to invite him along to one of the future shows and made a mental note to ask Tamiko.

'I'll keep an eye, if you want to go off anytime,' a voice said, interrupting his chain of thought. A middle-aged man was standing on the ramp of the next lorry along. 'I'm going to be here anyway. Got a lorry full of jumping ponies and I'm skivvy to my daughters for the day. Just give me your mobile number in case of emergencies.'

Daniel thanked him, and when Tamiko reappeared after fifteen minutes or so to get her black jacket and tidy up before competing, with her permission he took advantage of the man's offer, heading for ring two in Rolo's wake.

At the ringside he caught up with Hana and Jahan, and together they watched Tamiko's opening round. They stood close to a triple bar and the thudding, grunting, leather-creaking power of the horses as they passed was awe-inspiring. Jahan shrank back the first few times it happened but when he began to trust that the animals would stay on their side of the rail, he held his ground and watched with big fascinated eyes, ice cream from the cone in his hand running over his fingers unchecked until his mother noticed.

When Tamiko and Rolo entered the ring, Daniel was amazed once more that such a slight girl could control a horse of his size. They circled in the centre of the ring, her face a mask of concentration and Rolo looking like a coiled spring, until the bell rang and they could begin.

The round was impressive. Tamiko kept the horse collected, his stride rounded and neck arched, until three strides before the first jump and then with an explosion of exuberant power, he took off, giving the poles an easy twelve inches of clearance. On landing she checked him again, guiding him towards the next fence, and Daniel could see the part the borrowed martingale played as Rolo attempted to evade her restraining hands. He found himself holding his breath and tensing as they approached each jump, willing them to safely reach the other side, but as the round progressed, Rolo became steadily more eager. At the second last their luck failed. Getting too close, he tipped the pole with his front feet and the chance of a clear was gone.

Tamiko left the ring to a smattering of sympathetic applause and Daniel found he could breathe again.

'Wow! That make me so tense,' Hana said. 'I don't know how she does it. Did you see Aunty Tami, Jahan?'

Rejoining Tamiko outside the ring, Daniel expressed his admiration for her performance but she shrugged it off.

'I let him go too fast at the end. He is not easy with uprights. He gets too strong and is not careful.'

'Next time, maybe.'

She flashed her brilliant smile.

'Yes, there is always a next time.'

It was a long day, which passed for Daniel in a blur of horseflesh, saddles, bridles, leg protectors, studs, rugs and hurried cups of coffee. By the time all the horses were loaded into the lorry for the return journey, he was feeling mentally drained and pretty physically weary, too.

'Daniel, thank you. You have been amazing,' Tamiko said as she climbed into the cab and pulled the door shut. Between them sat Hana and the sleepy Jahan, and at the top of the windscreen, three large rosettes were proudly displayed.

'I enjoyed it,' he said truthfully, starting the engine. 'I didn't realise quite what I was letting myself in for when I agreed to drive the lorry, but it was fun.'

Tamiko instantly looked apologetic.

'I have asked too much. I'm sorry!'

'No, it was fine. As I said, I enjoyed it. Kept me out of mischief. Besides, I could hardly sit there and watch you struggle, could I?'

'Usually there is Inga. I don't think I realise before, just how much she does. That's odd,' she added as they rolled and rocked across the field in the convoy heading for the gate.

'What is?'

'Well, that looks like Boo's box up there,' she said, pointing towards the front of the queue. 'But it's turning right.'

'Where does she live?' Daniel asked, slowing to let another lorry join the line ahead of him. He glanced towards the road in time to see a huge cream-coloured lorry pull away. There was a jumping horse and a name emblazoned on the side, but it was too far away for him to read it.

'Not far from us; near Bath. Which is a good thing because I forget to give her back the martingale I borrow and will have to drop it in.'

'Perhaps she wants fuel or something,' Daniel suggested. 'Or maybe it's not her box at all, just one that looks like it. Too late to catch her now, anyway.'

The drive home was uneventful. Jahan slept the whole way and Daniel amused himself by finding tongue twisters that were rendered even more difficult by the girls' Japanese accents. After struggling with 'Red Leather, Yellow Leather' and 'She Sells Sea Shells' to the accompaniment of much giggling, they turned the tables by trying to teach him phrases in their own language. Daniel was pleased to see the sisters relaxing in each other's company.

After unloading Rolo and Babs, he set off wearily on the last leg of the day's journeying, to return Samson to his own yard.

It was a relief to hand over responsibility of the big chestnut to Inga, who appeared from the feed store as he switched off the engine, and he didn't protest too vehemently when she turned down his offer to clean the lorry before he left.

'I'll do it tomorrow. I don't mind. It's always my job after a show,' she assured him. 'Thank you for looking after Sammy.'

Transferring to the Mercedes, Daniel headed back to the cottage, looking forward to a good meal and a quiet evening in.

Taz jumped into the back, turned round several times and collapsed with a deep sigh. It hadn't been a good day for him; too many people and horses, and not enough running free. With resignation, Daniel reflected that the first part of his quiet evening had better be spent exercising the dog.

He turned into Tannery Lane, marvelling at how soon a place could become familiar and impart the feeling of coming home, but such thoughts were rudely banished by the sight of a van parked untidily in front of the cottage and a man hammering on the door with his fist.

# FOUR

The man's blood was obviously thoroughly up, because his assault on the door didn't falter following Daniel's arrival upon the scene. Tall and fairly strongly built, he was battering the painted wood alternately with his fists and feet, shouting all the while.

Daniel got out of the car, his mind automatically taking in details of the man's appearance. Loose-fitting jeans and a leather jacket over a pale grey hoody; was this the 'stalker' that Tamiko had seen and who he'd pursued at the shopping centre? He couldn't be sure, he hadn't got a clear enough view of that man.

'Open the door, bitch, or I'll break it in!' the man in the hoody shouted.

'Oi! What the hell do you think you're doing?' Daniel demanded, having to raise his voice quite considerably to make himself heard.

The man paused in his onslaught just long enough to say over his shoulder, 'Piss off!'

'Do you want to tell that to the dog?' Daniel enquired, heading for the rear of the Mercedes, where Taz was already voicing his eagerness to be of assistance. Once out, with Daniel's hand in his collar, he strained to be at the man, his front feet bouncing with every warning bark.

The man wasn't a fool. He stopped kicking the door panel and turned to face Daniel, revealing a dark-eyed, olive-skinned face with several days' growth of stubble.

'I got every right to be here,' he said, eyeing the dog with respect. His accent was strongly Midlands. 'My girlfriend's in there with my kid. She's stole him from me!'

'Children aren't possessions,' Daniel pointed out, quieting Taz. 'She's his mother. He needs to be with her.' In his head he was executing a mental about-turn. This couldn't be Tamiko's stalker, his own words had confirmed his identity as Samir Jafari, the abusive ex-partner of Tamiko's sister, Hana, but he could still be the watcher at the shopping mall.

'He's my son! He belongs with me and I'm not leaving without him!' Now Taz was quiet, he recovered some of his confidence.

'I think you'll find you are.'

'Piss off! Who are you, anyway? It's none of your fucking business!' Jafari's voice rose and he spat the words viciously. Taz started to bark again.

Taking his phone from his pocket, Daniel said loudly, 'I'm calling the police.'

'Call the bloody cops, then. I don't care. I've as much right to the boy as she has.' He turned and started to hammer on the door again. 'C'mon, bitch! Open the fucking door!'

Out of the corner of his eye, Daniel caught sight of someone peering round the front door in the next house along. He didn't mind an audience. An independent witness might be valuable if things turned nasty. He put his phone away, certain that Tamiko's first action would have been to call Jo-Ji.

Finding that he was making no impact on the door, Jafari swore again and cast about for a weapon. He found, beside the steps, a heavy iron boot-scraper and with this in his hands immediately began to make serious dents in the wooden panels.

Daniel decided that the time for talking was over.

'Put that down right now or I'll send the dog!' he shouted and Taz, recognising his old cue, became frenzied with excitement.

Jafari ignored him, perhaps rendered reckless by his own rage, or perhaps thinking it an empty threat.

Daniel repeated his warning to no avail and then, with a low-voiced, 'Get him!' he loosed Taz. Suddenly silent, the dog crossed the space to his target in a flash and fastened his jaws unerringly around the right sleeve of Jafari's leather jacket, pulling him off balance and causing him to drop the boot-scraper with a clang on the concrete step.

Jafari screamed in fright.

'Get 'im off me! Get 'im off!'

'Stand still and I will,' Daniel promised.

'I will. I will! Just get 'im the fuck off!'

'Taz, out!' he commanded and felt a swell of pride when the German shepherd immediately let go and stood back a pace, his eyes fixed with intimidating intensity on Jafari's face. It had been over a year since the dog had done any bite work and he had performed it with textbook precision.

Keeping an eye on Taz in his turn, Jafari backed up against the front door and rubbed his forearm.

'That dog's fuckin' dangerous. He tried to kill me! I'll report him and he'll be shot.'

'Rubbish. You were never in any danger. He's a trained police dog.' The words were confident but even so, Daniel felt a twinge of unease. He had been allowed to keep Taz following his retirement only after an assessment of his safety in public. Had he just put the dog at risk? No right-thinking officer would say so, but there were a scary number of health and safety jobsworths out there, and in addition to that, Daniel was very aware that he was back in the jurisdiction of his nemesis, DI Paxton.

Jafari's next words accentuated that fear.

'But you're not the fuzz, are yer? Or you wouldn't have threatened to call them,' he said, leaning towards Daniel with an evil sneer. 'So if you're not a copper, that's not a copper's dog.'

Taz interpreted his movement as a threat, and began to bark once more, but he obediently fell silent at a word from Daniel, who was saved the necessity of replying by the sound of an oncoming police car. Hoping against hope that it would be Jo-Ji, he warned Jafari not to move and waited for its arrival.

When it arrived, blue lights flashing, the first person that emerged was not Jo-Ji but another, less welcome face from Daniel's past; Paul 'Jono' Johnson, recently promoted, Daniel had learned from Jo-Ji, to sergeant. In the time before Daniel's fall from grace, he and his wife, Amanda, had counted Jono and *his* wife as friends, and although Daniel had never felt as close to the couple as Amanda had, he hadn't been prepared for their total rebuttal of his friendship when his career hit a brick wall.

From the other side of the vehicle, a young PC appeared, hesitant and a little tense.

'Sergeant Johnson. Constable Redman,' Jono said by way of an introduction, hitching his trousers up as he came forward. 'Right. What's going on here?' Round-faced with rather weak blue eyes and razor-cut gingery-blond hair under his cap, he'd put on a good deal of weight in the nine months or so since Daniel had last seen him.

'His bloody dog attacked vehicle!' Samir told Jono, pre-empting any attempt by Daniel to explain the situation.

'This man was trying to batter the door down with a boot-scraper,' Daniel countered. 'He was making threats against the women inside.'

'Daniel!' Recognition dawned in the sergeant's face, and from his demeanour, the feeling of discomfiture was mutual. 'What are you doing here?'

'I'm staying with Jo-Ji – that's Joey Matsuki in the dog unit – and his fiancé, Tami. This is their house. I've been out and I just came back to find this man trying to gain entry using that boot-scraper.'

'And did your dog attack him?'

'He detained him on my command, as he was trained to do. There was never any danger,' Daniel stated calmly.

Jono favoured him with a long look but made no comment. Taking out his pocket book, he asked Jafari his name and address, noting them down.

'Is that your vehicle?' he said then, indicating the white van.

'It belongs to a mate.'

'Name of . . .?'

'Assim Kahn. He lent it to me. He knows I've got it.'

Jono unclipped his radio and relayed the vehicle's registration number to his control.

'There's nothin' wrong with it. It's insured and everything,' Jafari protested.

'Then you haven't got anything to worry about then, have you?' Jono said pleasantly. 'You got your driving license on you?'

Jafari took his wallet from a back pocket and found the card, which the sergeant inspected.

'You're a long way from home,' he observed, handing it back. 'What are you doing here?'

'There's no law against travelling.'

'There is, however, a law against battering someone's door down,' Jono pointed out. 'I repeat, what are you doing here?'

'My partner's in there. She's abducted my son. I've got every right to see him,' Jafari asserted.

'It seems to me that if she'd wanted to see you, she'd have opened the door.'

'I told you – she abducted my boy. She's not just going to give him back because I ask, is she?'

'So you were going to take him back by force, were you?' Jono enquired.

'No!' Too late Jafari saw the corner he'd been backed into. He spread his hands. 'What am I supposed to do?'

There was a click from the front door lock and then the door opened a little and Tamiko peered anxiously out.

'Ah. Miss Yoshida?' the sergeant asked.

'That's right.'

'It was you who reported the disturbance?'

'I did.' Tamiko glanced apprehensively at Jafari.

'Do you know this man?'

She nodded. 'He's the ex-partner of my sister. She came here to get away from him because she was scared. Are you going to arrest him?'

'That depends—'

At that point his radio crackled into life and he turned away, but not before Daniel heard control verifying the ownership of the van in the lane.

'But he's threatened to kill her!' Tamiko protested when Jono turned back.

'Is that right?' Jono asked, looking at Jafari, but he, predictably, denied it vehemently.

'Oh, what a surprise,' Daniel muttered.

'He's hit her before,' Tamiko said.

'When was this?'

'I'm not sure. Some weeks ago, in Manchester where they lived.'

'And did she report it?'

'I'm not sure. Yes, I think so. She is very scared of him. She leaves because she is terrified of what he would do to her or her son.'

'Well, if she didn't report the abuse, then I'm afraid it's just her word against his,' Jono said, shaking his head resignedly.

'But you can see what he's like!' Tamiko persisted, her eyes imploring.

'I'm sorry. Where is your sister now?'

'In the house. She won't come out.'

'We can charge him with criminal damage with regards to your front door.'

'So you will arrest him, yes?'

'I'll take him in, he'll be charged and the court will order him to pay for repairs and to stay away from your sister.'

'Oh, that is no use!' Tamiko threw her hands up in despair. 'The law is stupid! Do we have to wait until my sister is harmed by this man?'

'Can I go now?' Jafari put in.

Jono shook his head.

'No. I have to ask you to come down to the station with me. My colleague will take a statement from Miss Yoshida and her sister.'

The younger officer, who had been hovering on the sidelines, now stepped forward, patently relieved to have been allotted a relatively simple task.

'You're *asking* me?' Jafari repeated. 'And what if I don't want to go to the station?'

'Then I *will* arrest you. The choice is yours,' Jono said patiently.

'Ah, this is so fuckin unfair! Always you believe the woman.'

'Well, *she* wasn't the one bashing the hell out of the front door, was she, sir?' the sergeant observed placidly, placing his hand on Jafari's arm to steer him towards the waiting police car.

He shook it off.

'What about the van?' he demanded.

'Give the constable the keys and he'll lock it.'

'And then what? How do I get back here to pick it up? Will you bring me?'

'No, I'm afraid you'll have to find your own way back. I can give you the number of a taxi, at the station.'

'That'll cost the bloody earth!'

'Quite likely. Shameful, isn't it?' the sergeant agreed. 'Now, are you going to come quietly, or do I have to arrest you for non-cooperation?'

Jafari gave in, but he shot a venomous look at Daniel and the dog as he passed.

'Aren't you going to arrest him? And what about the fucking dog? He's dangerous! He needs shooting!'

'Let me worry about them,' Jono said, guiding him safely past.

Taz rumbled under his breath and Daniel twitched his collar to shut him up.

It was over half an hour later when the police car bearing the two officers and Hana's unhappy ex-partner disappeared down the lane. Going back into the house, Daniel found Hana in the kitchen looking white and shaken, Jahan clinging to her side as he had on the night they arrived. Empty mugs stood on the table but Tamiko refilled the kettle and made yet more tea.

'Will Taz be in trouble for attacking the man?' she asked anxiously.

'He shouldn't be,' Daniel said, with a fair degree of confidence. 'It was necessary force. Taz wouldn't have gone in if I hadn't told him to and he stopped when I told him to. If anyone is to blame, it's me, not the dog.'

Jono Johnson's final words to him had been that the dog's part in the affair would be reported but with the evidence in the statements the girls and the neighbour had given, he had no anticipation of any problem. Daniel hadn't detected any malice in the sergeant's bearing, but he was clearly awkward in the company of his ex-colleague, and Daniel found he was glad he didn't have to depend on Jono's intervention on his behalf.

'*Why* didn't they arrest Samir?' Hana wanted to know. 'He should be locked away!'

'Because apart from his temper tantrum with the front door, they haven't got anything to arrest him for,' Daniel replied.

'But he's a bully! He's hit me before.'

'Well, you say you reported it, so it'll be on record and they'll take that into consideration.'

'But his van's still out there. What if he tries again when he comes back for it?'

'I don't think he will. He knows I'm here and he won't fancy a second taster of the dog. But anyway, I expect it'll take quite a while to process him at the station, especially being a Saturday evening, and hopefully Joey'll be back before long.'

When Jo-Ji did turn up, he did so with Jafari in the passenger seat, and watched while he turned the borrowed van round and drove away.

'Why did you help him?' Tamiko demanded crossly. 'Me, I would have made him walk.'

She and Daniel were sitting in the kitchen; Hana and Jahan had already gone to bed, exhausted after a long and eventful day.

'I was coming this way, and it gave me a chance to have a word with him,' Jo-Ji told her. 'Not that he was very forthcoming. He's convinced he's the injured party in all this.'

'I wouldn't waste time talking to him!' Tamiko declared. 'Did you see what he did to our door? If Daniel hadn't come back, he would have broken it down.'

'Did they say anything about Taz at the station?' Daniel wanted to know.

'Not a lot. It's in the report but I wouldn't worry too much. Ropey'll put in a word for you, if necessary.'

'What if he comes back and Daniel isn't here?' Tamiko asked, still worrying about Jafari.

'Well, I'm off for the next couple of days,' Jo-Ji said. 'I think the best thing we can do is try and find somewhere your sister can go, where Jafari wouldn't think of looking, then maybe we can all relax again, yes?' He put his arm round her shoulders and pulled her towards him, but she remained anxious.

'Do you think it was him all the time? The man who was watching me, I mean.'

'I wondered about that. Your sister left him some weeks ago, didn't she? Perhaps he came here hoping she would eventually turn up. After all, he was onto her fairly quickly when she did.'

'Did you ask him?' she said. 'What did he say?'

'I did. He told me to eff off. Not much help. But he's been cautioned, now. He knows if he turns up here again making a nuisance of himself, he'll be arrested. As for me – I'm going to let Dex and Bella out for a pee and then get to bed.'

With Jo-Ji at home to keep an eye on Hana and her son, Daniel was free to ride out with Tamiko again the next day. Being a Sunday, she had no clients, and they were able to set off soon after breakfast. Although it was a short and steady outing, more to stretch limbs and muscles that had worked hard the day before, Daniel thoroughly enjoyed it, beginning to feel quite at home in the saddle.

Tacking up, Tamiko had remembered the borrowed martingale again, and resolved to return it the following afternoon on her way to visit a client.

'I didn't know you did home visits,' Daniel said.

'Mostly, I don't, because with the cost of petrol, I have to charge a big amount, but some people prefer to have treatment in their homes and don't mind to pay, so I go. I see some nice houses,' she added with a smile. 'My client, tomorrow, has much money.'

'I'll come with you.'

'No, really, there's no need. I'll be OK now we know who was watching.'

'We *think* we know,' Daniel demurred. 'But even if it was Jafari, he's still out there and he's not thinking straight. There's no knowing what he might do. Jo-Ji will be here to keep an eye on your sister; it'll be better if I come with you.'

The rest of the day passed uneventfully, and the next afternoon found Daniel and Tamiko on their way to Bath in Tamiko's Peugeot. Daniel had offered to drive her there, but she had laughingly told him that she had a reputation to uphold, which slur on the condition of his Mercedes he took with a show of injured feelings.

'No. You shouldn't have to use your petrol for my work,' she told him, adding with a certain amount of pride, 'and I have advertising for my business on the car.'

The front doors of the navy blue Peugeot did indeed carry the name of 'Tamiko Yoshida, Holistic Therapist', on them, so Daniel gave in and settled into the passenger seat.

The property that Boo Travers called home was a substantial Georgian manor house, the roof and chimneys of which were just visible from the road over a laurel hedge of impressive proportions. A stone set into the wall was inscribed with the words Rufford Manor, which had then been picked out in gold. No obvious lack of money here, either, Daniel thought.

Tall, black, wrought-iron gates stood open, and Tamiko drove in. To the left, the gravel drive swung away between the laurel hedges towards the house, while a fork to the right led downhill towards a five-bar gate under a brick arch, which appeared to form the entrance to the stableyard.

Heading for this, and parking in front of the arch, Tamiko collected the martingale from the back seat of the car and continued on foot, letting herself through the gate and quickly disappearing from Daniel's line of sight.

Alone in the vehicle, he switched the radio on and ran through the pre-set channels. Finding little to his taste, he turned it off again, and sat tapping his fingers. In deference to the hair-free state of Tamiko's vehicle, he had left Taz with Jo-Ji, and now felt ridiculously bereft. The dog was so much a part of who he was and everything he did; Daniel felt incomplete when he wasn't there.

Suddenly Tamiko was back, hurrying and looking a little flustered.

'Sorry I was long time. There is no one there so I decide to put it in the tack room and write a note to her. Then a man comes who is her brother, so I can give it to him.'

'Couldn't you have texted Boo?' Daniel enquired.

'I don't have her number,' Tamiko said, reversing and turning the car. 'I don't really know her very well.'

'But you knew where she lived.'

'Once I came here with Natalie, a few months ago, to see a horse she was buying. Now I must hurry not to be late for my client. It is five more miles.'

Daniel looked sideways at her, a time or two, as she drove, then finally asked, 'Did something happen at Boo's to upset you?'

She shook her head.

'No, not really. It was just that the man I saw was quite angry.'

Daniel frowned.

'Angry? Why should he be?'

'He saw me come from the tack room and ask me who I am and what I do there. I told him I return the martingale and he asked how I get in. He tell me the gates should not be open and I should not come in, but how was I to know that?'

'They were electric gates,' Daniel said. 'Presumably someone left them open by mistake, but that's not your fault, is it? You say it was Boo's brother?'

'Yes. When he ask my name, I say "But I do not know you either", then he tell me.'

'Good for you!' Daniel said. 'You weren't doing anything wrong. Don't worry about it.'

Tamiko's client lived in another Georgian property, but this one was a stately town house standing in beautifully manicured formal gardens in a leafy street on the edge of Bath.

'The problem is there is not always a place to park,' Tamiko said, driving slowly past. 'That is the house of Stella, but there are no spaces on the road here.'

Daniel glanced in through the gateway as they passed and saw a narrow, bricked parking area in front of the house that was already taken up by a sports car and a motorcycle. On the front steps he caught a glimpse of a woman with short blonde hair, in biking leathers and a T-shirt, apparently deep in conversation with an older woman.

Tamiko drove to the end of the road with no luck, and then turned the car in a side road and drove slowly back. As they approached the house once more, they saw a motorcycle emerge from the gateway and pause at the road edge.

'Maybe you can get in now,' Daniel said and Tamiko put her indicator on.

The biker did a quick scan of the road, nodded to Tamiko and pulled away smoothly, leaving the way clear for her to drive in between the gateposts and park.

'I must go, I'm a little late.'

Taking a hold-all from the back of the vehicle, Tamiko said a hasty goodbye to Daniel and hurried towards the impressive, pillared front entrance where she was met by the neatly dressed, grey-haired woman Daniel had seen when they drove past. The woman glanced incuriously in his direction and moments later, she and Tamiko had disappeared inside.

Having been informed that he would be left to kick his heels for at least an hour, Daniel locked the car and went for a walk, once more keenly feeling the absence of the German shepherd at his heels. The area was well kept, expensive-looking and exclusively residential. Daniel had to walk over half a mile to find a small enclave of retail outlets and amongst them a café where he could buy a coffee. He was back at the house and waiting, ten minutes before Tamiko re-emerged.

'It is strange,' she said when they were back on the road. 'I find out my client was first wife of Boo's husband, Dennie Travers; the one that died. I didn't know it before but I mentioned they have names alike. Stella is Stella Travers-King although she mostly just calls herself King, now. When I tell her I have been to give back the martingale, she tells me she is not at all a friend of Boo. She says they were married for twenty-five years when Dennie left her to marry Boo. I think she is very bitter. She got quite upset and called her a bitch. It was very awkward. I wished I hadn't said anything but some clients like you to talk while you are doing a treatment. I think some they are lonely.'

'You weren't to know,' Daniel said. 'It happens. Poor you – you've had quite an afternoon of it, haven't you?'

The following day, Tamiko had no early clients, so she and Daniel took the horses out in the cool of the morning, riding through the lanes, down a grassy bridleway and into the woods beyond. As Taz was more than happy to run at the horses' heels, it was a great way to see the countryside and exercise him thoroughly at the same time.

Tamiko was very companionable now she had shed her initial shyness and he was discovering a sense of humour lurking under the often deadpan exterior. This morning, however, something was troubling her and after a while, he invited her to share her thoughts.

'It's Hana,' she admitted. 'Last night while we talk, she had several messages on her phone and she seemed . . .' She paused, searching for the right phrase. 'Not there?'

'Absent-minded? Pre-occupied?'

'Yes. She wasn't listening much to what I say. I ask her if it is Samir on the phone and she finally say yes. I tell her to ignore him and she say she will, but I'm not sure.'

'Why didn't she say something before? Was he threatening her?'

Tamiko shrugged.

'I'm not sure. She wouldn't let me see the messages. She say she will delete them but I don't think she has.'

'You don't think she'd go back to him?'

'I don't know. I do know she is worried about where she will go and what will happen to her and Jahan. I think she hoped they could stay here but now she realises it wouldn't work. The house is too small, for one thing. I'm worried that if Samir makes promises to her, she might believe him because she wants to believe him.'

'Because it's easier,' Daniel said.

'That's it!' Tamiko seemed relieved that Daniel understood. 'My sister isn't very strong. She's always needed someone to lean against. For a long time it was me but then, when I met Jo-Ji, she looked for someone else, and Samir was there. If she thinks she can't be with me, I'm afraid she'll go back to him.'

Daniel sighed.

'It's a common pattern in abusive relationships. It's sad but sometimes, however much you try, you just can't save people from themselves.'

'But the little boy! Jahan. He's such a sweet child and she adores him. How could she put him at risk? After the way Samir behaved the other night, too.'

'Do you want me to try and talk to her?' Daniel made the offer reluctantly; he had a strong feeling Hana might resent his intrusion. 'Or maybe Jo-Ji would be better.'

'Could you? Hana has always been jealous of Jo-Ji. She feels he took me away from her.'

'OK. I'll see what I can do.'

Any thoughts Daniel may have had about tackling her sister immediately upon his return to the cottage were frustrated by the news, somewhat apologetically imparted by Jo-Ji, that Hana had gone out and taken Tamiko's car.

'I slept in,' he admitted. 'I woke up when Karen arrived, and heard her talking to Hana before her first client came, and then fell asleep again. Sorry.'

'But where has she gone? And to take my car without asking. I can't believe she is so stupid!'

'I asked Karen if she knew anything but she didn't. Apparently Hana said she wouldn't be long, and she's left Jahan with her.'

'She *is* planning to come back, then,' Daniel put in. 'That's something, I suppose.'

'Well, I hope so.' Jo-Ji was a little more cautious.

Tamiko rounded on him, eyes flashing.

'Oh, no! I know you don't think much of my sister, but even *she* wouldn't run away and leave Jahan behind!'

'Unless she thought it was best for him, perhaps,' Daniel suggested cautiously.

'How long is she gone?' Tamiko wanted to know.

'Only about half an hour, I think, from what Karen said. I guess all we can do is wait and see.'

'I'd offer to go looking for her, if we had any idea where she might have gone,' Daniel said.

'You don't think she's gone to meet Samir?' Tamiko asked anxiously.

'It crossed my mind.'

'Surely even she wouldn't be that stupid,' Jo-Ji said.

'I find out last night he sends her text messages,' Tamiko told him. 'I'll try to ring her, now.'

Daniel wasn't very surprised when neither her call nor a text was answered, and with the arrival of Tamiko's first client, all attempts to reach her sister had to be shelved for the time being.

Halfway through the morning, Jahan had grown tired of sitting quietly with a book in Karen's small treatment room, and Daniel offered to take the small boy for a walk with Taz. Even though he gave the boy a piggy-back for the greater part of the expedition, progress was slow as Jahan was entranced by the woods they passed through and wanted to be set down to explore. By the time they returned, Karen had gone home and Tamiko's last client had left, but Hana still hadn't returned and the mood in the cottage was tense.

Tired, Jahan began to be fretful at the absence of his mother and wasn't soothed by their promises that he would see her soon. Tamiko made him a hot chocolate and turned the TV on.

'I hope she doesn't do anything stupid,' Tamiko said quietly, coming back into the kitchen. She picked up her mobile from the table, located a number and called it.

'Well, she already has,' Jo-Ji stated uncompromisingly. 'She doesn't have a car of her own so, for a start, she almost certainly hasn't got any insurance, and come to that, we don't even know if she's got a driving license. But if you're right, and she has gone to meet Samir, she must be absolutely crazy.'

'She still doesn't answer her phone,' Tamiko said worriedly, adding softly, 'What if Samir has hit her again? Attacked her? He has a temper. We don't know if she could be lying somewhere, badly hurt.'

'Surely she'd be sensible enough to meet him somewhere public, wouldn't she?' Daniel said, equally quietly. He cast a look at Jahan but the boy seemed engrossed in a program about a wildlife park.

'I hope so, but . . . I don't know. She is trusting too much, my sister. But how will she know where to go? Here it is all new to her.'

'I can't believe she'd even think of meeting Jafari, after what happened the other night,' Jo-Ji said. 'I suppose we must just be thankful she had the sense to leave the kid behind.'

Daniel had been thinking about what Tamiko had said.

'What if she went back to the shopping centre? It's the only place she knows and it's well signposted. It might be worth me going out there to see.'

Jo-Ji was just agreeing to this plan when the doorbell rang.

'Oh, thank God!' Tamiko exclaimed, hurrying to answer it.

'Tami, wait!' A glimpse of a familiar pattern of blue and green squares through the sitting room window made Daniel urge caution, but she was too swept up in her relief to heed him.

Throwing the door open, she came face to face with a tall, middle-aged police officer.

'Miss Yoshida?' At her nod, the man took his peaked cap off and tucked it under one arm. 'Detective Sergeant Walters. I'm afraid I have some bad news. Do you have anyone with you?'

Tamiko gasped.

'Oh no! My sister! Please tell me what happen. What has he done?'

'I'm afraid your sister has been involved in a serious accident and has been taken to hospital. I can take you there now, if you'd like that.'

'Oh, my God!' Tamiko's voice caught on a sob and Jo-Ji, reaching her side, put his arm round her.

'How?' he asked. 'I mean – what happened?'

'It was a road traffic accident. The car she was driving was hit by another vehicle. I'm sorry.'

A little behind them, Daniel felt a small hand catch at his trouser leg and looked down to see Jahan's dark head peering through the open doorway.

'Where's Mummy?' he asked in a small voice.

# FIVE

The drive to the hospital seemed endless. Tamiko and Jo-Ji left straightaway in the waiting squad car, but Daniel offered to stay behind and lock up, following on a few minutes later with the boy and thus giving the other two time to see how the land lay.

The officer had no detailed information as to Hana's condition, except that she was in a bad way, but his grave face implied that things were indeed extremely serious. They had told Jahan only that his mother was poorly and had gone to see a doctor, which had provoked tears and renewed demands to see her. However, placed on a cushion and strapped into the passenger seat of Daniel's car, he sat in silence throughout the journey to the hospital save for the occasional, doleful sniff. Daniel had a feeling there might have been many times in his young life when being quiet and unobtrusive had been the safest thing, and the thought saddened him.

The hospital and its environs were familiar to Daniel. In his ten years at the Bristol Met, his duties had frequently taken him there and, as now, those occasions had rarely been pleasant.

Parking the car with doubtful legality in a nearby side street, he lifted the little boy onto his hip and headed for the main entrance and A&E.

Inside, there existed the usual bustle and highly charged atmosphere of A&E departments everywhere. Daniel headed for reception, still carrying Jahan. When he enquired as to Hana's whereabouts, the permed and heavily made-up woman behind the plexi-glass wanted to know if he was a relative. Daniel said he was and after favouring him with a doubtful look, the woman gave him directions.

Heading for the door she had indicated, Daniel was aware of a dozen or more minor casualties dejectedly nursing various parts of their anatomy or merely looking miserable. As he lifted his hand to press the door release, he suffered a shock as his glance fell on a pretty young woman with a cloud of dark hair, holding a wad of blood-stained fabric to her face. She was deathly pale and leaning against an older woman, who stroked her shoulder lovingly.

As the door hissed open Daniel was for a brief moment held immobile by the searing clarity of the flashback that hit him. The incident that had led to his resignation had ended in such a way, and it had haunted his dreams for months.

A doctor hurried past, turning sideways to avoid him, and he pulled himself together. That was then; this was now, and the drama of the present was too great to indulge in guilt trips into the past.

He hurried on down the shiny corridor, his soft-soled shoes squeaking on the polished vinyl tiles. Jahan was clinging to him tightly, the thumb of his free hand stuck into his mouth for comfort. They rounded a corner to find Tamiko standing outside a cubicle with drawn curtains.

'Hi. How is she?' Daniel asked, but Tamiko just shook her head and shrugged, the strain showing in her eyes.

'Nobody tells us anything. We see her for a few minutes but then the doctor comes and we have to leave. They say she needs surgery.'

'Where's Joey – er, Jo-Ji?'

A brief smile touched her face. 'It's OK, I know you call him Joey. He's gone to fetch me a coffee. It's not that I want it but he needs to do something.'

'Where's Mummy?' Jahan asked, looking at Tamiko.

'The doctors are looking after her. We have to wait here,' she told him, finding a smile for the boy and stroking his arm.

'Is Mummy poorly?'

'She is, Jahan-chan, but the doctors will make her better,' Tamiko said.

'I want to see her.'

'In a minute, maybe.'

To Daniel's surprise and relief, the little boy seemed to accept this and subsided into silence, once more.

Beyond the curtain, there were sounds of activity and much urgent discussion. From other cubicles came occasional sounds of moaning and demands for attention or help. Occasionally a curtain would twitch aside and a nurse would come bustling out, heading down the corridor on soft-soled shoes, gaze determinedly centred so as not to invite attention from the scattering of anxious relatives waiting for news. To one side an elderly man was lying on a trolley, eyes closed in a white face and skeletal hands clasping the thin blanket that covered him. The atmosphere, as always, was a mixture of fear, worry, boredom and frustration; the soundtrack the continual, monotonous beeping of countless electronic monitors, the trilling of telephones and the murmur of voices discussing other people's destinies.

Jo-Ji reappeared with two lidded, paper coffee cups but even as Daniel greeted him, the mood beyond the curtain underwent a sudden change. There was a flurry of activity, the vocal exchange became more urgent, and a man's voice barked a series of orders including a demand for theatre space. This was obviously not met with the desired response, because moments later he was heard to snap, 'I don't care! We don't have time for that. Tell them we're on our way.'

Tamiko turned a shocked face to her fiancé and, anticipating Hana's emergence from the cubicle, Daniel carried Jahan away down the corridor that he might be spared a view that might upset him further. Glancing back, he saw the trolley bearing the boy's mother, attended by nurses and at least one doctor, being wheeled away with a drip stand pushed along beside it, before it passed from sight round a corner, with Tamiko and Jo-Ji hurrying in its wake.

'Shall we go and find you a chocolate drink?' Daniel asked the little boy, who nodded solemnly in reply, and he set off for the café. At the entrance to the department, they met DS Walters going in the other direction. He showed every sign of walking straight past them until Daniel hailed him.

'They've taken her to theatre,' Daniel said. 'Hana – Miss Yoshida, that is. I gather things have become critical. I imagine it'll be some time before she'll be well enough to be questioned.'

'I saw you at the house,' Walters said. 'You are . . .?'

'Daniel Whelan. A friend of Joey and Tamiko's. This is Hana's son.' Daniel would have liked to question the officer about the circumstances of the accident but the boy's presence precluded that.

'Where's Mummy?' Jahan said, hearing his mother's name.

'She's with the doctors,' Daniel said bending down. 'We're going to get a chocolate drink, do you remember?'

'Daniel Whelan . . .?' the sergeant said on a reflective note. 'Not *PC* Daniel Whelan?'

'Not anymore,' Daniel responded flatly, turning away. 'We'll be in the café if you want us.'

It was in fact Tamiko who found them in the hospital café, over an hour and a half later, by which time Jahan had consumed not one but two hot chocolates and a doughnut, and was now leaning sleepily against Daniel.

'Any news?' Daniel asked quietly, folding up the paper he'd been reading.

Shaking her head wearily, Tamiko slid into a seat on the other side of the table. 'She is still in the operating theatre. They say she has injuries to the head and much bleeding. Jo-Ji is waiting there, talking to the Sergeant Walters. I come to see if you are OK with Jahan. Jo-Ji will text if there is news.'

'Has Walters said anything about the accident?'

'Not much. He says it was very bad. A bigger car – a 4×4, they think – hit her from the side. My car it is very broken – smashed. They are looking for people who see what happen. He tells us there will be another one, soon, who will answer our questions.'

'An FLO – Family Liaison Officer.' Daniel nodded. 'I'll get you a drink. You look shattered.'

She shook her head. 'I'm not thirsty.'

'You'll need energy, though. Have something sweet.' Daniel made as if to move.

'No.' Tamiko put out her hand. 'Don't disturb him. I'll get it, and for you?'

'Thanks. Another latte. Better make it a decaff this time or I won't sleep for days!'

Placing the drinks on the table a minute or two later, she slid into the seat opposite Daniel, bowed her head and rubbed her face and eyes with her hands.

He reached across and touched her arm.

'You OK?'

She looked up. 'Yes . . . No. I feel so guilty, Daniel.'

'I don't suppose it will help to say that people nearly always do in this situation, but it's true. It's also nearly always irrational, but that won't help either. But think about it; what more do you think you could have done?'

She shrugged.

'I don't know. Listened a bit more? I think maybe if I try harder to stop Hana getting involved with Samir at the start . . . I never liked him. I knew he was no good for her. If I play the big sister and tell her no, none of this would have happened.'

'And you have a crystal ball, do you? Besides, *could* you have stopped her? I'm sure she knew you didn't like him but people have a right to live their own lives and make their own mistakes; it's difficult to accept, but true. You didn't ask her to follow you to England in the first place.'

'But I'm her older sister. I should have look after her.'

'She's not a little girl anymore. She's a grown woman, Tami. You tried to help her but she went her own way. You have nothing to feel guilty about.'

Tamiko sighed.

'You are right, I know it, but I can't stop thinking there must have been something I could have done. If she didn't go to meet Samir today . . .'

'You weren't even there when she left. Besides, we don't know for sure that's what she did,' Daniel pointed out.

'But where else?'

He shook his head.

'I don't know. Hopefully she'll be able to tell us herself.'

'But what if she can't – what if . . .?' Tamiko's eyes filled with tears.

'All we can do is wait,' Daniel told her gently. 'Don't torture yourself.'

It was another two hours before there was any news, by which time Tamiko's nerves were stretched to breaking point. On the advice of a nurse, they had all relocated to a family room, where comfortable chairs, magazines and a drinks machine were available. There was also a selection of toys for Jahan to play with, of which, after an initial period of uncertainty, he took full advantage.

Daniel, Jo-Ji and Tamiko sat in silence watching him, having long exhausted the unrewarding cycle of suppositions surrounding Hana's accident.

It was a testament to the state of her nerves that when the door finally opened, Tamiko visibly jumped.

Tall and fiftyish, with thinning grey hair and a deeply lined face, the surgeon who stood in the doorway had clearly come straight from the operating theatre. His hands looked soft and slightly reddened – vigorously scrubbed, Daniel supposed.

'Miss Yoshida?'

'Yes?' Tamiko stood up. 'Please – how is my sister?'

'We've managed to stop the bleeding and I think, for the moment, she's stable, but you must understand that the force of the collision must have been considerable. Unfortunately the impact appears to have been from the side where the whiplash effect is most dangerous. At the side the neck is largely unsupported by muscle and therefore extremely susceptible to damage. Your sister's injuries are complex and she will need further surgery.' He paused and rubbed one eye wearily with the heel of his hand. 'It's striking a balance between the treatment she needs and what her body can sustain at this point.'

Tamiko was frowning as she tried to take in what she was being told.

'But she will be all right?'

The surgeon compressed his lips and lifted his hands in a gesture of helplessness.

'I'd like to be able to reassure you but the truth is, we just don't know. It's too early to be able to make any predictions. She has youth on her side but sometimes that's just not enough. I'm sorry. We can only wait and see.'

'Can I see her?' The tremor in Tamiko's voice showed how close she was to breaking down. Jo-Ji moved close and put his arm round her shoulders.

'Yes.' The surgeon nodded. 'But she is very sleepy and needs to rest. She may not show any signs of response. Please be quiet and don't agitate her.' He stood aside and motioned to where a nurse stood waiting. 'Melinda will take you down when you're ready.'

'Thank you,' Tamiko hurried forward but turned in the doorway as Daniel spoke her name.

'Shall I bring Jahan?'

She looked across to where the boy sat, surrounded by discarded toys, his big, dark-lashed eyes following her every move.

'Yes, I think so. To see might help him understand – unless . . .?' She shot a questioning look towards the surgeon, who nodded.

'It's up to you. You know the child, but I think it is probably a good idea.'

The room to which Hana had been transferred was part of the intensive care unit. Another nurse stood beside the bed, intent upon the monitors, but when they were shown in she stood back to let Tamiko draw close to her sister.

From his position near the door, Daniel could see little other than medical paraphernalia. A frame kept the sheets raised off the lower part of Hana's body and a myriad of tubes and sensors ran from the bed to various drip stands. At the head of the bed the ubiquitous bleeping monitors bore witness to a life on hold.

Tamiko leaned over the bed and kissed her sister, her gleaming black bob swinging forward to hide her face. Jo-Ji held his fiancé's hand, comforting by his presence.

After a bit, Tamiko motioned Daniel forward and, with a word of encouragement, he led Jahan towards the bed. A small plastic footstool stood against the wall and Jo-Ji moved it closer so the boy could be lifted to stand on it.

Silently Jahan stared at his mother with wondering eyes, from his viewpoint not seeing, as Daniel did, a face that told the before and after story, but only her good side, where the sweep of her lashes lay against the smooth skin of her cheek, and only the swathes of bandage that hid most of her dark hair told of the damage within. The other side of her face was almost unrecognisable with a swollen, discoloured eye, bruised and abraded cheekbone and a badly cut lip just visible through the oxygen mask. Her olive complexion was pallid and a brace supported her damaged neck.

Jahan put a small hand towards her and pointed. 'Mummy asleep,' he said turning to Tamiko.

'She is, darling. She has to sleep much, so she can get better,' Tamiko told him, her eyes filling with tears.

'How about we leave Mummy to sleep and go and find some ice cream?' Daniel suggested, and was relieved to see Jahan's attention instantly diverted by the idea. In his time on the force he had seen the devastation caused by countless RTAs and he knew from sad experience that the outcome of side impacts was rarely good. The surgeon's words had confirmed his suspicion that Hana's neck was broken. She was lucky to have survived this long; most didn't. As he turned away, he caught Jo-Ji's eye and saw the same knowledge there.

As the afternoon wore on, Daniel began to worry about Taz, shut up in the cottage, and when a kindly nurse offered to make up a bed for Jahan, who was finding it increasingly difficult to stay awake, he sought Tamiko out at her sister's bedside and announced his intention of returning home to let the dog out.

'Do you want me to see to the horses, too?' he asked.

'Daniel, would you?' she exclaimed in quick gratitude.

'Of course.'

'Can you remember how . . .?'

'I'll manage. Don't you worry.'

It was a relief to leave behind the emotionally charged atmosphere of the hospital and emerge into the warm breeze of the August evening. As always, there was a moment of readjustment as the sounds of the city replaced the electronic rhythms of the intensive care unit; it took that fraction of a second to realise that outside, life continued as normal, oblivious to the heartache and drama within the hospital walls. Daniel often thought that brief period of transition was like coming out of a cinema after a deeply absorbing film.

He reached his car, removed a parking ticket from beneath the windscreen wiper, then slumped into the driver's seat, pulled the door shut and closed his eyes. The penalty notice wasn't unexpected and hardly important in the scheme of things; an insignificant pinprick in a day of raw hurt.

On his own, he could finally allow his mind to run along the avenues it had been pulling towards, ever since news of Hana's accident had reached them. Because of having to keep Jahan occupied, Daniel had had no chance for more than a word or two with Jo-Ji, and that in Tamiko's hearing, but he would have laid a sizeable bet on Jo-Ji's thoughts running along the same lines. Was Hana's accident just that – an accident – or had Samir Jafari, unable to accept that she would actually leave him, lost control and taken his revenge? If Tamiko's sister was to be believed, it would have been by no means the first time he had resorted to violence when his will was crossed.

Daniel sighed and started the car. Until they had more details, conjecture was pointless. The police had first-hand knowledge of Jafari and doubtless they would be pursuing the same line of thought. Indeed, if there was sufficient cause to suspect that the collision was anything but accidental, they might already have pulled Hana's ex-partner in for questioning.

That they hadn't became immediately obvious on Daniel's return to the cottage, because the first thing he saw was Jafari's white van parked in the lane and the man himself standing in the front garden peering into the ground floor windows.

When Daniel parked and got out of his car, he could hear Taz's deep voice from inside the cottage, warning the trespasser, in no uncertain manner, that he'd better stay away.

As Daniel approached, Jafari turned to meet him, spreading his hands in a placating manner.

'I ain't done nuffing,' he said, before Daniel had a chance to demand what he was doing there. 'I just wanted to talk.'

'You were told to stay away. She doesn't want to see you,' Daniel stated.

'Ah, but that's not true. She does. I've seen her and she's realised she was wrong. She's gonna come back with me.'

'You've seen her? When?'

'Earlier this morning. She gave you the slip, didn't she? Didn't you wonder where she'd gone? She was with me, wasn't she? You tried to stop her but I knew she wanted to come back to me. She don't know nuffing else, does she? She's lost without me.'

'Then why did she run away in the first place?' Daniel asked, his mind busy with a dilemma. 'And where is she now?'

For the first time, Jafari showed doubt. 'She came back to get the boy,' he stated.

'When did you last see her?'

'This morning, I told you! Why all the fuckin questions? She wants to be with me and there's nothing you can do to stop her.'

'True. But if that's the case, what are you doing here?'

'Come to pick her up, didn't I?'

'She's not here.'

'Why? Where is she? What have you done with her?' He started to bristle with suspicion.

Either Jafari was a consummate actor or he was completely ignorant of what had happened to Hana that morning. Daniel didn't know him well enough to be sure, and although on the surface he appeared to have all the subtlety of the proverbial bull in the china emporium, he suspected there might well be a strong vein of cunning in the man. It was just possible that his presence at the cottage, demanding to know her whereabouts, was part of a bluff to conceal his part in the 'accident' that had all but killed her, but Daniel thought it unlikely. He decided to trust his instincts.

'I'm afraid Hana has been involved in an accident,' he said, watching the other man closely. 'I'm sorry. She's been taken to Bristol Hospital. I'm afraid she's in a bad way.'

'You're lying! I just saw her this morning.'

'It must have happened on her way home, then. We've been at the hospital all afternoon.'

'And the boy? Where's my boy?'

'He's at the hospital, too. He's OK. He wasn't in the car with her but of course, if you saw her this morning, you'd know that.'

'What hospital? Where is it?'

'Bristol.'

'If I find out you're lying . . .' Jafari didn't complete the threat, but his narrowed eyes and tight lips conveyed the message.

'For God's sake, man! Why would I lie about something like that?'

'To keep me away from her.'

'What – for all of an hour or two? What would be the point?'

Casting him a glance of deep dislike, Jafari muttered something unintelligible, pushed past Daniel and headed for his van.

'The police are there, waiting to talk to her,' Daniel called, just to be sure Jafari didn't entertain any ideas of causing trouble at the hospital. With that thought in mind, he took out his mobile and called Jo-Ji to warn him of Jafari's impending arrival, before addressing himself to the business of seeing to the animals.

It was mid-evening before Daniel returned to the hospital, by which time he had brought the horses in from the field and fed them, exercised all the dogs, and even fed the cats, who managed to put aside their lingering distrust of him just enough to accept the food he put down, although Shinju still watched him closely with her deep-blue Siamese eyes and wouldn't settle to eat until he had left the kitchen.

At the hospital he found everything much as he had left it, the warmth, noise and emotional intensity wrapping around him like an unwanted blanket as soon as he entered the building.

He found Tamiko still at Hana's bedside. She greeted Daniel with an attempt at a smile and the information that her sister's condition was unchanged, and said that Jo-Ji was checking on Jahan.

'Did Jafari turn up?' Daniel asked softly.

'Yes, he did. He wants to see Hana but they don't let him in. Then he wants to know where Jahan is but Jo-Ji had warn the police and nurses, and they keep him away. The police now take him to ask questions about the accident.' She raised worried eyes to Daniel's. 'You don't think it was him who hurt Hana, do you?'

'Actually, I don't. I would swear he was genuinely shocked

when I told him what had happened. But I could be wrong, and obviously the police have to question him. At least it keeps him out of the way for a bit,' he added. 'Can I get you anything? A coffee, or tea? Something to eat? You look exhausted.'

'No, thank you. I had a drink not long ago. Are the horses OK?'

Daniel opened his mouth to answer but was forestalled by a low moan from the girl on the bed.

'Hana!' Tamiko breathed, getting to her feet and leaning over her sister. 'Hana, can you hear me?'

'Tami . . .' Daniel spoke her name in warning, though he didn't follow it up. His eyes were on the monitors and even as he registered that the displays were changing, Hana's breathing altered, becoming uneven and harsh. Her body gave a slight jerk, the visible side of her face flinched, and then the displays flat-lined and an alarm sounded.

'Hana?' For a moment Tamiko was uncomprehending and as the sound of hurrying footsteps approached the door, Daniel took her arm and drew her away from her sister.

'No!' she struggled against him, hitting out at him.

'Tami! They need space,' he said urgently, catching at her free hand.

Suddenly the room was full of people and noise, the bed was surrounded and a nurse was there, insisting that they stand back and give the medics room. A young doctor bent over Hana.

'You need to wait outside,' the nurse said, firmly but kindly, and with Daniel's help, shepherded Tamiko through the open door and into the corridor beyond.

For Daniel there was a kind of inevitability about what followed. He had seen it all before, even if he hadn't been so closely involved on previous occasions. The frantic but controlled activity of the hospital staff, the sounds beyond the door as they tried to restore life, the way that everything happened in double-quick time, yet seemed also to be in slow-motion.

Tamiko was staring at the closed door with wide, scared eyes and with his arm around her shoulders he could feel her trembling violently. There was nothing to say; reassurances were meaningless. In the next few minutes her sister would either live or die; they both knew it, and words of comfort would change nothing.

It was ten minutes before the door opened, and the doctor's expression was all that was needed to tell them that Hana had lost her fight for life.

'No! . . .' Tamiko began to sob and Daniel squeezed her shoulders.

'I'm sorry,' the doctor said. 'There was nothing we could do. There was just too much . . . . . . It was hopeless.'

'But she's so young, . . .' Tamiko said through her tears, as if that fact would prove his statement false. 'She's my little sister.'

'I'm sorry,' the doctor said again. He looked tired and a little dispirited. 'She had too many injuries. Internal injuries. We tried but there was nothing we could do.' A pager clipped to his breast pocket began flashing and he glanced down but ignored it.

'But it was so quick. A minute ago she was OK. She even make a noise. . . .'

'The machines were keeping her alive. I'm sorry. Had she survived, it's very likely that her brain would have been damaged. There really was nothing we could do.'

Tamiko took a shuddering, steadying breath. 'Can I see her?'

'In a minute. The nurse will tell you when. I'm so sorry,' he repeated, and with a brief, sad smile, took a step backwards and then round them, disengaging himself from one tragedy and moving on to try and prevent another. Moments later he was striding away down the corridor, responding to his pager as he did so.

Tamiko turned to look up at Daniel. Her eyes were swimming with unshed tears.

'What am I going to do?' she asked brokenly.

'Come here, love,' he said softly and gathered her close, shaken by the strength of his wish to protect and comfort her. She was still trembling and as she clung to Daniel she began to sob again silently. He stroked her back, resisting the urge to kiss the top of her head; saying instead, 'Shall I text Joey?'

Still clinging, she nodded, and he freed up one hand to remove his phone from the back pocket of his jeans.

They were still in the corridor when Jo-Ji appeared, less than a minute later.

'I was on my way,' he explained. 'I saw the doctor. Darling, I'm so sorry!'

'Oh, Jo-Ji,' she cried and left Daniel's embrace for that of her fiancé. Jo-Ji held her tight, rubbing her back and touching his lips to her hair.

The door behind them opened and two nurses came out, a third pausing in the doorway to tell them it was all right to go in now, if they wanted.

Over the nurse's shoulder Daniel could see Hana, free now of the tubes and wires, her face still and calm.

Tamiko went hesitantly forward, Jo-Ji half a step behind, holding her hand. Daniel watched as they approached the bed and then he turned away. This was a family affair.

The nurse gave him a small, sad smile and sighed. 'It never gets any easier,' she said. 'Especially when they're so young. It's such a waste.'

Daniel nodded. 'I used to be a policeman.'

'Then you'll know,' she said, nodding, and touched his arm briefly as she moved away.

Because he wanted one and there wasn't anything else he could usefully do, Daniel went in search of a decent coffee, returning a little later with a tray bearing three lidded cardboard cups.

Jo-Ji and Tamiko were still with Hana. Tamiko was by the bed, holding her sister's hand in silent misery, but as Daniel hesitated in the doorway, Jo-Ji left her side and came over.

'Is Jafari still with the police?' Daniel asked, low-voiced. Jo-Ji nodded.

'Have you heard anything?'

'Not so far. They won't talk to me, of course. Investigators are on site and Walters did tell me they were concerned about the circumstances of the accident.'

'In what way, exactly?'

'Well, it's a hit-and-run, so they're looking for witnesses. We can't discount the idea that it might have been deliberate.'

'Mm.' Daniel proffered the tray of drinks. 'I may be wrong, but however much I dislike Jafari, I'm inclined to believe that he knew nothing of this till I told him,' he said finally.

'Well, I hope you're wrong,' Jo-Ji said. 'Because if it wasn't him, I don't even want to consider the alternative.'

'I know. Hana was driving Tami's car, and from a distance they

don't look dissimilar . . .' Reluctantly, Daniel voiced what they
were both thinking.

'Yeah.' Jo-Ji looked bleak.

'Shit.'

'Yeah.' Jo-Ji nodded.

They both knew that if the crash hadn't been accidental and
Jafari was cleared of blame, then far from having come to a
tragic end, their troubles might just be beginning.

# SIX

'Well, he's finally sleeping.' Tamiko came into the
kitchen where Jo-Ji and Daniel were drinking beer
over the debris and remains of take-away fish and
chips. 'I'm not sure he really understand what is happening, but
I think maybe that is good.'

'Come and sit down, love, you look shattered,' Jo-Ji said. 'I'll
make you a cup of tea. Daniel?'

'Please.' It was nearly midnight and Daniel was feeling tired
himself, and he hadn't anywhere near the same level of emotional
involvement that Tamiko had. She had hardly eaten anything.
He drained his glass and gathered up the greasy paper, wrapping
it round the inevitable surfeit of chips and dumping the lot in
the bin.

'Recycling . . .' Tamiko protested faintly.

'Not tonight,' he stated.

Silence fell, broken only by the chinking of a spoon against
china as Jo-Ji stirred the tea. It had been an evening of long
silences.

'I keep thinking about Jahan,' Tamiko said finally. '*Kawaiso
ne* – poor little boy. He have so much trouble for such a short
life.'

'Well, he's lucky to have you looking out for him,' Daniel
responded. 'I was very impressed with the way you took charge
at the hospital. That nurse was left standing with her mouth
open!'

'To be honest, so was I,' Jo-Ji told him. 'I have known Tami for four years and *I've* never seen her like that.'

'Well, somebody has to do something!' she exclaimed. 'That stupid woman who say he must wait for a social worker. And then what? Couldn't she see that what he needs most is people he knows, hot food and a bed?'

'I was very proud of you,' her fiancé stated. 'And the image of you standing toe to toe with that nurse and wagging your finger at her is one I shall treasure for years to come.'

Daniel nodded. The amply proportioned ward sister had dwarfed Tamiko's diminutive form but she had in no way allowed the woman to dominate her, informing her that if the social worker wished to see the child, she was welcome to visit him at the cottage – tomorrow.

'I was just so angry,' Tamiko said in a smaller voice. 'About everything. And then that woman . . . Was I rude?'

'No. Don't worry.' Jo-Ji put her mug of tea on the table and kissed the top of her head. 'Drink this and get to bed.'

'But I won't sleep,' she protested. 'How can I? There is so much we have to think about – to decide. What happens to Jahan now? What if Samir—'

'One day at a time,' Jo-Ji said sitting beside her and putting his arm round her shoulders. 'What is that saying you're so fond of?'

'Yes, I know. "*Ashitawa ashitano kazega fuku*",' she murmured, translating for Daniel's benefit, '"Tomorrow it will blow tomorrow's wind". It is true; I say it many times to others but now I find it not so easy to follow. My sister I already miss very much and I worry so much about her little boy. I don't know what to do. It is all seeming such a mess.'

'Jahan isn't just *your* problem,' Daniel told her. 'You've got Joey to help you and, if there's anything I can do, you have me, too. Things will sort themselves out eventually. I'm so sorry about Hana.'

'If only she hadn't gone to meet Samir, she would still be here,' Tamiko said, tears filling her eyes once more.

'I'm sorry. I feel a bit responsible for that,' Jo-Ji admitted.

'But you couldn't know,' she exclaimed. 'It wasn't your fault. But why is he again being questioned? They don't think – I mean, it was an accident, wasn't it?'

'It's routine.' Jo-Ji and Daniel had agreed not to tell her of their suspicions just yet. 'But given his history, we have to check Jafari's movements, just in case.'

Tamiko shook her head. 'He's a bully and I think maybe he has hit her one time, but surely he wouldn't try to kill her?'

'It depends what she said to him when they met, this morning,' Jo-Ji said. 'If she didn't tell him what he wanted to hear, who knows . . .? But Daniel got the impression they had come to some agreement, so let's hope he's in the clear.'

'How awful it would be for Jahan, when he's older, to find out that his father had killed his mother,' Tamiko suggested.

'I honestly don't think it'll come to that,' Daniel said gently. 'Jo-Ji's right. This is getting us nowhere. We're all too tired to think straight. We should get to bed.'

Tamiko pushed her chair back. 'I'll just go to see the horses first.'

'I can do that,' Daniel offered.

'No. It is for myself I need to see.' Perhaps aware that her tone had been sharp, she added, 'I'm sorry. That was rude. I just feel that, after everything, I won't rest until I have seen that they are OK. I need something to be right. To be normal.'

'I'll come with you, then,' Daniel said.

Tamiko looked as though she were going to protest further, so he added, 'Taz needs to stretch his legs.' He didn't want to have to explain to her at this point that until they knew for sure who had driven their car into the side of Tamiko's car, he and Jo-Ji were going to make sure that she was never out of their sight.

The next morning brought authority in the burly person of DS Walters and a female colleague with auburn hair, who Jo-Ji greeted as Sue, and who was introduced as the Family Liaison Officer assigned to Hana's case.

Jo-Ji answered the door and brought them through to the kitchen where Daniel and Tamiko were sitting having a late breakfast after an early ride. No matter what the human tragedy, the animals still had their needs and Tamiko had wanted to ride, to clear her head. She had cancelled her clients for the day, but Karen had just arrived and Jahan had followed her upstairs to her treatment room where he was happily, if somewhat messily, engaged with a colouring book and crayons while she worked.

'What news?' Jo-Ji asked. Rostered on duty, he had been given compassionate leave to be with Tamiko.

'We haven't yet found a witness who saw the collision, but we're going to put a notice out at the roadside and see if anyone comes forward,' Walters reported. Bald-headed, with just a shadow of a ring of hair at the lower edge of his scalp, he had a slightly avuncular air about him.

'Was it – do you think it was Samir?' Tamiko asked.

'No. He's in the clear. He did meet your sister at the shopping centre, as he said, but at the time of the collision he was refuelling at a garage on the Bath road. They have him on CCTV.'

'That's convenient for him,' Jo-Ji observed dryly. 'Do we know if he's down here alone? If he *was* with her yesterday morning, he'd have a pretty good idea of her route home. He could have had someone waiting at a convenient point while he established his alibi at the petrol station. What about this Assim Kahn character that owns the van?'

'I can't really discuss the investigation with you, you know that,' Walters told him, apologetically. 'But of course, we're checking everything out.'

'So where did it happen?'

'That's the interesting thing,' the sergeant said, naming a rural B road, southwest of Bath. 'Not the most ideal spot to set up an accident, one would think.'

'I know that road,' Tamiko said. 'We use it the other day, when I drop off the martingale and visit my client, do you remember, Daniel? But why would she have been there? That's not the way home.'

'We have no way of knowing,' the FLO spoke for the first time. 'It's possible she just took the wrong road.'

'There are road works on that stretch of the road,' Walters added, unbending a little from his strictly procedural stance. 'She was stationary at the lights. We believe that the vehicle that hit her was travelling in the opposite direction and it looks like it just swerved into her, pushing her car into a tree at the side of the road. I'm sorry, miss,' he added, as Tamiko flinched at his words.

'So it doesn't *look* as though it was premeditated,' Daniel put in. 'Not an ideal choice of location, one would have thought. On the other hand, it's a strange place to lose control – on a straight road.'

'There was mud on the road but it seems the vehicle that hit her made no attempt to stop,' Walters said. 'The collision was heard by a farmer in a nearby field and it was him that called the ambulance. He reported that the other driver drove away straight after the incident.'

'His vehicle must have taken a bit of a battering,' Jo-Ji observed. 'Did no one see it further along the road?'

'That's what we need to find out,' Walters said. 'But forensics think the vehicle probably had bull bars fitted. It may have come off relatively lightly. We are working to trace it. It could hold valuable DNA evidence.'

'Unless they've torched it,' Daniel responded.

'Yes. Unfortunately that's often the case,' Walters agreed. 'We do, however, have a couple of mobile phone traces for that area at the time of the collision. One of them is your sister's phone but if we can track the others down, we might have our man – or woman, of course.'

'He uses his phone after driving into my sister?' Tamiko asked bitterly.

'Not necessarily used it,' Jo-Ji told her. 'Phones are talking to the nearest masts all the time – we can pick up those signals and triangulate a position for any given phone at any time, even if it's not actually being used. People don't realise, they're like little trackers that we take with us everywhere.'

'Anyway,' Sergeant Walters said, 'I just need to ask you a few more questions about your sister's recent movements and her relationship with Samir Jafari, and then Constable Reece will explain her role as the liaison officer. Basically, she'll be your first point of contact from now on; anything you want to know, any worries – yes, well, I'll let her explain.'

Jo-Ji had barely closed the door on the departing backs of his colleagues when another car drew up in the lane outside the cottage, and a plump young woman in an over-tight skirt and cream blouse climbed out and began to make her slightly unsteady way up the path on impractically high heels.

In her mid twenties, with a friendly smile and a broadly Bristolian accent, she introduced herself as Cara Siddons and produced ID that backed up her claim to be a social worker.

Tamiko immediately assumed a defensive stance, but having met Jahan and asked numerous questions of Jo-Ji and his fiancée, good sense miraculously prevailed, and Cara announced that although the situation would have to be reviewed, she was satisfied that the boy was in the best place for the time being. Reams of paperwork followed and countless forms had to be filled in and signed before the social worker stood up, twitched her skirt into place over her curvy behind and departed with a cheery wave and a clop of stiletto heels.

'Thank God.' Tamiko heaved a sigh and looked at Jo-Ji. 'I hope no one else come now.'

'You've been brilliant,' he said, slipping one arm round her and ruffling Jahan's hair with his free hand. 'Both of you.'

'So what happen now?' Tamiko asked. 'My head is . . . . . .' She made a circling movement with her hand and looked at Jo-Ji for help.

'Whirling? Spinning? I'm not surprised.'

'But what I must do and I wish not, is phone my parents,' she said. 'I don't know how I will tell them. I can hardly believe it myself. Hana was my father's favourite. Even her name means that – favourite. He will be very sad.'

It was mid evening; the day had been a long one, taken up with all the dreary formalities that follow a death, but now animals and humans had been fed, Jahan had gone to bed, and it was the first time Daniel, Jo-Ji and Tamiko had had the opportunity to relax.

After a day of dealing with the authorities and endless conjecture, the three of them had talked themselves out but although the TV was on, the volume was turned low and none of them were really watching. Outside the open window, a blackbird's alarm call sounded in the dusky lane, possibly pinpointing the location of one of the cats, and in the kitchen, Taz was stretched out on the cool, tiled floor, apparently asleep but not so deeply that he didn't open his eyes whenever Daniel so much as shifted his position on the beanbag.

After fidgeting for a while, Tamiko stood up and disappeared across the hall into the room Jo-Ji used as his study. For several minutes, the two men could hear her rummaging and eventually, Jo-Ji called out to ask if she needed any help.

'No, I'm fine. I have find it now,' came the muffled reply, and in due course Tamiko reappeared carrying a large white box which bore the insignia of a local removal company. She placed it on the carpet and knelt down in front of it.

'What have you got there?' Jo-Ji asked.

'Just some things. Family things. I realise today that Jahan has never know his grandparents – never seen a picture, even – so I thought I find photograph that is still packed since we came here.'

Daniel and Jo-Ji watched with lazy interest as she tore the tape from the box and delved inside, lifting out a number of keepsakes wrapped in newspaper, followed by three large photograph albums. Sitting back on her heels, she began to leaf through the first of these, absorbed in her memories and occasionally turning the book round to show Daniel pictures of Japan, her childhood home and family.

'This one is my whole family when I was about twelve years,' she said at one point. 'That is me sitting in the front; my mother, my father, my sisters – that is Hana, pulling a face at the camera – and my two brothers. My uncle and aunt stand at the back. We are a big family. Ah, in this one you can better see my parents. My mother, she is beautiful, I think.'

Daniel looked at the small faded print, seeing a middle-aged woman with a familiar, heart-shaped face.

'You are very like her,' he commented, without thinking.

Tamiko blushed a little, delving into the box once more.

'Somewhere, I have a copy of that photo in a frame, which is bigger,' she said, as Daniel carried on turning the pages of the album. Jo-Ji, who had almost certainly seen them before, took his phone from his pocket and began to scroll through his messages.

'Ah, here it is,' Tamiko said presently, holding up a silver frame. 'Tomorrow I will show it to Jahan.'

She laid the photograph on top of the leather-bound albums and began to replace the other items in the box.

'One day I hope we will have a house that is bigger and these things can be seen,' she said wistfully, then paused, frowning. 'Oh! . . .'

Jo-Ji looked up. 'What is it?'

'That is strange. This man I have seen somewhere.'

She had smoothed out a sheet of the newspaper wrapping and was pointing at the picture.

'Who is it?'

'I'm not sure,' Tamiko bent closer to read the text. 'It says, a businessman. Oh, Dennis Travers! He must be the one who was husband of Stella, in Bath, who I give massage to.'

'Well, you can't have seen him recently,' Jo-Ji observed, returning his attention to his phone. 'He died a couple of years ago. Boating accident. It was big news at the time.'

'Perhaps you saw a photograph at Stella's house?' Daniel suggested.

'Maybe,' she said doubtfully. 'But I don't think so. She was angry when she spoke of him. I don't think she'd have a photo for people to see.'

'Well, maybe he just reminds you of someone,' he said. 'Can I have a look?'

Tamiko handed him the newspaper and he looked at the rather grainy photograph, which showed a suited businessman cutting the tape at the opening of a building that the text named as a new youth club. According to the glowing encomium that accompanied the photo, Dennis Travers (46) had been a philanthropist of no common order, making generous gifts to various good causes. Either he was indeed a candidate for canonisation or he had a friend on the editorial staff of the paper, Daniel thought cynically, looking more closely at the man in the picture.

Dennis Travers, at the time managing director of Travers-King Construction, appeared to be of average height and build. In a black and white photograph it was difficult to judge hair colour but it appeared to be either fair or greying, and receding at the temples. He wore a benign smile, as did those around him, and peering closely, Daniel, who had a good memory for faces, also felt the man looked vaguely familiar and mentally scanned the new acquaintances of recent days.

'You're right. Actually, I think he looks a bit like Boo Travers' son. The one we saw at the show,' he told Tamiko. 'Hmm. There's a thought . . .'

'You are right! Stella tell me she finds that Dennie had been cheating on her long time,' Tamiko said. 'You are thinking maybe Harrison is Dennie's son?'

'It makes you wonder, doesn't it, but if that's the case, your Stella has good reason to be bitter. I'd say Boo's son must be getting on for thirty, from what I remember.'

'Poor lady. I wonder how long she knows he cheats.'

'It might have come as a complete surprise,' Jo-Ji put in. 'You'd be amazed at how long a relationship can go on without one partner knowing anything about what the other is doing.'

'Especially if they don't *want* to know,' Daniel added.

'You make me worried, now,' Tamiko joked, looking at her fiancé, but Jo-Ji just laughed.

'You'd catch me out straightaway,' he told her. 'I'm a hopeless liar.'

The next couple of days were taken up with arrangements for Hana's funeral. Jo-Ji had returned to work and the FLO contacted them with the frustrating news that there was as yet no trace of the hit-and-run vehicle, though they were fairly certain that they were looking for a 4×4, possibly a Land Rover.

With no available DNA evidence and no witnesses, the investigation appeared to have stalled. Of the mobile phone signals that had been picked up at the time and place of the accident, two had been traced and their users cleared but the third remained unaccounted for and was no longer emitting a signal. It seemed that whether the crash had been intentional or not, the driver had been very thorough in covering his tracks.

A mood of depression descended on No. 5 Tannery Lane, not helped by Jahan, who, after asking for his mother a couple of times, had retreated into his own world, showing no emotion and not offering to talk unless spoken to.

'I wish he would cry or be angry,' Tamiko told Daniel as they exercised the horses, early on Friday morning. 'It's not natural for a little boy to be so quiet.'

'I think it's probably a survival strategy. I get the feeling he's learned that keeping quiet is the safest bet. I don't think he's had a very happy life, so far.'

'Yes, I agree,' she said, nodding sadly. 'The only thing he show any interest in since Hana's accident, is the horses. He want to know if he can go to watch the horses jumping again, but I have to tell him, not for a while.'

'Are there no shows coming up?'

'Well, yes. There is one on Sunday that I have entered, but it doesn't seem right.'

'I understand what you mean,' Daniel said. 'But there's nothing you can do for your sister now except look after her little boy, and if you think going to a show would cheer him up, then why not go?'

Tamiko frowned. 'I don't know . . . What would people think?'

'Realistically, most people won't know. If you meet friends there, you can explain. Wear a black armband, if you like, as a mark of respect. It's your call, but personally I think it would be good for you, too. There is nothing more to be done until the funeral and sitting around feeling miserable won't achieve anything.'

Tamiko looked thoughtful.

'I don't mean to interfere,' Daniel added. 'But, whatever you do, do it for yourself and Jahan. Don't worry about other people – it's none of their business.'

'No, you don't interfere. I am grateful. I will think about it,' she said then. 'Now we should hurry to get back so Jo-Ji can go to work.'

# SEVEN

Half past seven on the Sunday morning found Daniel, Tamiko and Jahan en route to an agricultural show near Oxford. Tamiko had agonised for a long while about the morality of attending the show but when she tentatively mentioned it to the boy, Jahan's eager reaction swiftly banished any remaining doubts. They had given him such minor tasks as he could safely carry out during the preparations and now he sat between them, wide-awake despite the early start, with a light of expectation in his coal-dark eyes.

On the monitor, three horses could be seen in the rear of the lorry: large, placid Samson unconcernedly pulling at his haynet, Rolo, head high and showing the whites of his eyes, and Natalie's young horse, Raffa, who was leaning against the partition for support but appeared otherwise calm. On this occasion, Natalie's groom, Inga, was travelling with them in the living area to the rear of the cab, for which Daniel was extremely grateful. Remembering Rolo's excitable behaviour at the Devon show, he had not relished the idea of having to cope with him, Natalie's youngster, *and* Jahan.

Once the showground was reached, Inga immediately proved her worth as a groom, swinging into action with an efficiency that made Daniel wonder how Tamiko had put up with his own fumbling efforts with such good humour, the week before. Finding his presence around the horsebox surplus to requirements for the present, Daniel offered to take the boy off to see the sights and duly set off with Jahan's hand held firmly in his.

It was not so many years since he had led his own son in such a way, but at that age, Drew had been a far livelier youngster. Jahan walked obediently at his side, never lagging behind or pulling towards something that had caught his attention; only his quick dark eyes showing the depth of his excitement. Looking down at him, Daniel decided the boy must have inherited whatever family gene had brought Tamiko halfway across the world to indulge her passion for horses.

According to a map of the showground, the secretary's tent was on the far side of the horse rings, and as Tamiko had asked him to fetch another copy of the ring plan to replace one she had lost, Daniel headed that way.

Horses were being led or ridden all around them as the first classes of a busy day got underway. Although it was a mixed agricultural show, the horses had been assigned a field of their own, presumably to minimise the risk to spectators, and the concentration of horseflesh in that one area could have been daunting to a less interested child. To one side of the field a small city of equine-themed trade stalls had been set up on a grid pattern, and already a good number of people were browsing along the alleyways.

'What colour horses do you like the best?' he asked the boy as they paused beside a ring where a dozen gleaming hunters were being shown in-hand.

'The white ones,' Jahan replied, instantly.

'They are beautiful, aren't they? Did you know that most white horses are born very dark brown, and that proper horse people always call them grey, not white?'

'That one's white,' Jahan said, pointing to a very light grey pony in one of the showing rings.

'It is, but it's still called grey. The only true white horses are called albinos, and they have pink skin under their white coats.'

'Actually, that's a myth,' a voice said close behind Daniel. Surprised, he turned to find Boo Travers standing there, her auburn fringe lifting in the light breeze. She smiled, showing perfectly even, white teeth. 'There *are* no true albino horses. You occasionally get an albino foal born but they never survive. It's actually called Lethal White – a defective gene. Something to do with the nervous system, if I remember rightly,' she added. 'Hi, again. Daniel, isn't it? We met last week. Is Tami here, then? I didn't think – that is, I'd heard there'd been an accident, is she OK?'

'She's fine. Well, still in shock and grieving for her sister, of course, but she's doing amazingly well. Where did you hear about it?'

'Oh, you know – the riders' grapevine, I guess. Nothing much stays a secret for long. Her sister – God, that's awful! She must be devastated. What happened exactly?'

Daniel frowned and shook his head slightly, casting a brief significant glance down in Jahan's direction.

'You should talk to Tami,' he suggested quietly, adding in a brighter tone, 'this is her nephew, Jahan. He wanted to come along to see the horses, didn't you, Jahan? And we thought it would do us all good to get out.'

'I like the grey ones,' the boy announced, the reference to Hana apparently having passed him by, as Daniel had hoped it would.

'So do I,' Boo confided, bending towards him. 'I've got a grey one in my horsebox. He's called Frankie Foo and he's very friendly. Maybe you can come and see him later.' Straightening up she said to Daniel, 'Tell Tami I'm so very sorry, and I'll catch up with her later,' and with a wave of her hand, turned to walk away across the showground, her slim figure neat in navy-blue corduroy jodhpurs.

Daniel watched her go with narrowed eyes. She was undeniably attractive. Had she really been the 'other woman' in her eventual husband's life for the best part of thirty years? She would surely not have lacked other offers and from the little he had seen of her, Daniel found it hard to believe she'd be content to play second fiddle for such a long period of time. She gave the impression of being a woman who would know what she wanted from life and find a way to get it, but he acknowledged that opinion was built on very little substance – his copper's intuition cutting in – and that had been wrong before now.

A tug on his sleeve recalled his attention to his small charge.

'Can we go and see the lady's grey horse?'

'Not now, Jahan. We're supposed to be finding the secretary's tent for Aunty Tami, remember? Come on, let's go.'

With Inga in attendance, Daniel found he had little to do to help apart from looking after Jahan, which wasn't onerous. Tamiko had a very successful morning, both with her own horse and the two belonging to Natalie, and watching her performances with his semi-educated eye, Daniel felt that she was a horsewoman of some considerable skill. Although diminutive in stature, she seemed to have developed a strong rapport with her equine partners that completely counteracted any disadvantage her size might have conferred on her.

'I worry that my sadness might upset the horses and make them difficult,' she confided to Daniel as they had a quick lunch in the horsebox. 'But it is the opposite. It's as though they have make me calmer. Or perhaps they are not feeling me as much as I thought,' she added with a small shrug.

'I think they are very in tune with you. By the way, have you seen Boo Travers? We ran into her earlier, didn't we, Jahan?'

'We're going to see the grey horse,' the boy responded, waving sticky fingers. 'The lady promised.'

'We were talking about grey horses and she invited Jahan to go and meet hers,' Daniel clarified.

'That'll be Frankie. He's lovely. Mind you say thank you,' Tamiko told her nephew. 'Yes, I see her in the distance but not to talk with.'

'She'd heard about the accident but I have a feeling she may have thought you'd been involved. Anyway, she asked if you were OK, and said she'd catch up with you later.'

'Well, it *was* my car, so I suppose it would be easy for someone to have the wrong idea,' Tamiko said. 'I hope she doesn't come. I don't want to talk about it.'

'I'll warn her if I see her first.'

With this in mind, straight after lunch, Daniel took Jahan by the hand once more and began to walk down the rows of horseboxes and trailers, searching for the one driven by Boo Travers. From the Devon show, he knew it was cream-coloured and, according to Tamiko, had 'Rufford Manor Showjumpers' and a picture of a horse painted on the side, so in spite of the large number of vehicles, Daniel was confident of locating it fairly easily.

Knowing Boo had arrived early, as they had, he started his search at the front of the field, and for safety, hoisted Jahan onto his shoulders and held his ankles. There were a lot of horses coming and going and a rider in a hurry could easily overlook a small boy.

He quickly spotted the lorry at the far end of the second row and headed that way, but it seemed he had timed it badly, for as he walked down the side of the horsebox, he could hear voices involved in an angry exchange at the rear and paused, not wanting to intrude.

'I don't care!' That voice, though low and furious, was recognisable as Boo's. 'It doesn't change the fact that I specifically told you not to come looking for me here! What if one of my friends sees you? How am I supposed to explain that?'

'Tell them I'm your lover,' a second voice suggested with amusement and the hint of a Scottish accent. 'What's the big deal?'

'The big deal is that I don't want you hanging around.'

'The way I see it, you don't have much choice, so you may as well get used to it.'

'I thought you were supposed to be visiting a friend in Oxford – though it beggars belief that you'd have any!' Boo returned.

'She was out.'

'I don't blame her!'

'Ooh, but you're a little spitfire, aren't you, my love?' the soft tones said with evident appreciation.

'If you call me that once more, I swear I'll drive off and leave you here!' Boo said furiously.

'We both know that isn't going to happen, don't we?' The Scotsman dropped the lilting charm. 'So you might just as well suck it up and treat me nice. It won't be forever.'

'Don't you touch me!'

Daniel decided it was time he made an appearance.

He strode forward, saying chattily to the boy, 'This looks like it might be the right one. What d'you think?'

As they rounded the rear of the lorry, the quarrelling pair fell abruptly silent and turned to face him, Boo looking flushed and annoyed, the Scotsman, with his hand on her arm, merely curious. Behind them a horse stood tied to a ring on the tailgate, partially tacked up.

'Hi, Boo. I hope you don't mind, but you did say Jahan could come and see your horse.' Daniel stopped and looked from one to the other, affecting discomfiture. 'Oh, I'm sorry. Are we interrupting something?'

Boo smiled brightly, disengaging her arm. 'No, not at all. We're all finished, here. Cal was just leaving.'

Not above average height, her male companion was, however, built like a power-lifter, the black vest and denim waistcoat clearly chosen to display his tanned muscles and tattoos to advantage. His face was lean, hard and deeply tanned, with a dark moustache that drooped to the jawline each side of his thin-lipped mouth, and the ghost of a scar that ran through one eyebrow. What Daniel could see of his hair under a denim baseball cap was grizzled and pulled into a rather wispy ponytail at the back, and he wore an earring, but he was emphatically not the kind of man you would tease about being girly, if you had any sense.

'I was, an' all,' the man agreed. 'I've got an appointment with the beer tent. I'll see you later, m'darlin'.' He blew a kiss at Boo.

Stepping towards Daniel, he put a hand up to tweak Jahan's foot and gave an exaggerated wink. 'Take my advice, little one. Don't be in a hurry to chase the ladies, but when you do, treat 'em rough and don't take no for an answer. They love it!'

'You're delusional!' Boo hissed at his departing back, but he merely raised a hand and carried on, whistling under his breath, and she uttered an incoherent groan compounded of deep annoyance and frustration.

'Er, I should probably mind my own business . . . . . .' Daniel said, glancing significantly in the direction the Scotsman had taken.

'Oh, Cal's just a family friend. Well, friend is putting it too strongly – more an acquaintance, really.'

'Of your brother's?'

'My brother?' She frowned.

'Sorry, I'm being nosy. Tami said she met your brother when she dropped the martingale back the other day.'

Her brow cleared. 'Oh, of course. No, my brother was just visiting for a couple of days. Cal was actually a friend of my father's. My dad died five years ago, but Cal won't take the hint that I don't want him hanging around. Since Dennie died he seems to think I need looking after. Having said that, he's not usually as bad as that. I think he's been drinking.'

'Army mate?' Daniel had recognised one of the tattoos.

'Er . . . yes, that's right.' She transferred her attention to Jahan who had begun to wriggle on Daniel's shoulders, bored with the direction the conversation had taken. 'Now, have you come to see Frankie Foo, little man?'

Jahan agreed that he had, and the next few minutes were taken up with unloading the grey horse from the lorry so that the little boy could stroke him and then, which clearly thrilled him to the bone, be lifted onto his broad back.

'And now I must put him away and finish getting Rocky ready, because we're due in the ring soon,' Boo said after a while. 'Are you going to come and watch me jump?'

Jahan nodded, his eyes still round with wonder as he watched the big grey being led back up the ramp and into his stall.

'Are you going to be all right? Or would you like me to hang around in case your friend comes back?' Daniel asked.

'What, Cal? No, that's all right. I'm not scared of him. He just winds me up, that's all. I said I'd give him a lift home, so I can't really avoid him.'

'Personally, I'd leave him to find his own way home, if I were you, but I know it's none of my business.'

'Thanks for your concern, but I really can take care of myself,' Boo told him, and there was just enough steel in her voice to dissuade Daniel from further comment.

He put up his hand. 'Well, thanks for letting Jahan sit on Frankie – he's absolutely made-up,' he said.

'My pleasure.' The attractive smile was back, and Daniel could almost have believed he had imagined the Keep Off signal.

He took Jahan's hand and turned away, then remembered his promise to Tami.

'Oh, and I meant to say—'

Daniel's abrupt change of direction surprised her and she reacted sharply. 'What?'

'Just that I passed on your message to Tami, and she's grateful for your concern but really can't face talking about it at the moment.'

Boo's countenance relaxed into sympathy. 'That's OK. I understand. I know what it's like. Thanks.'

As Daniel and Jahan walked away, the little boy tugged at his hand.

'Mrs Boo is a nice lady, isn't she?'

'She is,' he agreed. 'Weren't you a lucky boy to sit on Frankie?'

Boo Travers *might* be a nice lady, Daniel reflected as they made their way back onto the main showground, though he wasn't a hundred percent certain on that one, yet. However, one thing he did know; she was a woman with a lot on her mind, and he wouldn't have minded betting that the beefy Scotsman had a lot to do with it. The strain showing on her face when she had thought Daniel was no longer looking had belied the airy confidence in her words.

In the horsebox, on the way home, with Jahan having succumbed to contented exhaustion, Daniel outlined his encounter with Boo to Tamiko.

'It obviously wasn't the man you saw at her stables, that time,' he said, having described Cal to her.

'No. I tell you before, that was her brother,' Tamiko said. 'He wasn't at all like this man you describe. His hair was light-coloured, um . . . blond with a beard that was more brown, or orange?'

'Ginger?' Daniel suggested.

'Yes, ginger. And even though he was cross with me a bit for being there, he was not at all like this Cal who sounds like an arsow.'

Daniel smothered a laugh. 'A what?'

She flushed slightly. 'An arsow. Do I not say it right? It's what Jo-Ji says sometimes when people behave very stupid.'

'No, you're fine. You just surprised me, that's all.'

Tamiko's flush deepened. 'It is perhaps not a very ladylike thing to say?'

'Not very but it doesn't bother me,' Daniel assured her. Then after a period of silence, 'I shouldn't make a habit of copying everything Joey says, if I were you. The language of the police locker room can leave a bit to be desired.'

'Excuse me.' Inga leaned through the door from the living quarters. 'I'm sorry, I shouldn't have been listening, but did I hear you talking about Steven – Boo Travers' brother?'

'If that's his name, yes. Tami saw him the other day, when she went to drop off the martingale she'd borrowed.'

'Oh. I didn't know he'd come home. I, um . . . used to know him quite well, before he went away.'

From the pink tinge to her complexion, Daniel inferred that she had probably known him very well.

'Did you say he had fair hair?' she asked Tamiko. 'It was darker when I knew him.'

'So, where's he been?' Daniel asked.

'He emigrated: Australia.'

'Well, that could explain the hair. Sun bleached, perhaps.'

'Of course, you're right. But I wonder why he didn't call me when he knew he was coming. Do you know if he's still here?'

'Boo said he was just visiting for a couple of days. She gave me the impression he wasn't there anymore, sorry.'

'Oh.' Inga's face registered her disappointment, then she said brightly, 'It's been four and a half years, I expect he's moved on with his life – married even. Sorry. I didn't mean to interrupt.'

'Perhaps Boo has another brother,' Daniel suggested. 'It seems a long way to come for such a short visit.'

'Perhaps he comes to see her son who is ill,' Tamiko said.

'Yes, that's probably it,' Daniel agreed. 'Anyway, this guy I saw was a friend of her father's, according to her, but it was almost like he had some hold over her, from what I overheard. She obviously doesn't like him – and didn't mind telling him so – but it's as if, for some reason, she can't get rid of him. Interesting.'

Tamiko glanced sideways. 'You are wearing your policeman's hat.'

He smiled. 'It's a fixture. Sorry, just thinking aloud. What we should be doing is celebrating all these rosettes.' He nodded towards the half dozen bright ribbons displayed along the top of the windscreen.

'I am pleased, very pleased, but there is also a guilty feeling.'

'No, there shouldn't be. Hana would be pleased for you. Just enjoy.'

'Natalie was very pleased with the way Raffa went,' Inga told her. Samson and Raffa's owner had been at the ringside with a party of friends to see her horses jump. Daniel had been briefly introduced by Tamiko and his impression had been of a pretty, plumpish, blonde-haired woman in a strappy sundress, slightly high on alcohol and the company of friends. 'She wanted to know if you are still going to the fundraiser tomorrow night and if she could have a lift,' Inga added.

'I suppose so. I had forgotten about it,' Tamiko said. 'It's to raise a fund for an injured rider we know,' she added for Daniel's benefit.

'If you go, will there be room for me?' Inga asked. 'I have no car at the moment.'

'Yes. Sure,' Tamiko told her, the query having apparently decided her. 'We can pick you both up at seven. That's if Daniel . . .?'

'Of course. No problem.'

Daniel found himself reflecting on Tamiko's observation about his policeman's hat, later that evening, when he borrowed Jo-Ji's

computer to catch up on correspondence. Jahan was in bed and
Tamiko dozing on the sofa, and after dealing with personal emails
from Drew and Fred Bowden, and the inevitable accumulated
dross of an Internet account left idle for a few days, he found
himself pondering the possibility of finding any information on
Boo Travers' Scotsman online.

The problem was that he didn't even have a full name for the
man. Cal, she had called him, but he had no way of knowing
whether that was a first name, like Callum, or a nickname derived
from his surname. For Boo's father, whose supposed buddy the
overbearing Cal had been, he had no information at all.

Wishing he had the police's national computer network to call
on, he decided that the only search route open to him was through
Boo herself, and with the limited information he held on her, he
started with the electoral rolls. That none of it was any of his
business, he freely admitted, but his curiosity had been piqued
and he knew from experience that it would keep niggling at him
until it was satisfied.

A search of the electoral roll found Belinda Travers living at
Rufford Manor, and gave him the names of three others, presum-
ably her children, living at the same address. Her eldest son,
Harrison, who Daniel had already met, was presumably living
elsewhere, but of the three, the two females bore the surname
Travers, and the male was listed under the name Spencer Allen.

Was this the son with leukaemia, he wondered? And did it
mean that Spencer wasn't Dennie Travers' son or merely that
he'd declined to alter his name when his mother and father had
finally married? If this was the case, was it safe to assume that
Allen had been Boo's maiden name, or had she perhaps been
married before?

The website refused to divulge any more information
without him spending money so he abandoned it in favour of
a genealogy site, where he took advantage of a free trial
subscription to search for possible matches for the birth of a
Belinda Allen, somewhere between forty and fifty years previously. Even doing a countrywide search there were mercifully
few entries and taking a punt on one registered in the Bath
area, he came up with one registered forty-six years ago with
a mother's maiden name of Lightfoot. Thanking providence

that it hadn't been Smith or Jones, Daniel then searched for
a marriage between Allen and Lightfoot in the Bath area, in
the five years previous to the birth, but drew a blank. Widening
both his search area and time period, he got lucky. A David
Harrison Allen had married a Carol Anne Lightfoot in
Cirencester, some twelve years before Belinda had been born,
and unless the fact that Boo's eldest son was also called
Harrison was a huge coincidence, Daniel felt fairly confident
that he was on the right path.

Trying a search for births, surname Allen, in the period before
and after Belinda's birth, he found one other male birth to a
mother with the maiden name of Lightfoot. His name was Steven.
That then, would be the brother that Tamiko had seen at Belinda's
home; the one who Inga had claimed to know. There were no
others that he could find.

Trying a new direction, he did a general search for Boo's
father, David Harrison Allen, and scanned through the military
records. This was doomed to disappoint because closer inspection
revealed that there was nothing more recent than the Second
World War. Scrolling on down, he found two mentions of his
man in newspaper archives, one of which was an obituary dated
seven years previously, from which he learned that Boo's father
had been a well-respected solicitor and town councillor who had
passed away in a nursing home at the age of eighty-five and been
survived by two children.

Apart from serving in the second world war, long before Cal
would have been born, there was no mention in the biography
of any army career; it looked like David Allen had always intended
to study law. Either he had the wrong man or Boo had lied about
her father's connection to the Scotsman. He was inclined to
suspect the latter, as the ages of the two men would have been
so widely divergent. The second article merely concerned a town
planning issue in which he had been involved.

Daniel sat back and gazed at the screen, thoughtfully. With no
recent army records available to view, it seemed he was snook-
ered, unless he could persuade someone to search through military
records for him. But even if he could find someone willing to
do so, what could he give them to go on?

Returning to the search page, he singled out newspaper archives and entered the keywords 'Wessex Light Infantry' and 'Cal', clicking search, without much optimism.

The computer screen blinked, went blank and then threw up three results: one regional paper and two national dailies. With quickening interest, Daniel clicked to view the first result and let his breath go in a long, low whistle.

'Well, well,' he breathed. 'Whadda y'know?'

Zooming in on the grainy image, he read of the dishonourable discharge from the WLI of twenty-three-year-old Corporal John McAllum, known as Cal, and nineteen-year-old Private Dennis Travers, both recently stationed in Wiltshire. It seemed that the two of them had been involved in an illegal and highly suspect bookmaking business, based at an unnamed licensed premises near their barracks, which had subsequently led to a civilian trial. The paper was dated some thirty-three years ago.

It seemed that Boo Travers' connection with the Scot wasn't through her father, as she'd claimed, but by way of her dead husband. But why had she lied? Had Dennie been involved in other nefarious business with the Scotsman before he died, that had somehow left Boo inextricably linked to Cal?

Daniel read through the other two reports but learned no more, except that it had apparently been the opinion of the court that Private Travers had been led on by his older co-conspirator, and should therefore be treated more leniently. Because of this, the nineteen-year-old had been spared a custodial sentence, being required instead to complete a term of community service.

Daniel turned the computer off and sat back in his chair. It seemed his copper's instinct had been true, after all. There was some mystery attached to Boo's relationship with McAllum, but he was no nearer to knowing what it was. Presumably Dennie Travers had turned his life round after his first, ill-starred venture into criminality, as he had risen to become MD of Travers-King Construction, but had he remained friends with his army buddy? Having had the benefit of meeting the Scotsman face to face, Daniel felt it was unlikely. He wasn't the kind of man a socially climbing businessman would want to be seen to associate with. So was it blackmail, then? Had McAllum had some hold over Travers? A hold that continued to exercise some power over his widow, even after his death?

Daniel got to his feet. It was time to go out with Tamiko to let the dogs have a last run and tuck the horses up for the night. Turning the light off as he left the room, he was aware that far from satisfying his curiosity, he had set it ablaze, and he could no more leave the mystery unsolved than he could stop breathing.

# EIGHT

The next morning brought a phone call from the social worker assigned to Jahan's case, with the unwelcome, but not totally unexpected news that, as the boy's father, Samir Jafari was claiming the right to have custody of Jahan.

Jo-Ji, who took the call, was quick to raise concerns about Jafari's fitness to be a father, citing Hana's claims of abuse, and was assured that full checks were being carried out.

'You should know, as well, that the kid is absolutely terrified of his father,' Jo-Ji told them, and received the promise that it was Jahan's interests that everyone had at heart.

'So they might have,' he said darkly, as he put down the phone. 'But if Jafari's name is on the birth certificate, they'll have the devil's own job stopping him taking the poor kid. We'll just have to hope Hana really did report Samir and wasn't just saying it to please us.'

'They can't make him live with his father if he doesn't want to, can they?' Tamiko looked anxious and Jo-Ji put his arm round her shoulders.

'They'll have a fight on their hands if they try,' he told her. 'If she did report him, as she claimed she did, it'll be on record, even if she retracted it later. If it's there, I should imagine we'll be OK.'

'But then what will happen to Jahan?'

'We'll have to wait and see, sweetheart. One day at a time. Everyone wants the best for him.' He broke off as Jahan appeared, cuddling the sleepy Siamese cat, Yasu, with whom he had formed a bond that appeared to be mutual.

'Yasu says he's hungry,' he announced.

'Yasu is telling you lies,' Tamiko said assuming a severe expression. 'He has just eaten a big breakfast. If he eat anymore he'll be too fat and lazy to move. He needs to go outside and catch the mice.'

'Shall I take him out?' Jahan asked.

'Tell you what – I'll come with you,' Daniel said, the possibility that Jahan's father might attempt to snatch the boy at the forefront of his mind.

'And I must get on. I have clients soon,' Tamiko said.

At seven, that evening, driving his own rather scruffy Mercedes, Daniel pulled up at Natalie's front door. With her leg encased in a plaster cast, Natalie could only sensibly be installed in the front passenger seat, her crutches stowed beside her, while Tamiko and Inga took the back seat. Taz had been left with Jo-Ji, who had volunteered to look after Jahan for the evening.

Away from her giggling friends, Natalie proved to be a pleasant enough companion, although Daniel soon became aware that the sidelong glances she sent at him under her heavy lashes were openly flirtatious.

The venue for the fundraiser, the function room of a town centre hotel, was already filling up in a promising fashion by the time Daniel's party got there, a quarter of an hour after it started. Tamiko had explained that Marcus Stenhouse, an accomplished and popular rider who had been the mainstay of many national teams, had been badly injured in a crashing fall, the previous autumn. He had been left partially paralysed but hope had been offered him in the shape of a groundbreaking but expensive operation in the USA, hence the fundraising event.

Plied with champagne or orange juice according to preference and driving status, the guests were being entertained by the light strains of a string quartet, whose efforts were competing for attention with the speakers of two TV screens that were showing, on a loop, recordings of some of Mr Stenhouse's most notable successes. In one corner, a photographer was offering to take a photograph of anyone or couple who cared to pose for one; someone else had brought along a selection of riding and eveningwear; and tickets were being sold for a raffle with some impressive prizes.

The walls were covered with boards bearing newspaper clippings and photographic evidence of the man's show jumping career, and there was to be a charity auction of promises, Natalie told Daniel, leaving one of her crutches by the door and claiming his arm for support, thereby presumably thinking to assure herself of an escort for the evening. Daniel caught Tamiko's eye and could tell by its twinkle that she was laughing at him.

They moved round the room as a group, accepting the canapés that were on offer and dutifully buying raffle tickets.

Several people stopped to speak to his companions, one or two offering their sympathy to Tamiko, but the only person Daniel knew was Boo Travers, who was attending with her son, Harrison. Of the Scotsman, there was unsurprisingly no sign. At such an event he would have stuck out like a nun in a knocking shop.

From the evidence on show, Daniel could see that the so far absent Marcus Stenhouse, who had sent his apologies and was expected to put in an appearance at any moment, had indeed been a *force majeure* in the show-jumping world, and was as popular as Tamiko had stated. However, endless photographs of people and horses he didn't know soon began to pall on Daniel and he found himself watching the clock. He had a suspicion that the late arrival of its focus had been carefully calculated to encourage people to stay longer at the fundraiser and spend their money.

'Oh, look! There's Boo Travers!' Natalie exclaimed, pointing at a photograph of four riders lining up for a prize-giving. 'Have you met Boo? She's a sweetie! Boo, have you seen this?' she called out, seeing her across the room.

Daniel dutifully looked at the photo. It was dated some six years previously, and the winning team of riders were named as Marcus Stenhouse, Sally Porter-Hughes, and Steven and Belinda Allen.

'My God, I look two stone heavier in that photo!' Boo exclaimed, coming over in response to Natalie's call. 'That was the last time I jumped old Barney Bear. He retired after that. God, he was a fabulous horse! You remember him, don't you, Harry?'

Coming up to the group more slowly, her son shrugged.

'You know me. One brown horse is much like another,' he said. 'But I remember the party we had afterwards!'

'Harrison takes after his father,' Boo said rolling her eyes. 'Works hard and parties hard, with no time for anything else.'

'Oh, I don't think you can say that about Dad!' her son put in with a wink in Daniel's direction. 'I have got three siblings, after all!'

'Cheeky sod!' his mother said fondly.

'You're not a rider, then?' Daniel asked. Wearing black jeans, a white T-shirt and a casual jacket, it was easy to see that Harrison kept himself fit one way or another. He might be stocky; he certainly wasn't fat.

'No. I'm more into water sports – anything in, on or under it, really.'

'So, what's your line of work?'

'Er, construction,' Harrison said, and as Daniel's gaze dropped instinctively to his hands, he added, 'No, not the actual building part, more the surveying and planning.'

'Like your father,' Daniel suggested, taking a punt.

'Same company. Did you know him?' Not a blink. It seemed his parentage was an open secret.

'No. Only of him. Newspapers and suchlike.'

'Yeah, he was pretty hard to miss,' Harrison said with a note of pride. Someone hailed him and with a word of apology to Daniel, he turned away to greet them.

Tamiko was leaning close to the picture of the prize-giving, frowning.

'This is not your brother, *is* it?' she asked Boo.

'Ye-ah.' Boo sounded surprised. 'It *was* six years ago, but he hasn't changed that much. Of course, he's in Australia now.'

'But the man I saw at your house . . .?'

'Oh – I see. No, that was my other brother – er, my half-brother, Ricky. He was staying for a few days, but he's gone home now.'

Daniel had been watching her closely.

'Where is home?' he asked.

Boo rounded on him with a quizzical look. 'For Ricky? Dorset – Bournemouth, actually. Why do you ask?'

'Sorry. No reason. Just naturally nosey.'

Her eyes narrowed, but Inga forestalled any further comment by asking her if she'd heard from Steven lately.

'Not for a month or two,' Boo told her. 'You know what men are. You knew he'd married?'

Inga shook her head. 'No, I didn't,' she said. 'But I'm not surprised.'

'Yes, he met her when he'd been out there a couple of months and they got married last year. He's running a jumping yard and she's riding for him.'

'That must be nice.' Inga's smile was brittle and Daniel felt sorry for her.

'Boo? Hi – I thought it was you!' a slightly husky female voice exclaimed with obvious pleasure, and Inga moved aside to allow the newcomer to join the group. 'I haven't seen you for an age and you didn't return my call.'

'It must be at least a fortnight,' Boo joked. 'Sorry about the call, it must have slipped my mind. How are you, anyway?'

'I'm good. Busy as always. How's Spencer?'

'Oh, you know. Up and down.' The words were spoken lightly but the shadow of pain that crossed her face was unmistakeable. 'He keeps fairly cheerful.'

'He's amazing. Well, you know where I am. If there's ever anything I can do.' The woman was of slightly more than average height, fairly stockily built and wore her fair hair very short. This, combined with a straight nose and determined chin, gave her a slightly mannish look, not greatly mitigated by her choice of clothing. Daniel guessed she was in her late-thirties and mentally filed her as probably ex-forces.

He smiled and put out his hand. 'Hi. I'm Daniel.'

'Chris.' The woman's grasp was firm, as he had expected. She looked round at the others.

'Sorry,' Boo said, belatedly. 'This is Chrissie Haynes, who saved my bacon a few months ago when I ran out of fuel on the way back from a show. Chris – Daniel, Tamiko, Natalie and Inga.'

'All I did was drive to the nearest petrol station with a can,' Chris laughed. 'Not exactly heroics!'

'But it was a foul night and no one else had even bothered to stop,' Boo said.

'You weren't on your bike, obviously,' Daniel said.

'My bike?' She looked bewildered.

'Yes. Didn't I see you somewhere, recently, on a motorbike?'

'I think you must be mixing me up with someone else,' she said.

'Maybe,' Daniel said. 'Sorry. So, what do you do?'

'Chris does clever IT stuff,' Boo said. 'When she's not riding or rescuing stranded people.'

'So, you're a rider, too?' Daniel said.

'Well, after a fashion,' she said. 'Nowhere near Boo's league. I actually hadn't ridden in years when I met her, but we got talking and she encouraged me to start again. She kindly said I could borrow one of her horses and we've been riding out together occasionally, ever since.'

'Nothing kind about it,' Boo retorted. 'It's nice to have the company now Spence doesn't come out so often. By the way, Tamiko and Natalie ride, too.'

'Not at the moment, obviously,' Natalie pointed out, gesturing at her plaster cast. 'But I have a jumping yard. Inga is my groom.'

'Oh, and this is my eldest, Harrison,' Boo said as her son reappeared at her side.

'Hi,' Chris said.

'Hi.' Harrison looked at her with narrowed eyes. 'Haven't I seen you before?'

'Oh, God! Not another one,' his mother protested.

'No, I have. You did some work at TKC, didn't you?'

'TKC?' Chris repeated blankly.

'My father's company; Travers-King Construction. A couple of years ago, wasn't it? I remember seeing you around. Internet security or some such, isn't it?'

'Oh, yes. Of course. I did. I remember now.'

'Really?' Boo asked. 'You never said. That must've been when my husband was alive. Did you meet him?'

'D'you know, I never made the connection,' Chris told her. 'How mad is that? I suppose I've had so many other contracts since then, it just didn't occur to me. I may have met him. I meet so many people in my job.'

A stir amongst the crowd nearest the door made everyone turn that way and the babble of conversation dropped to a hum of anticipation. Watching Chris, surreptitiously, Daniel thought she looked profoundly grateful for the interruption.

There was a cheer and a burst of clapping and a powered wheelchair appeared in the doorway. The guest of honour had arrived and all else was forgotten as everyone in the room gravitated towards Marcus Stenhouse and Daniel's party were separated from Boo and her son. Still keeping an eye on Chris Haynes, Daniel saw her drift towards the bar. She interested him. When he'd mentioned the bike, she'd pretended surprise, but he was an old hand at reading faces and he was pretty sure that what he'd seen was wariness.

After a couple of minutes and on the pretext of fetching drinks for the ladies in his party, Daniel restored Natalie's crutches to her and followed Chris Haynes. She didn't look overjoyed at finding him next to her at the bar. He gave his order to the barman and then asked her conversationally, 'Does Boo know you're friendly with Stella Travers-King?'

'Travers-King?' Again the wariness.

'The woman I saw you talking to in Bath.'

She frowned slightly but responded in the same casual tone he had used.

'Oh, was that her name? No. Why on earth would I? All I did was buy a bracelet from the woman on eBay.'

'But knowing Boo as you do, you must have made the connection.'

'Not until now. She called herself King when I contacted her about the bracelet. What's it to you, anyway? I don't believe I caught your surname.'

'Whelan,' Daniel said. 'Daniel Whelan.'

The barman placed the drinks on the bar and Daniel handed over a note.

'And how do *you* know Boo,' Chris asked. 'I don't believe I've ever heard her speak of you.'

'I don't imagine you have. I don't really know her. I'm a friend of Tamiko and her partner, temporarily driving the horsebox while Natalie is out of action. I only met Boo a couple of weeks ago.'

'So, why all the questions?'

'Just naturally nosey, I guess,' Daniel said with a smile and a wink, pocketing his change and picking the drinks up from the bar.

Any hopes that Daniel may have had that the arrival of its main player would hurry the fundraising event to its conclusion were soon extinguished. After all the greetings had been exchanged, the raffle took place in what seemed like slow motion and then the auction began. Had it just been Daniel and Tamiko, they could have slipped out whilst this was getting underway, but Natalie had set her heart on bidding for several lots and so they had to stay to the bitter end.

Shortly after the auction started, Daniel saw Chris Haynes make her way to the door, and telling Tamiko he was going to look for the Gents, he followed her out into the foyer. It had been a possibility that she was bent on the same purpose, but as he paused in the doorway, he saw her disappearing through the outer door to the car park. Again he followed, this time moving into the shadows at the side of the building. All cars leaving the well-lit car park had to pass close to the hall and he had a fancy to see what Ms Haynes was driving. A few minutes later, he was back with the others.

On the way home, Daniel asked the question that had been on his mind since their earlier conversation with Boo.

'So, did you ever meet Boo's half-brother, Inga?'

'Not that I remember,' she replied. 'I don't think he was ever spoken of. But I was never really involved with the family, as such. Steven lived near Salisbury and I used to meet him there mostly.'

Back at the cottage, when the horses had been seen to and Tamiko had gone to bed, Daniel begged for the use of Jo-Ji's computer again.

'I'll start charging you soon,' Jo-Ji joked. 'Time you were dragged kicking and screaming into the twenty-first century and got yourself a smartphone or a tablet.'

'I've got a smartphone – well, semi-educated,' Daniel joked. 'But I can't get a reliable signal in this neck of the woods, and besides, it's so bloody fiddly. I'm not the world's best typist, as it is, but trying to do anything on my phone takes forever.'

'No probs. I don't mind, really. Fancy a beer?'

Daniel did, but he had checked his email, answered one from his son and was again searching the genealogy site when Jo-Ji made his reappearance.

'Sorry. Got side-tracked. The cat brought a mouse in and let it go. I've had to pull the dishwasher out and everything.'

'Find it?' Daniel asked, his attention still on the screen.

'Eventually, and then instead of being grateful, the bloody thing tried to bite me! Anyway; here's your beer.'

'Thanks.'

'Doing your family history?' Jo-Ji asked, looking at the screen.

'Not mine. Boo Travers'.'

'Who's she? Should I know her?'

'You might know *of* her. She's the wife – widow – of the businessman who disappeared. You remember, we were talking about him the other night.'

'Oh, yes. Dennie Travers. So why the interest?'

'I don't know. Something's just not right.'

'Oh, is this something to do with the bloke you saw at the show?' Daniel had mentioned the encounter with the Scotsman, but Jo-Ji hadn't seemed particularly interested.

'Yeah, partly. I don't know – I can't put my finger on it. I just get the feeling she's in trouble.'

Jo-Ji put his head on one side.

'Do you fancy her?'

'What, Boo? No. That is, I hadn't thought about it. She's attractive, yes, but that's not what this is about.'

'OK. If you say so,' Jo-Ji said with a half-smile.

'And it's not only McAllum. There's some mystery about her brother – the one Tami saw that time. Now Boo claims he's her half-brother, but looking at her mum's records, she married at seventeen and, as far as I can see, stayed married until she died eleven years ago.'

'OK. Stayed married on paper, but you don't know what happened in real life. They could have separated and she might have had a dozen other kids.'

'Boo said his name was Ricky. I've looked for a Rick, Ricky or Richard Allen born to a Carol Anne Allen or Lightfoot – which is her maiden name – within the likely period, and come up with absolutely zilch. The trouble is, he could have taken his natural father's name, in which case I'm stuffed.'

'Or he could be a half-brother on her dad's side,' Jo-Ji pointed out. 'If *he* had an affair and the kid took his mum's name, you likewise won't have a hope in hell of finding him.'

'I know, it's a bugger, isn't it? It's all so bloody complicated!'

'A chap at work's doing his family tree – bores us rigid with it – and he's always complaining that he can't find records he's looking for, even when he knows they should be there,' Jo-Ji said. 'But even if this Boo *is* lying – does it really matter? Lots of families have dirty secrets. I doubt she's a master criminal.'

'No, probably not. It's just bothering me.'

'You're bored,' Jo-Ji stated flatly.

'No, I'm not,' Daniel said quite truthfully. 'Tell me about Dennie Travers again.'

Jo-Ji sighed. 'This is why you were such a good copper,' he said. 'You're like that bloody dog of yours. Once you get on a trail, you won't stop till you find your man. OK. Local businessman; partner in Travers-King Construction, based in Bristol; drowned after falling overboard from an expensive yacht during a party to celebrate his wedding anniversary, if I remember rightly.'

'His wedding to Boo, that would be.'

'That's right.'

'So his family would all have been there.'

'I imagine so.'

'Whereabouts did it happen?'

'Off the Kent coast. That's why I don't know all the details – it wasn't our baby.'

'How long had he been married?'

'I've no idea.' Jo-Ji sounded exasperated. 'You've got the computer – look it up in the newspaper archives if you want all the gory details. I'm sure there'll be plenty; it's the kind of thing they love. I'm going to bed. Back to work tomorrow.'

'OK. Thanks Joey. And thanks for the beer.'

'More in the fridge if you want it,' Jo-Ji said as he went out the door.

Intent once more on the computer, Daniel didn't even hear the door shut.

Following Jo-Ji's suggestion, he entered 'Dennie Travers overboard' on Google and within a fraction of a second was faced with pages of search results. Pulling a notepad and pen close, he opened the first newspaper article and set about making notes.

Half an hour later he sat back, took a swig of his beer and reviewed what he'd learned. Just over two years ago, Dennie Travers, aged forty-nine, had chartered a forty-metre motor yacht to host a party to celebrate the twenty-fifth anniversary of meeting his eventual second wife, Belinda Travers, to whom he had then been married for three years. With no expense spared, he had taken his family and over sixty guests out to the exact spot where he had apparently proposed to her on their return from a Caribbean cruise.

At eight o'clock in the evening, shortly after toasting each other – one of the papers even had the name and price of the indecently expensive champagne – Dennie had apparently tripped and gone overboard whilst fooling about on deck with his eldest son, Harrison.

Upwards of thirty shocked partygoers witnessed his fall, but even though the alarm went up immediately and an inflatable lifeboat was launched within minutes, Mr Travers had disappeared. It was reported that the sea was choppy and the sky overcast, that night. Currents were known to be particularly strong in the area and it was believed that Dennie might well have hit his head as he fell and been unconscious when he went into the water. His son, who was one of the crew of the lifeboat, was said to have been distraught. Coastal lifeboats and a helicopter were sent out but the currents and the onset of night hampered the search.

Daniel tapped the pen on his teeth, wondering whether Cal had been on the boat, but moments later, he admitted that that suspicion was unfair. As far as he knew, John McAllum had been a friend of Dennie Travers' younger days. He had no reason to suspect that the Scotsman harboured any grudge against the businessman, even if he perhaps felt that Dennie had got off lightly for the crime they had both committed. Thirty odd years was a long time to wait to get even, and if their relationship had soured because of that long-ago incident, it was hardly likely that Dennie would have invited the man on his celebratory voyage.

Whatever the case, all the papers seemed clear on one point; it had been Harrison who had been closest to his father when the accident had occurred, so whether or not his ex-army partner-in-crime had been on the boat seemed irrelevant. Unless you believed that he was, for some reason, in league with Harrison Allen . . .

Speculation was pointless, and, as Jo-Ji had observed, did it really matter? It wasn't his concern.

In spite of this, a few moments later, Daniel was busy scrolling through records for the marriage of Dennis Travers and Stella King, which when found, gave his age at time of marriage as twenty-two, and hers as twenty-nine. Both their fathers were listed as deceased; Stella's described as a company director, Dennie's as a banker.

A general search threw up newspaper reports of the wedding, which had been a lavish affair by all accounts. In the absence of her father, the bride had been given away by her grandfather, Aubrey King, who was apparently the founder of King Construction, as it was then. Dennie Travers had taken on his wife's name and presumably, at some point in the future, King senior had bestowed upon his grandson-in-law a partnership in the company. It seemed the youthful miscreant had done very well for himself.

Using his age and name, Daniel then searched for a birth record for Dennis Travers, even though the on-line results would provide no details of his father. In the event, it told him more than he expected. There was only one Dennis Travers in the four-year search window the site used. Dennis S Travers had been born in Aldershot fifty-two years previously and his mother's maiden name was also listed as Travers. Presumably the father was no longer in the picture, or perhaps, Daniel thought cynically, Edith Travers simply hadn't known who the father was. Aldershot was, after all, a garrison town.

If Dennie had indeed gone off the rails during his teens, it was not altogether to be wondered at; single mothers had not been socially accepted in those days and the boy might have had a difficult time growing up, especially if his mother had acquired something of a reputation. It was not surprising that he had invented a deceased banker as a father for the purposes of his marriage certificate. It was all supposition, Daniel had to admit, but it had the ring of truth about it.

Another search, this time for John McAllum, threw up rather too many results, though narrowing it down to Scotland helped. However, Daniel had no idea whether Cal had actually been born in Scotland or merely to Scottish parents. He was forced to give up that avenue of curiosity and finally, stretching a stiff back, to admit that he was very little further forward. The mystery might very well be no mystery at all, and merely a product of his over-suspicious mind.

He stretched his cramped back muscles and glanced at the clock on the wall. Half past one.

Time for bed.

Time for one last search.

He typed Chris Haynes and IT into Google and it immediately gave him a website. She was indeed in internet security. There was nothing untoward about her professional profile, as far as Daniel could see. In her photograph she had longer hair and wore make-up, which made her almost unrecognisable as the woman he'd seen at the fundraiser. Having your hair cut was no crime, though Daniel reflected with an inward smile that he'd seen a few haircuts that were on the verge of criminal.

He switched the computer off and Taz, roused by the familiar quadruple note of Windows closing down, stood up from his position by Daniel's feet and shook himself, sending a shower of loose hairs to decorate the carpet.

'Yep. Time for bed, mate. Let's go,' Daniel told him.

The following day Tamiko and Daniel rode, as was their custom, in the cool of the morning before Tamiko's first client arrived, and then Daniel and Jo-Ji looked after Jahan until lunchtime, when Jo-Ji set off for his shift. The afternoon was rendered stressful by the necessity of the ongoing funeral arrangements. A date had been set for the Friday, but as Hana had had few friends that Tamiko knew of, it was going to be a very low-key affair.

'Tami, do you remember that silver Mondeo that was parked along the lane this morning when we rode out?' Daniel asked when Tamiko finally finished phoning. He was standing to one side of the window, looking out. Jahan was sitting on the floor by the sofa, playing with a selection of toy cars that Karen the beautician had brought for him.

Tamiko shook her head.

'I don't think I notice it particularly. Why?'

'Well, it's back. It wasn't there at lunchtime, when Joey went, but it's back, now.'

'Who do you think it is? Not Samir?' Her eyes widened.

'It's possible. It may not mean anything, but I don't feel like taking any chances. What do you say we ring Joey and ask if there's a squad car in the area that could just swing by.'

'I think so. That's a good idea.'

Daniel did so, giving Jo-Ji the car's registration number for good measure.

'How did you know that?' Tamiko asked, coming to stand beside him. 'The car I didn't even notice and yet you have his number. Can you see it from here?'

'Habit,' Daniel said. 'Anything out of place and I automatically log the details.'

It was around twenty minutes before the police car appeared, and about halfway through that time, at a moment when Daniel wasn't watching, the silver car disappeared. Jo-Ji had been in touch with the news that it was registered to a pensioner living on the outskirts of Bath, whose name meant nothing to any of them.

'Sorry. It may have been a false alarm,' Daniel told the two uniformed officers who came to the door to check on them. 'But it was there for several hours – either that or it went away and came back.'

'That's all right, sir. Better safe than sorry. We'll swing by again, later, if we're in the area.'

Minutes later, Jo-Ji called back.

'I just called the owner of that Mondeo – a Mr Graham Siddons – and he was at home. I asked him if he knew where his car was at that moment and he said parked in a residents' car park, along the road. I have a feeling he'll ring back in a minute. Anyway, I hear it's moved on, now.'

'Yeah, just before your guys got here. Bloody typical!'

'Well, keep your eyes open and don't let Tami or Jahan go out alone – even into the garden.'

'Grandmother; eggs,' Daniel said lightly.

'Yeah, mate, I'm sorry. It's what you're there for. See you later. I'll be back about eleven with any luck.'

The rest of the afternoon passed without incident. The car didn't reappear and as the heat of the day cooled into evening, Daniel took the chance of giving Taz his second run of the day, taking Tamiko and Jahan along with him. The horses had spent the day in the wooden field shelter to avoid the flies but as the temperature dropped they moved out into the open to graze on the short grass.

Jahan pointed as they walked past the gate into the lane. 'Jahan ride the horses,' he suggested hopefully.

'Not now, sweetheart,' Tamiko said. 'We're taking Taz for a run.'

Even though he thought they were quite safe with the dog around, Daniel kept their walk close to the village and habitation, but they didn't see Jafari, or the silver Ford, or indeed, anything suspicious.

By the time they returned to the cottage, clouds were building in the southwest and by ten o'clock, when Tamiko habitually settled the horses for the night, it was just starting to rain in big, slow, heavy drops that presaged a downpour.

'This is good,' Tamiko said, as she and Daniel let themselves out of the kitchen door and locked it behind them, leaving Jahan asleep upstairs in his bed. 'We need the rain. The horses will be happy to come in, now. I'm surprised they don't shout already. Babs doesn't like to get wet.'

Halfway down the garden path, when the security light came on in front of the stables, there was still no sound from Babs and Rolo, and Tamiko muttered something and started to hurry. Fetching two lead ropes, she gave one to Daniel and went to the field gate, where they would normally have been jostling for position, ready to come in.

'Where are they?' she said, anxiety sharp in her voice.

'We need a torch,' Daniel stated.

'Yes. In the feed store there is one. On the shelf over the bins.'

As Daniel went to find it, Tamiko raised her voice to shout the horses' names in the distinctive way she always did.

'I can't hear them. Rolo always calls,' she told Daniel when he returned with the torch. She opened the gate and they went through with Taz pushing at their heels, reacting with excitement to Tamiko's tone.

The torch was fairly powerful but its beam didn't pick up the hoped-for glow of the horses' eyes. It was obvious almost straight away that the paddock was empty and the reason wasn't difficult to divine. In the far right-hand corner there was a five-bar gate that provided access to the field from the lane. Normally it was kept chained and padlocked at both ends; now it stood open to the road and when Daniel and Tamiko reached it, they found that the heavy-duty chain had been cut through near the catch with bolt-cutters.

Tamiko looked at Daniel through the increasingly heavy rain, her face stricken.

'Oh my God! They've gone! They've been stolen!'

Daniel stepped out into the lane and without much hope swung the torch beam in the direction of the village and the main road, and then the other way, towards the farm and woodland. Here, against all logic, perhaps twenty or thirty feet away, the light picked out the ruby red gleam of two eyes looking back at him.

Tamiko clutched his arm. 'That's Babs! Her eyes always shine red. Oh, my God!' She took a few steps towards the mare. 'Come baby, come here.'

Daniel stayed back and watched her, keeping the torch beam steady. However biddable horses were from day to day, once they were high on the excitement of being loose in the world beyond their field, they could be extremely difficult to catch again. He was aware that what they really needed was a bucket with some food but he had no intention of leaving Tamiko out in the dark lane by herself while he went to fetch one.

The whole situation worried him. Why had somebody gone to the considerable trouble of cutting an industrial strength chain to get at the horses, just to let them go free? One possibility was that they had only been interested in the younger, more valuable horse. The other was that it was a trap – a decoy to get Tamiko and Daniel away from the house. If that was the case, was Tamiko the target or was it Jahan, asleep alone in the house?

Tamiko was close to the mare now. Babs had raised her head

high at her approach but thankfully not attempted to escape. A couple more steps and she would have her.

Then, walking in her own shadow as she was, Tamiko appeared to stumble, twisting her ankle and falling sideways. The horse, it's nerves already on edge, whirled round and with a clatter of hooves, disappeared into the darkness.

Tamiko let out a squeal of pure frustration, picked herself up and began to run in pursuit.

'Tami! No!' Daniel shouted, but now his torchlight showed only an empty lane. He swore out loud, torn between following her and the uneasy feeling that he ought to turn back and check on the boy. Who were they dealing with? If it was Samir Jafari, then the boy would almost certainly be the target, but would he really try and kidnap the child when he had just started proceedings through conventional channels?

And what of the other, unknown threat, who may or may not have caused the death of Jahan's mother? If their suspicions were founded in reality then it would be madness to leave Tamiko out here alone.

For Daniel, the whole situation was careering horribly out of his control but he was aware that by standing irresolutely in the dark lane he was protecting nobody.

It had begun to rain in earnest now, silver rods in the torchlight, quickly soaking through the thin cotton shirt he wore. He made a snap decision.

'Tami! Wait!' he yelled again, and loosely tying the lead rope over one shoulder and round his body he began to run after her, his trainers slapping on the glistening wet tarmac. Immediately Taz ran ahead, leaping and bounding; highly excited by the night-time jaunt. It was all a huge game to him.

After perhaps fifty or sixty yards, the road curved left with an even narrower lane forking right. Here, to his huge relief, Daniel nearly ran into Tamiko, who had stopped at the junction.

'I think Rolo is there too, but they both run and I don't know which way they go,' she panted. Her face, in the light of the torch was strained with anxiety; her dark hair wet and plastered to her skin. She pointed to the right fork. 'If I go this way – you go down there.'

'No! Tami, wait!' Daniel said urgently, catching her arm.

'Listen. I don't like this. Why did they get them out and then let them go? It could be a trap.'

'I don't know, but I can't just leave them out here,' she cried, trying to loosen his hold. 'Please, Daniel. Please! We can't leave them.'

'I'm going to ring Joey,' he said, tucking the torch under his arm and taking his phone from his pocket. He found Jo-Ji's name in its memory and made the call.

'That's good. You call but I go after them,' Tamiko insisted, still trying to twist her arm free.

'We need to stay together.'

'Then you must come. I'm not going back!'

With a final tug, she broke free and started to run again, the violence of her action sending the phone spinning from his hand. In his instinctive effort to save the phone, Daniel felt the torch slip out from under his arm. It clattered on the wet road and promptly went out.

Daniel swore. He could see neither the torch nor the screen of the phone, which should have remained illuminated for a few seconds at least, and it might take precious minutes to find them; time that would let Tamiko get further and further away.

'Taz. Go seek Tami!' he commanded sharply, and the German shepherd disappeared into the darkness.

Cursing the rain, his own clumsiness and the overhanging trees that were robbing the lane of any faint light there might have been, Daniel searched the wet tarmac around his feet for the torch, not knowing which way it might have rolled. If he had had his own torch, which was uselessly locked in his car back at the cottage, it would have remained where it fell. Experience had taught him the disadvantages of carrying cylindrical torches.

Why hadn't he asked Taz to find the torch before he sent him after Tamiko?

For once, though, luck was on his side, and as he moved cautiously forward, he kicked it with his foot. Within moments his fingers found the metal barrel and with a triumphant, 'Yes!' he straightened up, feeling for the on switch.

Directly in front of him, almost sensed rather than seen, stood a deeper shadow in the darkness, and before the realisation of danger even dawned upon him, Daniel was hit with a clubbing blow to the side of the head, which sent him stumbling and sprawling into the hedge at the side of the road. For the second time in as many minutes, the torch spun off into the darkness.

# NINE

The attack was so sudden and unexpected that for a moment, Daniel couldn't gather his wits. His ears were ringing from the blow and his cotton shirt was no protection at all against the sharp twig ends of the blackthorn hedge.

He had thought there was no light in the lane, but the deeper looming darkness of an approaching figure proved otherwise.

There was no time to wonder who he was facing. This was survival. The attack had been brutal, and his assailant clearly meant to follow it up. Without waiting to find out how, Daniel scrambled onto all fours and propelled himself in a low, rugby-style tackle at where he estimated his attacker's legs to be, catching him thigh-high and bearing him backwards, wildly off balance.

As they both landed heavily on the road, a definitively male voice cursed and its owner kicked out to loosen Daniel's hold, but he was already rolling away and the booted foot only caught him a glancing blow as he came to his feet.

He would have given anything to have the torch in his hand but he had no time to look for it, so he stepped forward and aimed a hefty kick at the shadowy form in front of him.

He felt it connect and a grunt told him that it had landed well, but the other man was clearly a tough proposition, for instantly Daniel felt his leg grasped above the ankle and the next moment he was on his back in the lane. He pulled the trapped leg towards him sharply to draw the man closer and kicked out with the other, this time with the satisfaction of sending his assailant staggering backwards.

Somewhere off in the darkness Daniel heard a scream and then Taz started barking. He knew that bark; it was the one that signalled a quarry found. When he'd been on police business it had signalled success, now it told Daniel that his attacker wasn't working alone, which meant Tamiko was in danger.

His first instinct was to run to her aid while he was free to do so, but even if he could outrun his man, it wouldn't be for long. Almost certainly his assailant would be close behind. Sooner or later, if he and Tamiko were to survive the night, Daniel would have to disable his attacker, even if only for long enough to get them both away to safety.

Even as he dismissed the notion, the moment for flight was past. It seemed his opponent was becoming annoyed, for he came charging back with a roar of pure aggression, like a power lifter attempting a world record.

Whether the roar was meant to intimidate Daniel or was just the result of temper, he didn't know. However, the man's anger made him unwary and Daniel was able to side step and aim a short punch at his torso that doubled him up, grunting in pain. Clasping his hands together, Daniel brought them down with all the force he could muster where he judged the man's neck to be, and heard and saw him drop to the ground.

Breathing hard, he stepped across the dimly seen figure and sat on him, pulling his arms behind his back. It seemed the man might have hit his forehead on the tarmac because although his ribcage still rose and fell under Daniel's weight, he made no attempt to struggle.

Daniel had no way of knowing how long the man would remain stunned, but some innate morality stopped him from slamming his assailant's head against the road again to ensure his continued immobility. Instead, he untied the lead rope that was still around his body and used it to tightly bind the man's wrists, fairly sure, even as he did so, that had their positions been reversed, he would have been shown no such mercy.

Shaking his head at his own unbending principles, he stood up and dragged the man's limp body to the side of the road where he wouldn't be run over by a passing car. From the weight of him, he was a big man – around ninety to a hundred kilos, at a guess, but without the torch, Daniel was no closer to knowing who he might be.

Even though Taz's urgent barking still rang through the night, he paused just long enough to swiftly go through the unconscious man's pockets, finding only what felt like a cigarette lighter, a few coins and some scraps of paper, which he pocketed without compunction. The mobile phone he took from the back pocket of the man's jeans had clearly suffered as a consequence of the rough treatment Daniel had dealt its owner, and something fell off it to clatter onto the tarmac. He touched the screen but it remained dark, so he slipped it into his own pocket along with the rest. It could still provide valuable clues.

In the absence of his own torch or phone, he kept the cigarette lighter out, intending to see what he could make out by the light it generated, but it was empty.

His frustration at this accumulation of bad luck was banished from his mind by the sound of shouting and renewed barking, away down the lane. Moments later, he had pocketed the lighter and was running as hard as he could down the road Tamiko and the dog had taken.

It was still raining but coming out from under the overhanging trees, it was possible to make out the outline of the hedge against the sky as he ran towards the sound of the dog.

As he drew close he could see the bulky shape of a horse, with the smaller vertical of someone holding onto it. Logic suggested that this was probably Tamiko, which relieved Daniel's most pressing care and as he slowed up he heard her say his name with an echo of his own relief.

'It's OK,' he told her, more as reassurance than from any belief that it was true. 'Are you all right?'

'Yes, yes. The man, he is over there!'

Beyond the horse, Daniel could see another figure backed into the hedge and effectively held there by Taz, who was voicing all manner of dire warnings, not six inches from the man's crotch.

'Good boy. Quiet, Taz!' Daniel said, moving closer, and the dog's barking subsided into a low growl that was no less menacing.

'You,' he said to the man by the hedge, 'who are you and what do you want?'

Predictably, the man didn't reply, apparently gaining confidence from Daniel's control over the dog and choosing instead to try a cautious step to the side.

'Stand still or I'll set the dog on you,' Daniel rapped out.

The man did as he was told, even raising his arms a little as a sign of surrender. One hand was clearly empty; in the other, he held something but Daniel couldn't make out what.

'What is that? Drop it!' he said sharply, afraid that it could be a weapon of some kind.

The man opened his fingers and let the object fall.

'Turn round and face the hedge and put your hands behind your back,' Daniel told him. 'Now, or I'll send the dog!'

Obediently, the man turned, and Daniel stepped forward, grasping one of his wrists and twisting it up, none too gently, to somewhere in the region of his shoulder blades.

Taz crowded in and had to be ordered off.

'Now, matey, you're not going anywhere, so perhaps we'll have some answers,' Daniel snarled with some satisfaction, pulling the man away from the hedge and starting to march him back down the lane. In the almost total darkness, he could make out little more than the outline of his head.

'Are you sure you're OK?' he asked Tamiko as he reached her.

'Yes, I'm fine,' Tamiko said a little shakily. 'He grabbed me but then Taz comes and he let go again. Taz was amazing! I've got Rolo but not Babs,' she added.

'I'm sorry, but we'll have to come back for her,' Daniel said. 'As long as you're OK. If you've got your phone, can you call Jo-Ji? He should be on his way home, by now.'

'Daniel, I'm sorry. I left it—' she started to say, but was interrupted by the sound of an approaching vehicle.

Any hopes that it was a car that might be flagged down for assistance were doomed almost immediately, as it became clear that it was being driven at speed.

'Get off the road!' Daniel shouted at Tamiko but before either of them had time to take evasive action, the vehicle was upon them, its lights dazzling, and instantly Daniel's precarious control of the situation was shattered.

Frightened by the speed of the car, Rolo swung his hind-quarters round in order to charge back down the road, and in so doing, cannoned into Daniel and his captive, knocking them both sideways. As he stumbled, trying to maintain his hold on the man, Daniel heard the screech of tortured rubber as the vehicle tried to break hard on the wet road and the next moment the smooth metal wing caught him a glancing blow and sent him spinning into the hedge for the second time that night.

He heard Taz yelp and then start to bark furiously. Away down the lane, the horse's hooves clattered on the road and, close by, someone yelled, 'Get in!'

For a fleeting moment, Daniel's erstwhile captive was outlined by the interior lights of what was almost certainly a 4×4, and then the door slammed, the engine roared and it was away down the road, its headlights illuminating the galloping form of a horse in front of it. Of Tamiko, there was no sign.

'Tami!' he shouted, his voice sharp with fear for her, and to his intense relief, heard her call from further down the road.

'Daniel! I'm OK. Where are you?'

'I'm here,' he called back, aware even as he said the words, that it was a singularly unhelpful thing to say in the circumstances.

Taz homed in on the sound of his voice, fawning around him and licking his face with more enthusiasm than Daniel appreciated.

'Yes, good lad. Give over now, will you?' Daniel said, catching the dog's collar and holding him at arm's length. He became aware that he was, in fact, lying in the shallow ditch at the foot of the hedge; a ditch that for the last few months had probably been dry but which was now running with icy water from the earlier deluge.

Feeling as if he'd just gone a few rounds with a sumo wrestler and then been dunked in a water trough, Daniel rolled over, climbed out and sat on the verge, doing a cautious mental inventory of his body parts. They all seemed to be in working order, if a little sore, and in due course he climbed to his feet.

'Daniel? Are you OK?' Tamiko had reached his side, and put her hand on his arm. He could feel her trembling.

'I'll live,' he said with a wry smile she couldn't see. 'But I may need your healing hands tomorrow. And you? He didn't hurt you? I heard you scream.'

'No, I am OK but I was so scared. He was suddenly there, in front of me. He grabbed me and tried to make me walk with him, but I struggled and then Taz came and bit him, and he let me go.'

'Bit him, did he? Well done that dog! I don't suppose you've got any idea who it was?' he asked without much optimism, and sensed rather than saw the shake of her head.

'It was so dark and I think maybe he wore a hood, no – what is it called? Something that covers the face.'

'A mask? A balaclava? Damn! Why, I wonder. Was it someone we would have known? Can you remember if he said anything, Tami? Anything at all? It could be important.'

'He said I should go with him quietly and I wouldn't be hurt, and then after, when Taz was here, he shouted at me to call the dog off,' she said. 'But I think, nothing else. Daniel – I was so frightened! Who were they? What did they want?'

'I don't know. I wish I did. But you were brilliant, Tami.'

'I had to let Rolo go,' Tamiko said then, miserably. 'He could be anywhere, by now.'

'Let's get back to the house, then we can take the car out and look for them,' Daniel suggested. 'I want to check Jahan's all right.'

'Oh, my God! You don't think . . .?'

'Unlikely, given the attack on us,' Daniel said, putting his arm round her shoulders as they began to walk. 'They had got us away from the house, so if it was Jahan they wanted, why complicate things by coming after us?'

Taz nudged his leg and he put his hand down to fondle the dog's wet fur but found instead a hard metal object pressed into his hand. Taking it, he instantly recognised the shape.

'Oh, good boy!' he said warmly. 'Tami, he's found a torch. It must have been what the man was holding. Good lad, Taz. Clever dog! Come on, we should hurry in case they turn round and come back for another pop at us. Can you run?'

'Yes, I want to,' she said.

'Great.' He switched the light on and taking her hand, set off at a jog, back down the road towards the stables and the house. Beside them, Taz bounded happily; it had been an unexpectedly enjoyable outing for him.

Daniel and Tamiko reached the house at almost exactly the same time as Jo-Ji let himself in the front door.

'Hi,' he said, seeing them come into the kitchen. 'You're late doing the horses. Everything all right?'

He came through to meet them and his slight frown deepened to shock.

'Christ! What happened to you two?'

At the sight of her partner, Tamiko's commendable self-control weakened and with a sob, she went towards him and was instantly folded in his arms.

'Oh, Jo-Ji, it was awful. We've lost the horses!' she said brokenly.

'Lost them?' Jo-Ji looked at Daniel over her head.

'It's a long story, but first I need to check on Jahan,' Daniel said, turning sideways to get past them and heading for the stairs. Taking them two at a time, he went along the landing to the room where the boy slept. The door was ajar to allow the light from the landing to enter, and pushing it wider, he could see the contours of the child's body under the bedclothes and his dark hair on the pillow. Jahan's breathing was quiet and regular. He was fast asleep and safe.

Daniel heaved a sigh of relief and leaned against the doorpost as the adrenalin that had been coursing through his veins for the past half hour began, all at once, to ebb, leaving him spent and shaky.

Leaving the bedroom door as he'd found it, he collected two towels from the bathroom and went back downstairs, where Tamiko and Jo-Ji were anxiously waiting.

'He's fine,' Daniel said wearily. 'Thank God!' He handed one of the towels to Tamiko, who took it and began to mechanically rub her wet hair.

'Daniel, what happened?' Jo-Ji asked. 'Tami says you were attacked.' He had his phone in his hand. 'I need to call it in but they'll want details.'

'It was a trap. Whoever it was used bolt cutters to cut the chain and let the horses out and then waited for us to go looking for them,' he said, rubbing his own hair and face. He touched a sore spot and the towel came away smeared with blood. 'Somebody knows the routine. The horses weren't far away. It's my guess they had only just opened the gate. If they'd done it too soon, it's possible someone else might have seen them and come to tell us. That wasn't what they wanted, at all.'

'So what *did* they want? And who were they, have you any idea?'

'I don't know. It was so bloody dark and raining, I couldn't see anything much,' Daniel said, wincing as he mopped his face again and saw fresh, dark blood. 'And Tami said her man was wearing a balaclava or something similar.'

'Are you OK? You look a mess,' Jo-Ji said, frowning.

'Nothing major,' Daniel said, dismissively.

'Nevertheless, we should get you patched up.'

'First things first. The horses are still loose. We need to get out there and find them.'

'Five minutes to get some dry clothes on won't make much difference. You're both wet through and Tami's shivering, aren't you, love?'

Tami nodded, miserably

'It's partly shock, I expect. She's had a horrible time, but she was absolutely brilliant,' Daniel said.

'Either way, she needs to be warmed up. Go on, love, go and change. You too, Dan. I'll call it in and see if there's a car in the area that can help look for the horses. I expect they'll send SOCO out too, but God knows how long it'll be before we see them. There was a major incident at Templemeads earlier and they'll be tied up there for ages.'

Tamiko went obediently upstairs but Daniel held back.

'I wasn't entirely honest, just then,' he admitted softly. 'I'm pretty sure what they were after was Tami. They split us up and she said the man who caught her tried to make her go with him. My guy was more interested in making sure I didn't go anywhere, as you can see,' he added, indicating his face.

'There were two of them?'

'Three, I think. I left my chappie pretty well trussed up, but within a few minutes I'm pretty sure he was in the Land Rover that nearly creamed the lot of us. Someone must have cut him loose. I'd swear he couldn't have done it himself.'

Jo-Ji ran his fingers through his black fringe and down the back of his head, his good-natured face deeply worried.

'It may just be a coincidence but Roy Bartlett's disappeared.'

'Roy Bartlett? Oh, the crack dealer you told me about. When did this happen?'

'A couple of days ago.'

'And you were going to tell me, when?'

'No, I only found out today, just before I came off duty. I would've told you if I'd known, of course I would.'

'Sorry. I guess I'm a bit on edge. Do you really think he's behind this?'

'I don't know, I really don't. My instinct is to say no. Not that he isn't capable of it, but from my dealings with him, I'd say taking Tami out permanently would be more his style. Subtlety isn't a word he'd be familiar with, and abduction would be far more risky – for him.'

'Oh, I nearly forgot!' Daniel exclaimed. 'I took these off my guy when I had him tied up.' He produced the phone and other items from his pockets and put them on the kitchen table. A half dozen or so coins jingled and settled beside the expensive looking cigarette lighter, the cheap, broken phone, and three rather soggy pieces of paper, two of which proved to be banknotes, the other a receipt for an Indian takeaway meal.

'Sorry, SOCO will no doubt curse me. I've probably compromised any forensic evidence there might have been, but I didn't have time to do anything else; I had to go after Tami. The phone's smashed but you might still get something from it or the receipt, maybe. There's the torch, as well. That belonged to the man who tried to snatch Tami. I'm afraid we used it on the way back, but it had already been in the ditch and Taz's mouth, so it was never going to be great. You might get a partial, I suppose, but if they wore masks, they may well have had gloves, as well.'

'Expensive lighter,' Jo-Ji said thoughtfully. 'Looks like gold-plate.' He took a thin plastic glove from his pocket, put it on and carefully picked the lighter up. 'Initials,' he said. 'GKS. Ring any bells?'

Daniel pursed his lips and shook his head. 'Not right away. Oh, actually – what was the name of the guy whose car was stolen? You know, the one that was sitting out here earlier.'

'Graham Siddons. Damn!'

'Yeah. Could be a coincidence, I suppose,' Daniel said. 'But I'm guessing not. But at least that proves that the man who stole the car and was watching the house, earlier, was the one who attacked me. No chance he's actually connected to this Siddons bloke?'

'No. I don't think so. I did take a look. Mr Siddons is sixty-nine; a retired bus driver; lives with his wife, plays bowls and goes off most weekends in his VW campervan to club rallies.'

'Not your average criminal profile,' Daniel agreed. 'Look, Joey . . . Um . . . Do we have to make a big thing of this? I mean, apart from this little lot, there'll be bugger all to interest SOCO out there after all the rain and the thought of half Bristol Met descending on us until the early hours is, quite frankly, beyond tedious.'

'I'll have to call it in,' Jo-Ji said. 'For one thing, how else do we explain these?' He gestured at the items on the table. 'And for another, it could have some bearing on what happened to Hana.'

'Yeah, I know. But what say we play it down a bit?'

Jo-Ji frowned, pushing his fringe out of his eyes in a characteristic manner.

'If I call for that car, they'll want all the details, you know how it works. I don't want them to think I'm trying to hide anything.'

'Who is hiding?' Tamiko had come downstairs again looking much warmer in dry jeans and a sweater.

'No one. Dan wants to play it down.'

'What?' She turned wide, anxious eyes on Daniel.

'The whole thing. What happened tonight,' Jo-Ji answered.

'Only to avoid hassle,' Daniel put in. 'Obviously we have to report it, but can't we just say two men tried to get you into a car but the dog scared them off?'

'With you looking like you've been in a car crash, I think they're going to know there was a bit more to it than that,' Jo-Ji protested. 'Look, you know how it is. They'll keep asking questions until one of you contradicts the other. I could get into trouble, here.'

Daniel held his hands up. 'OK, I give in.'

'I'll ask them to go easy on you,' Jo-Ji said, finding the number on his mobile.

'I think it is possibly, the horses may have come home by themselves,' Tamiko said. 'Shall I go and look before you talk to work?'

'I'll go,' Daniel said.

'But if they are still excitable, they might not come to you,' she said.

'Then we'll both go. From now on, you go nowhere alone – not even in the garden. Promise?'

Tamiko looked from Daniel to Jo-Ji for confirmation, her eyes huge in her heart-shaped face.

Her partner nodded. 'He's right, sweetheart. We can't be too careful.'

'You are scaring me. I don't understand what is happening,' she said. 'Who does these things, and why?'

'I wish I knew,' Jo-Ji told her. 'But we *will* find out, and when we do, they won't know what's hit them, I promise you that!'

The horses hadn't come back, and after a short argument, during which Jo-Ji was reluctantly brought to see that of all of them, he would be the least useful on a horse-catching foray, he was left to stand guard over the sleeping boy. Tamiko and Daniel took the car, the dog, two buckets of food pellets and carrots, and two more lead ropes, and drove slowly along the lane in search of the runaways.

They came across Babs first, not half a mile from home and grazing on the grass verge, outlined by the lights of another car that had stopped twenty feet or so on the far side of her.

Tamiko was all for getting out of the car as soon as Daniel pulled up, but he caught her arm.

'Wait! We don't know who's in that other car.'

She looked shocked.

'You don't think it's them?'

'Probably not, but we can't take any chances. I'll go. You lock the doors as soon as I'm out; get into the driver's seat and be ready to go in reverse as fast as you can, if anything happens.'

'Leave you here?'

'I'll be OK. They're not interested in me,' he said, with more confidence than he felt.

He reached for one of the buckets and a lead rope, but before he could get out, they saw the passenger door of the other car open and someone get out. The Merc's lights instantly picked out a fluorescent tabard and the shining blue and green Battenburg pattern on the car's door, and Daniel heaved a silent sigh. In spite of his assurances to Tamiko, he hadn't relished the idea of walking into the dazzling headlights of the other car, not knowing who might be waiting beyond.

'It's all right,' he said to Tamiko but she too had seen the telltale door markings and was already letting herself out of the other door.

Five minutes later, the bay mare was safely caught and Daniel was driving slowly back down the road with Tamiko following, leading her, and the police car at a safe distance, bringing up the rear. It had been decided that the only sensible course of action was to take Babs back to her stable before embarking on a search for Rolo.

Tamiko was anxious, very much afraid that the young gelding might have galloped a long way before stopping, but when they drew level with the lane where Daniel's own drama had played out, they saw more headlights and were astonished to see a Land Rover being driven slowly towards the junction with a horse apparently trotting alongside.

It turned out to be the neighbouring farmer who had warned Daniel to keep Taz away from his sheep, the previous week.

'Found 'im wandering about in the lane near ours when I got back from the village,' he grumbled, his arm trailing out the window, holding the gelding on a piece of orange binder twine. 'Well, now you're here, you can take 'im. I've got better things to do than chase around after other people's horses all night. Have to be up at five.'

Daniel clipped his lead rope on the chestnut's halter, while Tamiko thanked the farmer profusely, explaining that someone had let the horses out of their field.

'Well, that's as maybe,' he grunted, unwilling to relinquish the sense of personal injury. 'But I've got better things to do.'

Relieved of the horse, he backed up the lane at speed, turned round in a gateway and disappeared into the night.

'Scared we'd get the breathalyser out,' one of the policemen said with a grin. He glanced a little doubtfully at the horse Daniel was holding, which was now sidling restlessly. 'Do you want me to lead that?'

'How about I lead it and you drive my car,' Daniel suggested. 'He knows me.'

The policeman approved that idea with visible relief and they were soon on their way back to the cottage, once more.

# TEN

'So what now?' Daniel asked, the next morning, as they met, heavy-eyed, over the breakfast table. As he'd feared, the night had been a long and tiring one and even Tamiko had overslept that morning.

Only Jahan was bright and full of energy. The effect of the repression of his former life was gradually lifting and aside from occasional questions as to his mother's whereabouts, he seemed to have settled happily into life at the cottage. Daniel knew he wasn't alone in dreading the day when it would have to be explained to the boy that his stay must come to an end. Now, he had finished eating and was watching TV in the lounge. Tamiko was in the treatment room upstairs with a client.

'Had a call from work,' Jo-Ji said. 'The phone is new, un-registered and on a pay-as-you-go tariff. No surprises there. Only been used a couple of times and they're working on tracing those calls. Forensics managed to lift a couple of good prints but we don't have any matches. We can probably find out where it was bought and have a look at the in-store CCTV. The lighter has prints too, but Mr Siddons has confirmed that it's his, so some of those prints will no doubt belong to him. The paper money, once it was dried out, had hundreds of prints, as you might expect, but as yet, none to get excited about. The receipt is interesting. Nothing on the fingerprint side of things because it's been rubbing about in his pocket for a while, besides getting wet last night. The India Palace Restaurant and Takeaway is actually in Lynton, on the Somerset coast. Date: a couple of weeks ago. Enough food, you would have thought, for several people – interestingly ordered at midday, rather than in the evening when most people would be getting a takeaway, although not if you're on holiday, perhaps. We'll see if anyone there remembers them and have a look for local CCTV coverage, but I wouldn't hold your breath. I don't imagine either Lynton or Lynmouth is a crime hotspot.'

'Probably rules out Samir Jafari, then,' Daniel said thoughtfully. 'Not that I thought it *was* him. I'm pretty sure my bloke was a lot heftier, and anyway, it doesn't make sense for him to attack us.'

'Unless he was hiring local muscle,' Jo-Ji said, adding softly, 'but as you say, once he'd got you away from the house, he'd have gone for the kid. Besides, why try now, when he's already going through official channels?'

'We're missing something here, we must be,' Daniel said in frustration. 'The only thing that makes any sense is for it to be your matey, Roy Bartlett.'

'But I'm as sure as I can be that he wasn't in Devon ten days ago,' Jo-Ji said. 'So we're back to the hired muscle scenario – which admittedly, is very much his modus operandi. We suspected he had a huge network of dealers and suppliers when he went down but he didn't give us anything, so I imagine he's owed quite a few favours now he's at large again.'

'Anything on the torch?'

'No. You were right, the man was wearing gloves. Torch is standard issue – buy it in any camping or hardware store, or off eBay or Amazon. Hundreds of them sold every day. With the dry weather we've been having there was no joy with tyre tracks – the verges weren't soft enough. They found the rope you used to tie your man up and SOCO got excited about that, but unless his DNA's on record, it's not going to help us much.'

'If it's your mate Bartlett, it will be,' Daniel pointed out.

'True, but as I said, I can't imagine he'd actually attack you in person. He's not the physical kind and I certainly wouldn't describe him as hefty. Oh, and by the way, they picked up your phone, too. You should get it back soon.'

'Does it still work?' Daniel asked without much optimism.

'Amazingly, yes,' Jo-Ji said. He shook his head in perplexity. 'God, what a mess this all is! When I first called you, I wasn't even sure there *was* a problem, and then after Samir turned up, it seemed we had the answer. I never dreamed anything like this was going to happen.'

Daniel poured himself a second coffee, and sat back, trying to make some sense of the whole thing.

Jo-Ji's phone rang and he picked it up off the table and looked at it.

'Work,' he said, and answered it.

After a moment he frowned and said, 'Harrison Allen? No, it doesn't ring any bells . . .'

'Yes,' Daniel hissed. 'I know him. What about him?'

'Hold on,' Jo-Ji told his contact, then to Daniel, 'Two of the phone calls to that phone you found were from a phone registered to someone called Harrison Allen. Who's he?'

'He's the eldest son of Boo Travers – you remember, the family history the other night? But what the hell's *his* connection to all this?'

'Does Tami know him?'

'Only through Boo. We met him the other night, but she doesn't know either of them well.'

'OK.' Jo-Ji turned away again to talk to his colleague.

Daniel thought for a moment or two, then pushing back his chair, got up and went through to Jo-Ji's den. On the computer screen, bubbles floated and rebounded continually until Daniel moved the mouse to wake the machine up and then opened up the family history website again. He couldn't see what possible connection Boo Travers' eldest son could have to the attempted abduction of Tamiko but there apparently was one, and remembering Boo's reaction at the fundraiser, he wondered if it had something to do with the mysterious half-brother, Ricky. Perhaps if he could track him down, he might be some way to finding the answer. It was a slim chance but they weren't exactly over-burdened with leads.

Going to his saved searches he found David Allen's death record. He had remembered correctly, and not only had Boo's father died in Dorset, but the registration district was Bournemouth, so if Ricky lived there too, there was just an outside chance that he might have been the one who notified the registrar of his father's death. But that was always supposing that David Allen *had* been his father, and that he had recognised Ricky as his son.

There had been no mention of a third child on his obituary. There were a lot of ifs and maybes but Daniel knew from his years in the Bristol Met that ninety-nine percent of detective work involved the methodical following-up of every lead, no matter how obscure. Because of this, and even though he knew if he ordered a death certificate it would take several days to arrive and would probably reveal nothing of interest, he decided to do it anyway.

On a whim, he then Googled the name Harrison Allen and turned up hundreds of results. Refining his search by adding first Bath and then Bristol helped to focus it and scrolling down, he found something that made him shake his head in wonderment.

'Feel free to use my computer any time you like, mate.' Jo-Ji had finished his phone call and come to find Daniel.

'Sorry, Joey. But lookee here, this is interesting. It's the business section of the *Bristol Enquirer*. I found out the other night that Harrison Allen worked at Travers-King Construction but apparently he holds down quite an extraordinarily exalted position in the company for one so young.'

'And . . .?'

'Well, if he is, as the newspaper account of his father's accident said, the natural born son of Dennie Travers, who was the Travers part of Travers-King, and Dennie was still married to Stella King until just a few years ago, that's a monumental cheek! Not only was Dennie having an affair, he apparently introduced his bastard son into the company that was founded by his wife's grandfather and fast-tracked him to a position on the board, no less. I mean, this was a couple of years ago and the guy's only twenty-seven now.'

'When you put it like that it *is* a bit cheeky,' Jo-Ji agreed.

'There's a picture here from four years before that, too. He would only have been twenty-one but he's got more of a beard than he has these days. Probably thought it made him look older.'

'More likely trying to disguise his likeness to his father,' Jo-Ji said.

'You're right. Dennie would still have been married to Stella at that time. Look, there's a bit here about Aubrey King's death, too. If Dennie had been married to Boo for three years at the time he disappeared, he must have divorced poor old Stella before the funeral flowers had even wilted. Tamiko said she was very bitter and, to be honest, who can blame her?'

'But what possible connection can any of this have with Tami?' Jo-Ji wanted to know. 'Last night was pretty full on, from what you say, and if – which scares me witless – the crash which killed Hana is linked to all this, then someone has a serious grudge against her or, more likely, me. I've never had anything to do with any of these people, and until Dennie died, they weren't even on the police radar, as far as I know.'

'Which brings us back to Bartlett. But then, what connection has *he* got to Harrison Allen? They would appear to make unlikely bedfellows.'

'Extremely, I would have thought,' Jo-Ji agreed. 'None of it makes any sense, at all.'

'Do you know anything about an Internet security consultant called Chris Haynes?' Daniel asked. 'That's Chris as in Chrissie or Christine, not Christopher.'

Jo-Ji shook his head. 'Where does she come into this?'

'I'm not sure. Maybe not at all. It's just that she was at the fundraiser the other night, too. She's a friend of Boo's, but apparently she did some work for Travers-King in the past. Harrison remembered her.'

'Well, that's not surprising, is it?' Jo-Ji asked. 'I mean, if Boo's husband employed her, it's quite possible he introduced them to each other.'

'But that's just it – he didn't. Introduce her, I mean. It seems they met by accident when Chris Haynes stopped to help Boo on the road and the friendship developed from there. Apparently she had never spoken of her connection with the company until Harrison brought it up. Doesn't that seem odd to you? I mean Boo would surely have spoken of her husband at some point and you'd think that would have jogged her memory, if nothing else did.'

Jo-Ji made a face and shrugged. 'So what are you getting at?'

'I don't know. It's just another thing that doesn't sit right, and that's not all; I saw Ms Haynes talking to Stella Travers-King that time I went there with Tamiko. She was just leaving as we drove by but they appeared to be deep in conversation. When I mentioned it to her, she said she was picking up an eBay purchase.'

'Well, I suppose that's possible . . .'

'Possible, yes, but a bit of a coincidence, don't you think? I mean, she worked for TK Construction, she's become friendly with Boo, and I see her chatting cosily with Dennie Travers' ex-wife. Too many coincidences for my liking.'

'Even if you're right – and I'm not convinced – how does it help? You don't think she's anything to do with the attacks on Tami? I mean, she doesn't even know her, does she?'

Daniel shook his head. 'No. I haven't got the foggiest how she fits in to the picture or even *if* she does. Sorry, Joey. I'm not helping much, am I?'

'Not helping?' he repeated. 'And what do you suppose would've happened to Tami last night, if you hadn't been there, you daft bugger?'

'Yeah, well. Gotta earn my keep. So what happens about Harrison? I suppose it's hands off, for now.'

'I expect so. We don't want to go in half-cocked. But they'll be ferreting out every scrap of info there is to find about him, so if there are any dark family secrets, I imagine they will be dragged kicking and screaming into the bright light of day.' He slapped Daniel on the shoulder. 'Well, I'm off to work in a minute. You happy looking after things? We'll try and send a car out this way occasionally to put the wind up anyone who might be hanging around.'

'Yeah. No probs. I imagine they'll lie low and lick their wounds for a day or two, don't you? Er . . . can you look up a number-plate for me?'

'Let me guess . . . Chris Haynes?'

'I wrote it down, just in case,' Daniel said, handing a piece of paper over and smiling sweetly. 'Wouldn't hurt to know a little more about the lady, would it?'

The day of Hana's funeral dawned overcast and humid. Worried that Tamiko might be a target on a day when her movements would be predictable, a police car was sent to escort the black Daimler that picked up the funeral party, consisting of Tamiko, Jo-Ji, Daniel and Jahan.

Although it was doubtful whether the boy understood the meaning of the occasion, he seemed to assimilate the mood of those around him and remained solemnly quiet throughout the service at the crematorium, his hand in Tamiko's.

There was a pitiful turnout for the ceremony. From what Tamiko had said, Hana had had little time to make friends when she had shared lodgings with her sister, before Samir came along, and once he was on the scene, he guarded her jealously from any other influence. She had spoken of a friend in Manchester, with whom she'd stayed after leaving Jafari, but they had found no contact number for her amongst Hana's things and so had no way of letting her know about the funeral.

Samir Jafari was present at the service, but Jo-Ji made sure he was seated on the other side of the aisle, and aside from looking across at his son at frequent intervals, he behaved himself. This in itself wasn't surprising, when the major part of the small congregation were either police officers or social workers.

Daniel noticed that on the occasions when Jahan saw his father looking, he shrank back and must have gripped Tamiko's hand more strongly, for she looked down at him and smiled reassurance.

Following the service and the cremation, Tamiko, Jo-Ji, Daniel and Jahan went to a nearby pub, accompanied by two of Jo-Ji's colleagues, where they had sandwiches and coffee in the lounge bar. Tamiko and Hana's parents had been unable to make the journey from Japan, but arrangements were in place for their daughter's ashes to be flown back to her childhood home.

'It is sad that she was so much hoping when she arrive but she was never really happy here,' Tamiko had said with tears in her eyes, when the decision was made. 'I must take Jahan to visit when he's old enough to understand. That's if . . .' She didn't finish the sentence, but the worry was there in her eyes.

'We won't let him take Jahan,' Jo-Ji had told her.

Now as they watched the boy making friends with the pub's cat, Tamiko said, 'Did you see Samir watching him in there? Jahan was terrified.'

'I did, and I'm pretty sure the social worker noticed it, too,' Daniel said.

'Do you suppose . . .?' Tamiko hesitated. 'I'm thinking about it a lot, and I know it is not what we can afford, but would they let Jahan stay with us?'

'You mean, permanently? Adopt him?' Jo-Ji said.

'I'm sorry. Now is not the time to say this,' Tamiko said, glancing towards the two police officers who were sitting a little apart. 'I should not put you on the dot.'

'The spot,' Jo-Ji amended, mechanically. 'You haven't. I've been thinking about it, too. He's a sweet kid, but it would be a huge commitment. We'd need to think about it very carefully.'

After the emotional strain of the funeral, the next few days were mercifully uneventful. Tamiko wasn't riding at any shows that weekend but she and Daniel exercised the horses when Jo-Ji was there to look after Jahan. They kept to the fields as much as possible, away from the roads where dangerous chaos could be provoked by a vehicle driven with intent, but Daniel kept a sharp lookout and saw nothing untoward. It seemed that for the time being, at least, the enemy were indeed keeping a low profile.

The worrying thing was, as Jo-Ji confided in Daniel over a beer on the Saturday evening, if the motive was revenge, then it wasn't just going to go away. If they failed to discover the who and the why of the attacks, then the threat would remain, and sooner or later, when Jo-Ji and Daniel relaxed their guard or grew careless, the aggressor would succeed.

'We won't let that happen, mate,' Daniel told him. 'We'll keep pushing and prying by fair means or foul until we find a sore spot, and then we'll poke it with a sharp stick until the bastards are forced to show their hand. Then we'll have 'em. It's only a matter of time, don't you worry.'

'With anyone else, I'd say it was the beer talking,' Jo-Ji said. 'But with you I feel strangely reassured. Ready for another?'

'Too many more and it will be the beer talking,' Daniel warned him. 'OK. Just to keep you company.'

It wasn't until Wednesday morning that Daniel received an envelope from the General Records Office, containing the certificate he'd ordered.

The certificate recorded the death of David Harrison Allen, aged eighty-five. Cause of death was listed as coronary thrombosis, and the informant one Richard Allen Cardew, of 23a Penny Marden Road, Bournemouth.

'Bingo!' Daniel said. 'Ricky. At last, a stroke of luck.'

'So now you know he exists and Boo Travers wasn't lying, are you happy?' Jo-Ji asked, looking over his shoulder.

Tamiko, who was also in the kitchen, looked troubled. 'Why did you think Boo was lying, Daniel? I thought you liked her?'

'I kind of do, but even nice people sometimes make bad decisions, Tami. I thought she was hiding something – she still may be, which is why I'm going to Bournemouth this afternoon. You'll be around today, won't you, Joey?'

Jo-Ji nodded.

'Yeah. Day off, today. But what do you hope to find out by going to track down this guy? A love-child of Harrison Allen's grandfather – I mean, how relevant is he likely to be?'

'I don't know,' Daniel said. 'That's why I'm going. But Tami apparently spoke to him that time. Come on, mate. You're a cop, you know the drill. Chase down every lead – it's the only way.'

Daniel arrived in Bournemouth in the early afternoon and using the satnav he'd borrowed from Jo-Ji, quite quickly found himself driving down Penny Marden Road looking for number 23. Whoever Penny Marden had been, he reflected, looking at the unprepossessing properties that lined the street, he couldn't feel that she would be overly honoured to be associated with it, if she could see it now. It may, at one time, have been pleasant enough, but the building style of the 1970s wasn't one that improved with age, and now looked merely tired and rundown.

Number 23 was no better than the rest. Bricks below, ugly boarding above from which the paint was peeling, and big, plain windows with metal frames. At the side of the building a metal stairway climbed up to a door at first-floor level and once Daniel had parked his car with two wheels on the pavement, as several others had, he saw 23a painted crudely on the side wall.

A net curtain twitched in the window of one of the ground-floor rooms, and after Daniel had knocked without answer on the door of the upstairs flat, he gratified the watcher's curiosity by ringing their front doorbell.

The door opened a scant six inches on a security chain and a woman with implausibly red hair and eyes thickly lined with kohl peered through the gap.

'If you're looking for Ricky, he's at work.'

'Yeah, I thought he might be,' Daniel said, roughening his voice a little. 'Does he still work at the same place? Down at the er . . .'

'Yeah, down the builder's merchant.'

Daniel looked down the road with narrowed eyes, then back at the woman, who had put a cigarette between her lips and now shifted a baby onto her visible hip, so that it also looked at Daniel. It had wispy dark hair that had been pulled onto the top of its head and secured with a bow, and a nose that badly needed wiping.

'So, remind me, love, how do I get there from here? I usually come in from the Christchurch side,' he said.

'Hang about.' The woman closed the door and removed the chain, stepping out onto the street next to Daniel in order to point up the road. She wore a spangly pink T-shirt over black leggings, with a pink pair of the ubiquitous Crocs on her feet. At some point in her past she had plucked her eyebrows into extinction and pencilled in two thin black lines instead. Removing the cigarette again, she said, 'You go to the top and turn left by the kebab shop, then along to the end, past the pub to the main road. Turn left and it's along there on the right. You can't miss it.'

'Thanks, love.' Daniel turned away.

'Why don't you came back here when you've seen Ricky?' she called after him. 'There's only me and the kid here, mostly. I could do with a bit of company.'

Daniel sketched a kind of salute, before settling back into the car.

The red-head's assertion that he couldn't miss it might have been true if the directions she had given him had been accurate, but soon after the kebab shop, he realised that she had missed out at least one turning, and it was only by trial and error that he eventually found himself on the main road she had mentioned. From here, however, the builder's merchant was easy to locate, being a branch of a well-known franchise.

He parked in their car park and went through the door into the cool of the showroom beyond, where almost immediately an assistant in black jeans and a short-sleeved purple shirt asked him if he needed any help.

'Er, yes, I'm after a really heavy-duty locking system for a gate,' Daniel said, thinking on his feet.

'All our bolts and padlocks are along here,' the lad said, leading the way. 'What sort of gate is it?'

Daniel explained about the field gate and was shown a number of impressive locks, from which he selected one. He had noticed that, alongside the company logo, the lad had a name badge on his shirt, which said 'Darren'. Short of wandering around the showroom until he'd seen all the employees' badges, he was plainly going to have to take the direct approach.

Putting his debit card into the machine at the desk, he asked casually, 'Does my mate Ricky still work here? Ricky Cardew? I haven't seen him in ages and thought we might catch up when he gets off.'

'Yeah, Ricky. He's out in the warehouse. Do you want me to page 'im?'

'No, it's OK. I'll find him on my way out – if that's OK?'

'Yeah. No problem,' Darren said, handing him his receipt. 'You can't go in the warehouse, but go to the door and someone'll find him for you. Have a nice day.'

Daniel did as he had been told and an overweight teenager listened, shouted 'Rickay!' at the top of his voice and then shook his head and waddled off in search of him, hitching his trousers up, Canute fashion, as he went.

Daniel waited on the threshold of the warehouse, thinking that he might treat Taz, at present waiting in the car, to a run along the beach when his business with Ricky was finished. He wondered which parts of the local coast, if any, might be dog-friendly at this time of the year, while he absent-mindedly watched the neat and efficient movements of the three or four forklift trucks he could see coming and going between the towering shelving and stacks of building supplies.

After a minute or two, the young man with the trousers appeared from an aisle halfway up the warehouse and began to make his way back towards Daniel, who tried without success to make out from his expression what news he bore.

It was because of this preoccupation that he didn't immediately notice that one of the forklifts was not only coming towards him but directly *at* him, at its top speed of ten miles an hour. It wasn't until the machine, which was carrying a substantial pallet-load of something shrink-wrapped in plastic, was fifteen feet away and blocking his view of the youngster, that Daniel realised the driver was aiming straight for him with no apparent intention of stopping.

Someone shouted a warning, even as Daniel leapt swiftly to one side, caught his foot on something and stumbled backwards, sitting down abruptly. He was back on his feet in no time but was hindered in his instinctive move to follow the forklift by a concerned worker who had run across and now fussed round him, showering him with shocked apologies.

'Yeah, thanks, I'm fine,' Daniel said, pulling away. But it was already too late. Away across the tarmac, the driverless forklift truck was trundling to a halt as its erstwhile operator was racing, on foot, towards a line of parked vehicles that presumably constituted the staff car park.

As he watched, debating whether or not to make a run for his own car, Daniel saw the man jump on a bicycle and, pedalling furiously, disappear round the front of the main building, heading for the road. A massive, liveried lorry turned in, hiding him from view and with a sigh, Daniel gave up the idea of trying to follow. Even if the cyclist were still in sight by the time he reached the main road, it would be easy enough for him to disappear into a footpath or alleyway too small for Daniel, in his car, to negotiate. Besides, he only wanted to talk to the man, he wasn't trying to arrest a wanted criminal. Which begged the question, why had Ricky reacted in such an extreme manner to Daniel's presence?

'I'm really sorry, sir,' an assistant wearing a supervisor's badge was saying. 'I really don't know what that was about. He'll be up before the boss when he shows his face back here, I can tell you. That's *if* he does.'

'No, really. Not on my account,' Daniel said. 'He must have thought I was someone else. I'm fine. I'll catch up with him another day. But if he comes back before I see him, please tell him I'm a friend of the family. He's not in any trouble.'

The supervisor repeated his assertion that such behaviour couldn't be allowed to go unpunished, so Daniel waved a hand and walked away carrying his purchase, leaving the warehouse workforce fairly humming with speculation. The incident would be the topic of the week, he guessed.

He was just unlocking his car when a voice said hesitantly from behind him, ''E wouldn't mean to 'urt you, Ricky wouldn't.'

Daniel turned and raised an eyebrow. A thin, gaunt-faced lad with spots stood twisting an oily cloth between his hands. His badge labelled him as Neil.

'Don't be 'ard on 'im – when you find 'im, I mean. Darren paged 'im to warn 'im you was comin', see? An' I reckon Ricky thought you was a repo man. That's why 'e ran.'

'Is he a friend of yours?'

The lad nodded. 'I'm new 'ere an' 'ees bin good to me. The others, they can be mean sometimes. But Ricky's nice.'

'OK, Neil. Thanks for telling me,' Daniel said. 'And look, if I don't catch up with him today, tell him I'm not a debt collector. I just want to talk to him. Family stuff – no trouble. Will you do that for me?'

Neil scratched his chin with none-to-clean fingernails and nodded.

Unwilling to go to the trouble of coming back another day, as he'd suggested he might, Daniel decided to drive back to Penny Marden Road and see if Ricky eventually turned up there.

With the red-headed curtain twitcher in mind, he parked several doors further down the street and with words of apology to Taz, who was by now heartily fed up with the whole outing, settled down to wait, sipping a takeaway coffee that he'd had the fore-thought to purchase on the way back.

The coffee was long gone and Daniel's patience had almost followed it, by the time his quarry finally put in an appearance.

Riding his bicycle up the street, he stopped on the opposite side to his flat and scanned the building, giving Daniel the opportunity to observe him for the first time. His age was the biggest surprise. With David Allen having passed away seven years previously at the age of eighty-five, he had expected Ricky to be closer in age to his father's legitimate children, Boo and Steven, who were in their mid to late forties. The man on the bike he estimated to be nearer his own age – certainly closer to thirty than forty.

From his imperfect vantage point, Daniel couldn't tell if he favoured his half-brother and -sister, but he could see that he was of average height and had dark hair, receding at the temples. At some point he'd changed out of his purple warehouse overalls and now wore stonewashed jeans and a faded blue T-shirt, perhaps to make himself less recognisable to the 'repo men'.

Apparently satisfied after peering across the street for a moment or two, Ricky got off the bike and wheeled it across to the bottom of the steps, where he hoisted it onto his shoulder and started to climb.

Daniel let himself out of his car and praying that Taz would behave after his long incarceration, opened the back and hissed, 'Heel!' at him.

Taz launched himself from the car, totally ignored his command and proceeded to relieve himself against a lamppost for ten long seconds.

Daniel felt guilty. 'Oh, sorry, mate,' he muttered.

Partially hidden from Number 23a by the car, he looked to see if Ricky had reached his front door. It would be a great deal harder, he imagined, to persuade him to talk once he attained the relative security of his flat.

However, fate was on his side, for once. Ricky's red-headed neighbour had emerged from her ground-floor flat and was even now standing at the foot of the outside stairs, engaging him in a conversation that Daniel imagined probably revolved around a description of his own earlier visit. The baby with the snotty nose was nowhere to be seen.

Calling Taz to heel once more, he began to saunter up the pavement, for all the world as if he was merely out for an evening stroll, and because Ricky hadn't had a decent look at him at the warehouse and the redhead had her pink-clad back to him, he was able to get level with the house before either of them noticed him.

He stopped and said in a clear voice, 'Boo Travers sent me.'

The redhead nearly jumped out of her pink spangles. She turned, saw Taz and screamed, flattening herself against the wall at the foot of the stairs.

Taz joined in the fun, producing the most blood-curdling growl in his repertoire until Daniel told him to shut up. At his stern words, the redhead stopped screaming and whimpered. Taz did as he was told but kept her under strict surveillance.

Ricky, who had stopped halfway up the steps, retreated to the top and lifted his bicycle above his head, as if preparing to throw it down on Daniel's head.

He put a hand up to halt him. 'Ricky, don't! I'm not a repo man, I promise. I'm a friend of Boo's. She's your sister, right?'

'Half,' Ricky said, keeping the bike where it was. 'Half-sister. What do you want? She didn't send you. She doesn't talk to me, none of them do.'

'It'd be a shame to smash up your bike for nothing,' Daniel went on. 'I only want to talk. It won't take a minute. Come on, put the bike down. Even if you threw it, the dog could get to you before you got the door open.'

Slowly, Ricky lowered the bicycle.

Taz, who had been dividing his attention between the redhead and the man at the top of the steps, decided to concentrate on the woman again, and licked his lips.

'He's a bit funny about pink,' Daniel said wickedly, and the woman raised wide eyes to his face for a moment before looking back at the dog. 'Tell you what, I'll hold his collar while you get back inside, if you like,' he offered.

In less than ten seconds, the door slammed shut behind her.

'I wish I could get rid of her that easily,' Ricky said with the beginnings of a smile. His voice was a great deal more educated than his surroundings would have suggested it would be.

'Yeah, well, I didn't think we needed her,' Daniel told him with a friendly wink. 'Look, I just wanted to ask you a couple of questions, that's all, and you've answered one of them already. I won't go into details but I saw your sister with someone who she claimed was you but I wasn't sure, and I wanted to check.'

'Sure it wasn't Steven, her real brother?'

'He's in Australia, apparently.'

Ricky shrugged. 'Don't know then, but it wasn't me, for sure. They might have forgiven Dad his lapse – on the surface, at least – but they've never forgiven me for being born, even though it was me who gave up university and looked after him when he was getting old and unable to cope. They rarely came near him in the last few years, except sometimes on birthdays and Christmases, but he was still going to leave them his money. I was supposed to have the house but in the end, after the care bills and the nursing home and such, there wasn't much left of anything. They blamed me for that, too. I think they thought I'd taken it or something.' He shrugged again, the bitterness plain to see. 'To be fair, I always thought it was Steven more than Boo. He always was a selfish bastard! Anyway, I haven't seen either of them since Dad's funeral.'

'Thanks for that. Sorry I gave you a fright.'

'Yeah, well, I shouldn't have driven at you earlier, but I panicked. I suppose I'll have to start looking for another job, now.'

'I'll ring your boss and try and make it right,' Daniel promised, but Ricky wasn't hopeful.

'It's all health and safety, these days, and I broke just about every rule in the book today. Bill, my supervisor, won't let it go. He's never liked me. It sounds crazy but it's like he's got an inferiority complex and I think he feels threatened by me.'

'Because of your education?'

'Yeah, I guess. But I don't want his bloody job, anyway. I was only there 'cos I couldn't find anything else.'

'What were you reading at uni?' Daniel asked.

'Law,' Ricky said. 'Took after Dad, I suppose. Can't afford to go back now though.'

'I'm sorry I've buggered up your job,' Daniel said, genuinely so.

'S'OK. I was bored out of my mind, anyway. It's just . . . well . . .'

'You needed the money.'

'Yeah. It's a long story. Look, if you don't mind, I'm doing a shift at the pub, later . . .'

Daniel took a card from his back pocket and held it up. 'My number's on here. Give me a ring in a week or two, if things get bad. I can't make any promises, but I'll put some feelers out, OK?'

Ricky didn't move, it seemed he still didn't totally trust Daniel or maybe it was the dog, who was gazing up at him in that disconcerting way that German shepherds have.

'I'll leave it here,' Daniel said, wedging the card behind the bracket for a light fitting on the wall just above his head. 'Good luck, mate.'

He called Taz to heel and turned away.

Ricky called after him. 'Was that true – about the pink, I mean?'

'Nah,' Daniel looked back with a smile. 'I made it up. He's pretty much colour-blind anyway.'

# ELEVEN

Having mollified Taz with a long run along the beach at Hengistbury Head, Daniel headed back to Maiden Ashton in a thoughtful frame of mind. From his age and description, Ricky Cardew was quite patently not the man that Tamiko had had words with at Rufford Manor, even without his claim of non-acceptance by his half-brother and -sister. As to who that might have been, the seeds of an idea were putting down tentative roots into Daniel's psyche, and the first thing he did when he got back to the cottage was to fire up the computer and do a search for images of Dennie Travers.

There was no shortage. Scrolling through them, Daniel selected two of the clearest and most recent, one being from the newspaper coverage of his disappearance, printed them off and showed them to Tamiko.

Her response was disappointing.

'It could have been this man, I cannot say for sure. As I tell you, my man has a beard and wears sunglasses. I only see him for a little while.' She looked again. 'I'm sorry. I cannot be certain.'

'It's OK, never mind. I remember now, you said he had a beard. I should have expected it, it's the obvious disguise.'

'The whole thing's quite a leap in reasoning,' Jo-Ji said. They were at the kitchen table, drinking tea. 'After all, all you really know is that Boo lied about who it was Tamiko saw. There could be any number of reasons why she did that, most of them far less dramatic than her husband coming back from the dead.'

'But if he did fake his death, for a life insurance payout, or whatever, don't you think he'd do almost anything to keep his secret safe?'

'You don't seriously think he's been here all along?'

'No, of course not! But his son is dying. Isn't it possible he's been lying low somewhere abroad and came back to see him?'

'And you think the attack the other night was his attempt to silence Tami? You're forgetting something important, aren't you? Tami had never met Dennie, so she had no reason to doubt that the man she saw was Boo's brother. Therefore she presents no threat at all, so why would they take the risk of attacking her? I'm afraid you'll need to have something a lot more concrete than that before I'm going anywhere near the boss with the idea,' he told Daniel. 'You know as well as I do that if we go charging in with no more than a supposition, we could easily end up with egg on our faces, if not a complaint of harassment.'

'It's not without precedent,' Daniel argued.

'I know, but the way things are at work at the moment, anyone who puts their head above the parapet without a very good reason is liable to get it shot off. It's your friend Paxton throwing his weight around again. I think the powers that be are leaning on him about these budget reforms. And I've got an assessment coming up in a week or two; I don't especially want to draw attention to myself in that quarter, if I don't have to.'

Daniel had to sympathise. He knew exactly how it felt to be in DI Paxton's black books and it was something to be avoided. It was the inspector who had made his own position in the force intolerable, eventually forcing his resignation.

'I guess by now Paxton knows I'm staying here – I hope that isn't making things awkward for you,' Daniel said.

'He hasn't said anything, but then I don't see that much of him, day to day, if I can help it – the joy of being in the dog unit. But he'd be sure to get involved if I started peddling that kind of theory about the place and he'd want to know exactly how much you had to do with it.'

'But you know, if I'm right, it could explain everything.'

'Just get me some more, Dan. Something solid I can put before them. Something they can't argue with.'

'OK. I'll try. It's probably for the best, anyway. One whiff of interest from your lot and I reckon they'd be gone before old Paxton gets his arse off his chair.'

'Anyway, I've got that info you wanted on Chris Haynes,' Jo-Ji said, then. 'Ran her numberplate and yes, that's her real name; Christine Haynes. She's thirty-eight, ex-army signals corps, and now runs a business advising on Internet security. It's just her and a part-timer, as far as my contact could see. No criminal record – not even a parking ticket or speeding fine. In fact, not on our radar at all. I can give you her address, if you want, but I really shouldn't.'

'Leave it for now. I don't want to get you into trouble and to be honest, I don't think I'd get anywhere calling on her at home. I get the impression she's a pretty tough cookie. What I wouldn't mind doing, though, is having a word with Stella King.'

'Oh, you want to see Stella?' Tamiko said, hearing the name. She was by the stove, preparing food. 'I'm treating her again tomorrow afternoon.'

'That's lucky. The gods must be smiling on me,' he said. 'Now I've just got to think of a way to engage her in conversation.'

As it turned out, Tamiko engineered the opportunity. As before, she and Stella disappeared inside the house fairly promptly upon arrival, and Daniel, left to kick his heels once more, again went for a walk. When he returned just before the hour was up, Tamiko opened the front door and beckoned to him.

'Stella needs something from her attic,' she told him. 'It's too heavy so I tell her you would be happy to get it down.'

'This is very kind of you.' Stella greeted him in the hall, plain and sixtyish, with her trim figure dressed in casual trousers and a cream polo shirt with a Ralph Lauren logo on the pocket. 'It's only a box of books that I promised for the local charity bazaar, but it's rather heavy and I didn't want to go and undo all the good work Tami has just done on me.'

Heights were something of a bugbear for Daniel, but even though the house had three floors and the trapdoor to the attic was, necessarily, on the topmost one, the ceilings here were lower than they were downstairs and the climb held no great fears for him. The box was, as she had told him, pretty heavy, and he had to back down the ladder, sliding it down the uprights, but within a very short time it was safely on the floor and the ladder and trapdoor returned to their respective positions.

'Could I ask you to carry it downstairs for me, Daniel?' Stella asked, adding as they reached the hall, 'thank you so much. Well, the least I can do is offer you both a cup of tea. Would you like one?'

Daniel had only just drunk a large cappuccino at the café along the road, but he assured her that he would love one, and she sent the two of them into the garden while she prepared it.

'Well done!' Daniel told Tamiko, as they wandered out onto a beautifully sheltered patio, festooned with pots and hanging baskets.

'It was just lucky she mention it,' Tamiko said. 'She was telling me about this bazaar and mentioned the books up in the roof.'

'Perfect. I didn't think it would be this easy.'

However, when Stella came out carrying a tray with teapot and china cups, it soon became clear that it wasn't going to be easy.

'I saw a friend of yours the other day,' Daniel told Stella, when the obligatory remarks about the weather and the prettiness of the garden had been dispensed with.

'Oh, did you?' she responded with polite interest. 'Who was that?'

'Chrissie Haynes.' He used the familiar form of her name, hoping it would put his hostess at her ease.

She frowned. 'I don't think I know her. What made you think I did?' she enquired.

'Oh, sorry. It was just that I saw you talking to her when I dropped Tami off, last time.'

'Oh, the lady with the motorbike?' Stella said. 'Was that her name? I suppose it was. She just came to collect some jewellery she bought from me on eBay.'

'Oh, I see. Sorry. It was just the way you were talking, I assumed . . .' Daniel cursed inwardly. Either she was telling the truth, which he doubted, or the woman had been forewarned.

'Just passing the time of day, as far as I can remember,' she said. 'How do you know her?'

'She's a friend of Boo Travers' and she introduced me. We know Boo through the horse. She has showjumpers, too.'

'Tamiko said you were driving the lorry for her,' Stella said. 'If I were you, I would keep clear of Mrs Travers and her friends. The woman is a slut!'

The word cut the soft, gentleness of the afternoon scene like a machete, incongruous from the lips of one who had so far been well-mannered and polite. Daniel glanced at Tamiko and saw that she was visibly shocked, but for his own part, inside he was cheering. He had pierced the barrier Stella King had so carefully put up.

'To be honest, I don't know her that well,' he said. 'But I do know you two have . . . history, shall we say? I'm sorry, I shouldn't have mentioned her.'

'Not saying her name won't make her go away,' Stella stated. 'She's a parasite. She sucked the life out of my marriage and one day she'll pay for that. She thinks she's sitting pretty, but she's not. The bitch will get her come-uppance soon and all her scheming will be for nothing. I can wait. I've waited twenty-eight years.'

'Some would say she's had her come-uppance,' Daniel suggested. 'What with losing her husband and now her son being ill.'

Stella became tight-lipped. 'If that's what you believe.'

'He's got leukaemia, I'm told.'

'I'm sorry for the boy,' she said, stiffly. 'But only for his own sake. Tell me, how do you suppose you'd feel if you discovered that everything you thought you had was a sham and always had been? Nothing but lies. She ruined my whole life.'

It takes two to have an affair, Daniel thought, but he didn't think it would help to say so.

'It must have been so hard for you,' Tamiko said with genuine sympathy. 'I can see why you're bitter.'

Stella turned and smiled at her, back in control of her emotions. 'Thank you my dear. I'm sorry, I shouldn't have spoken like that. Will you have another cup of tea?'

Sensing that he had probably learned all he was going to, Daniel declined and presently, they were shown to the front door with slightly less grace than they had been invited in.

'I'm glad I make another appointment before,' Tamiko said as they made their way to his car. 'She was very angry – very bitter. I feel the tension when I treat her, this time. It is supposed to make her relaxed but I think she is tense again as we leave.'

'I'm sorry. I hope I haven't lost you a customer, but she shouldn't blame you. It was me who stirred her up. Feel free to disown me, when you see her again.'

On the way home, Daniel's phone rang, and after a glance at the display, he apologised to Tamiko, pulled in at the first opportunity and answered it.

'Daniel Whelan?' The voice was male and hesitant.

'Yep. Is that Ricky?'

'How did you know?'

'Bournemouth number. Don't know anyone else in Bournemouth.'

'Oh, OK. Look, I hope you don't mind. You said I could ring . . .'

'And I meant it. What can I do for you?'

'Well, I've been thinking about what you said – that you might be able to help me. Did you mean it?'

'Of course. Did you lose your job? I'm sorry. I rang the company to try and put things right but like you said, they weren't interested.'

'Yeah, well, it was no great loss but it did keep body and soul together, just. I wasn't going to ring but I've just been told that the pub where I've been doing evening shifts is about to close, so now I'm really up the creek.' He paused, then rushed on. 'I'll understand if you can't help. I don't blame you, it's just I kept wondering whether you really had something in mind or not. I mean, if you did it'd be stupid not to . . . well . . .'

'It's OK. Yeah, I did have something in mind, but I can't make you any promises. Tell me, would you be prepared to up sticks to Devon?'

'Listen mate, you've seen where I live. Would you be sad to leave?' Suddenly, there was a note of optimism in Ricky's voice that hadn't been there before, and Daniel hoped to goodness he wouldn't have to let him down.

'OK. As I said, no promises, because I haven't checked it out as yet, but whatever happens, I'm sure we can come up with something. Speak in a bit.'

When he cut the connection he found Tamiko regarding him questioningly.

'Ricky? Boo's half-brother, Ricky?' she asked. 'You're a good man, Daniel Whelan.'

Daniel shrugged to hide his discomfiture.

'Not really,' he said, starting the car and looking for a gap in the traffic. 'But if I break something I like to fix it. It's only fair.'

That night, the residents of No 5 Tannery Lane and, quite possibly their next-door neighbours too, were rudely awakened by a thunderous knocking on the front door, which set Taz barking furiously.

Daniel, who was still sleeping in the lounge, was on his feet instantly and moving swiftly to the window to see who was outside. A glance at his watch showed him that, although it was almost light, it was barely four o'clock in the morning and the figure at the front of the house was illuminated not only by the general glow in the sky, but by the motion-sensitive security light over the door.

It was Samir Jafari and he looked as though he hadn't been to bed. Staring up at the first-floor windows, he didn't at first see Daniel on the ground floor. As he watched, Jafari stepped forward to hammer on the door again and then bellowed, 'I want my boy! Give me my son!'

Taz stood inside the door and redoubled his efforts until he was told to be quiet. With a hand on the dog's collar Daniel unlatched and opened the door and had the satisfaction of seeing Jafari stumble backwards as he came face to face with the dog's impressive dental exhibition, at that moment clearly visible beneath raised lips.

'Hold the dog!' he shouted. 'Don't let the fuckin dog go! I only want to see my son.'

'Then come back in the daytime, when you're sober,' Daniel told him. 'And come with a social worker.'

'I've got every right to see him,' Jafari stated.

'Then there shouldn't be a problem, should there?'

'That bitch says they're going to take him away from me. They can't do that!'

'You'll have to take that up with them. Nobody's said anything to us.'

'I want to see him now!'

'For God's sake, man! It's four o'clock in the morning!' Daniel pointed out. 'Go away before I call the police. You're waking the whole neighbourhood.'

'Not before I see my son. You can't stop me.'

'I don't have to. He'll do it for me,' Daniel said nodding at the dog.

Jafari stood staring at the dog for several long moments, unshaven and bleary eyed, then said, 'Fuck you!' turned and walked unsteadily back to his van, which was parked untidily across the lane.

With a crunching of gears, he straightened it up and drove away, just as Jo-Ji came down the stairs to stand behind Daniel.

'I've called it in,' he said. 'Hopefully they'll pick him up for driving under the influence. That won't help his cause overmuch.'

'Is Jahan OK?'

'Tami's with him. He was terrified, poor little bugger! Crying his eyes out – afraid his dad was going to take him away. I told him you and Taz weren't about to let that happen, and he calmed down a bit.'

'Right, you're on hot chocolate duty. I'll take Taz up to see him,' Daniel said, ruffling the dog's fur. 'Good work, lad.'

Taz ran into the lounge to find a tug-toy, his reward for a job well done.

The next day, as Jo-Ji wasn't working until late, Daniel decided to take him at his word and try and get the proof he needed. After his early morning ride with Tamiko, he packed a digital camera into a backpack along with a bottle of water, a flask of coffee, a waterproof-backed blanket and a handful of dog biscuits. In his pocket he slipped a memory-stick-sized voice recorder, and wearing a lightweight pair of walking boots with grey jeans and a dark-green fleece, he put Taz in the back of the car and set off towards Bath.

According to the Ordnance Survey Explorer map he'd looked at over breakfast, the fields surrounding Boo Travers' home at Rufford Manor were bordered on one side by a large area of woodland. There was a public footpath marked on the map, running through the wood and out across farmland on the other side. Between the footpath and the boundary with the Rufford Manor land the wood climbed steeply to a ridge before dropping away again to the edge of her fields. Daniel wondered if a person climbing to the top of that ridge with a pair of powerful binoculars, such as he had in the glove compartment of the Mercedes, might be able to obtain a useful view of the Rufford Manor land and buildings. And if that was the case, and a person was very patient, might he see someone moving around who had no business to be there? As he had no better plan in mind, Daniel had decided to check it out.

The day was warm and sunny, and when he reached the gravelled pull-in that served as a car park for the path into the woods, Daniel found several cars there before him. Glancing at them as he parked, one in particular caught his eye and searching his memory, he identified the numberplate.

'Well, well, Ms Haynes. I wonder what you are doing here . . .?' he mused. It was just possible that she too had a dog and that her choice of footpath was coincidental, but Daniel didn't seriously entertain that possibility for long. He remembered his first mentor at the Met standing on his hind legs in the local bar one night and proclaiming loudly, 'I'm a police officer; I don't believe in fairies, Father Christmas or coincidences!' Although he wouldn't go that far, Daniel did think that Chris Haynes' presence in the woods adjacent to Boo Travers' land was probably stretching chance a bit too far.

Gathering his backpack and his binoculars, he let Taz out and, calling him to heel because of the road, walked along the line of vehicles towards the footpath sign.

Chris Haynes' car, a medium-sized 4×4, had a waterproof jacket and some files on the back seats, and the area behind them was empty apart from a rather less than clean blanket and a pair of Wellington boots. This in itself wouldn't necessarily have argued the ownership of a dog, but the clincher was the state of the side windows, which were almost opaque with dried-on nose marks.

'Maybe we've got it wrong,' he said to Taz, who stood watching him with his head on one side. 'You don't care, you just want to get in the woods, don't you? Call yourself a police dog? You should be helping me.'

Taz's answer was to jump at Daniel and then run ahead of him, tail waving happily, to where a sign and a dirt path flattened by the regular passage of feet marked the way into the trees.

He knew from the map that the path ran parallel to the Rufford Manor boundary for the best part of a mile before veering fairly sharply away to the right, following the lower ground. At this point, he would make his way uphill to the top of the ridge and hope to find a viewpoint from which to observe the property on the other side without himself being seen.

In spite of the half dozen cars in the car park, Daniel only met one group of walkers. As was his habit, Taz dropped back to his side as they approached, and regarded the two women with their assortment of children with supreme indifference. He treated their two golden retrievers with a similar aloofness, but bestowed upon a brindle and white Staffie, a look of such seething hatred, with all his hackles raised, that Daniel had to make a grab for his collar.

'Sorry. He was bitten once,' he explained to the mums, but they were too busy anxiously gathering their children to them to respond to his apology, and hurried past on the other side of the track.

Reaching the bend in the track, Daniel paused to survey the slope he intended to climb. It was steeper than he had expected, even though the contour lines on the map had shown it to be a considerable feature of the landscape. Bracken was thick at ground level, covering the rising land with a sea of green, whilst above, a mixed canopy of oak and ash, liberally interspersed with tall pines, spilled dappled sunlight onto the forest floor. There didn't seem to be a path of any kind to follow and Daniel had resigned himself to ploughing uphill through the undergrowth, when Taz, who had been casting about at the side of the track, suddenly became animated and dived into the bracken, nose to the ground, and disappeared.

Daniel moved the fronds aside. Sure enough, there was a narrow path of beaten earth barely six inches wide, which was clearly a regular byway used by wildlife, and although the ground was too dry – even after the downpour of a few nights before – for footprints, he could see evidence that something bigger had recently passed that way in the bent and bruised bracken stalks at intervals along the way.

'Steady, Taz. Wait for me,' he called in a low voice, and was rewarded by the sight, some thirty feet away, of the dog's head lifting above the greenery to look back at him.

Because of the limited visibility and because he didn't want Taz to initiate a full Search and Detain on what might possibly just be an innocent member of the public out birding or worse still, looking for a secluded place to have a pee, he told him to sit and wait.

Once he caught up, he took a tracking line and harness from his backpack, and put them on the dog. His tracking thus given the official stamp, Taz leaned into his harness eagerly. This was his business; this was what he lived for, and Daniel had to keep checking him in order to be able to keep up.

On four legs, Taz made nothing of the hill but Daniel, labouring in his wake, discovered to his cost that although they were following a path, it was by no means clear, and several times he stumbled over fallen branches and small, knotty tree stumps, or had to duck under fallen timber. The bracken was chest high and the atmosphere humid, pungent with the smell of it and buzzing with insects. He was sweating and breathing hard, and by the time he reached the crest of the ridge, he was sure that unless the person they were tracking was stone deaf, they would be well aware of his presence if they were anywhere within fifty yards of him.

At the top of the hill, the trees rose like a wave and dipped down the other side. A little way off, to one side, a stand of beeches kept the encroaching bracken at bay, and leading a very reluctant Taz off his track for a moment, Daniel took the opportunity to have a rest and survey his surroundings.

Taking a swig of water, he poured some into a special foldout drinking bowl for the dog, who drank thirstily.

Even though he had climbed a good three hundred feet, the outlook was disappointing, the slope being more gradual on this side of the ridge so that his view was blocked by the leafy tops of the neighbouring trees. It seemed he'd have to get closer.

Swinging his backpack into place once more he clipped the dog's lead back onto his harness and giving him the command to track on, they moved back to the narrow path and set off down the slope.

After only a couple of minutes of working his way downwards Daniel could see open sky ahead and before long the path came out of the trees and ran along the edge of a steeply shelving section of hillside. Below were open spaces of heath and grass, dotted with smaller trees and scrubby growths of blackthorn and brambles. At the foot of the hill, around a hundred yards away, was a thick bushy hedge interspersed with trees, and beyond it, pastureland. Rufford Manor land.

Although the narrow, animal path swung right to follow the contour of the hill, Taz didn't hesitate, but plunged straight on, over the edge of the escarpment and down.

'Hey, wait!' Daniel hissed, giving three quick tugs on the tracking line. It was his own way of telling the dog to stop, when he didn't want to raise his voice. Taz stopped obediently but with evident frustration.

'Sshh!' he said, to quieten the whining protest. 'We need to look before we leap, OK?' Safely off the skyline, it would be a good time to take stock of his surroundings. He had a pretty good idea who Taz was trailing, but even so, he didn't particularly want to blunder into her before he had had a chance to see what she was doing out there. If she was on the same mission as he was, it was quite probable that she would have hunkered down somewhere on this hillside to watch the valley below, and if she was tucked in the shade of one of the patches of scrub, he might not see her until Taz marked her position with a frenzy of barking as he had been taught to do.

He unbuckled the dog's harness and took it off and finding his own clump of blackthorn to sit under, took his binoculars from his backpack and fitted them with the anti-reflective lens covers that were invaluable for covert surveillance. The honeycomb filters lowered the light levels a little but it was an acceptable trade off to cut out the danger of attention being drawn to his position by sunlight flashing on the lenses. He began to sweep the hillside methodically from side to side with the glasses, from just below his position to the very bottom of the valley.

There, he could see that just outside the field boundary was a stony track following the line of the hedge along the bottom of the valley until it disappeared from his view into the trees to his left. Directly below him, a field gate opened onto this track, and getting his map out, he located the track, denoted by a faint dotted line alongside the boundary; easy to miss with all the contour lines. From the section he was looking at and tracking left, it appeared to lead eventually to the road on the side of which he was parked, but half a mile or so further on. With a sigh, he realised that if he'd spotted it earlier, he could have saved himself the climb over the top of the ridge.

Looking down the hill once more, his eye was caught by a movement and picking the binoculars up again he saw a figure in khaki cropped trousers and a grey-green T-shirt walking along the track towards the gate. By the short blonde hair, Daniel identified the walker as Chris Haynes, and at her heels trotted a terrier of indeterminate parentage.

As he watched, she reached the gate onto the Rufford Manor land, and with the briefest of glances around her, vaulted it in impressive style and disappeared from view. The terrier squeezed under the gate and followed her.

'Now, where are you going?' Daniel muttered, scanning the pastureland beyond the hedge. Off in the middle distance he could see the slate rooftop of the manor itself, partially hidden by the trees that surrounded the formal garden. Like him, Chris would have seen that it was impossible to find a good vantage point from the hill but surely the woman wasn't going to try to walk close enough to watch the house and garden. The risk of discovery would be very real with so much open land to cover.

As he watched, the trespasser came into view again and Daniel realised she was making her way towards a small wooden building that was tucked under the hedge not far from the gate. At first, it looked like a field shelter for stock but closer inspection revealed that it had doors in the end nearest the gate. They appeared to be padlocked.

Chris Haynes reached the building and hefted the padlock in her hand before bending down to put her eye to the door. Apparently unsatisfied, she then circled the building, perhaps looking for a window or a weak point. It was while she was hidden from Daniel's view and he lowered the glasses for a moment, that his attention was caught by movement on the periphery of his vision.

A Land Rover was approaching along the track outside the

boundary hedge. With his heart rate accelerating on behalf of the woman by the shed, he watched to see if it would stop at the gate or drive on by.

It stopped and a figure got out that, even without the binoculars, Daniel could identify as Cal McAllum, the Scotsman he had seen at the show. Wearing jeans and a leather waistcoat over a red vest, with shades and the same baseball cap he had worn before, he walked round the front of the Land Rover, took a key from his pocket and began to unlock the padlock on the gate.

'Shit!' Daniel muttered. By now, he imagined Chris Haynes must be well aware that she had company, but she was in a perilous position and could only hope to avoid detection by staying hidden at the far end of the shed. Daniel felt detached and useless in his position on the hillside, but until Cal was back in the Land Rover, he dare not move for fear his movement caught the man's eye. It crossed his mind to act as a decoy by showing himself, but it was by no means certain that unless he went close enough to reveal his identity, the Scotsman would do any more than note his presence, and Daniel didn't want to be forced to show his hand, if he didn't have to.

Lifting the binoculars again, he watched Cal pull the gate wide, return to the Land Rover and drive through, before getting out to close and lock the gate once more. Daniel couldn't see the woman and the dog, who were presumably hidden at the far end of the shed, and devoutly hoped that the Scotsman wouldn't see them either. He didn't imagine that the fact of her being female would earn her any leeway if he found her on Rufford Manor land, where he seemed very much at home.

The Land Rover was moving again now, disappearing behind the hedge, heading for the shed, and Daniel decided the time had come to move closer, just in case he needed to take a hand in proceedings. He stuffed the binoculars in the backpack and then, with a reckless disregard for the health of his ankles, he set off at speed down the slope with Taz bounding at his side.

He angled across the hill to keep the thickest part of the hedge between him and the vehicle, and once in the valley bottom, followed the track back, walking on the turf at the side of the stones and keeping Taz at heel, until he was level with the shed on the other side of the hedge.

Cal had driven the Land Rover inside the building and as Daniel listened, he killed the engine and, in due course, came out and closed the doors. He could just see the man's head and shoulders through a gap in the vegetation and as he replaced the padlock and turned away, it began to look as though Chris would be lucky. But then Daniel heard a muffled yap and with a sinking heart, saw the Scotsman freeze as he clearly heard the same. At the sound of the other dog, Taz was on full alert, too, and was inclined to rumble until Daniel twitched his collar and whispered an urgent, 'No!'

On the other side of the hedge, Cal started to move silently towards the back of the shed and Daniel lost sight of him. Moving quietly, himself, he shifted his position to bring the Scot back into view, and was surprised to see Chris Haynes walk out from behind the building with the terrier under one arm and meet him head on.

Her startled cry was masterly. If Daniel hadn't been sure she knew Cal was there, it would have fooled him. So, she had decided to try and brazen it out.

'Who the bloody hell are you and what are you doing in here?' Cal demanded.

'I – I'm sorry. I wasn't doing anything. That is, Nipper came in here hunting rabbits and I couldn't get him to come back.'

'This is private property. It says "Private" on the gate, can't you read?'

'I know. I can read, but Nipper can't,' Chris said, with a nervous laugh.

Cal wasn't amused. 'Don't try and get clever with me, woman! You should keep the animal on a lead if you can't control it.'

'He saw the rabbit run through the hedge and followed it. It's not my fault. I couldn't just leave him here.'

Cal took off his baseball cap and scratched his head, thoughtfully. Then he replaced it and stepped closer to Chris.

'You see, it's like this. I don't like trespassers, and I especially don't like dogs. If I see that little rat in here again, I'll shoot it. And that goes for you, too! BANG!'

Chris took a hasty step back, looking scared. 'You can't go round threatening people like that!'

Cal lifted his hands. 'Threatening? I didn't say a word, yer honour. Who's to say I did? The rat? Eh? Now get out, and don't come back!'

Chris began to edge round him, but as she passed him, Cal suddenly shot out a hand and stopped her.

'Wait! What's this?'

Chris had a camera and binoculars slung over her shoulder and he had caught hold of one of the straps. She had no choice but to stop.

'It's a camera.' This time Daniel felt her uneasiness could well be genuine, and wondered what pictures she had shot with it.

'I can see it's a fuckin camera! What have you been doing with it? And don't say taking pictures.'

'B-but I have. B-birds,' she stammered. 'I'm a birder, I've been trying to get shots of the buzzard up on the hill.'

'A buzzard? That's hardly rare enough to interest a real birdwatcher.'

'I know it's not rare. It's part of a study. No! Let go! What are you doing?' She tried to pull the strap out of his hand, but he had hold of the camera itself now and was fiddling with it. 'You can't do that!' she exclaimed, jerking it out of his hands, and almost in the same instant, without apparent thought, he back-handed her across the face, knocking her to the ground. The terrier, shaken from her hold, yelped and ran for the gate.

Daniel had seen enough. Stamping and scuffing on the stony track, he assumed an American accent and called out, 'Sweetheart? Honey? Have you found that dog yet? What's going on?'

'Yes, he's here!' Chris called, following his lead seamlessly. She scrambled to her feet. 'I'm just coming.'

It seemed that Cal shared Daniel's unwillingness to be seen, for with the imminent appearance of back-up and therefore a witness on the scene, he made no further attempt to detain Chris or her camera and within a very short space of time, she was climbing back over the gate and onto the track.

As she turned towards him, Daniel could see that the Scotsman's blow had bruised her cheekbone and drawn blood from her nose.

'What the hell?' he exclaimed, keeping in character. 'What happened to your face, honey?'

'Leave it, please,' she said. 'He's not worth it!'

'He?' Daniel demanded. 'Someone did this to you?'

'No, please. I shouldn't have been in there. Please leave it!'

'I'd listen to the lady, unless you want some of the same,' Cal remarked loudly from beyond the hedge, and then, when Daniel didn't reply. 'No, I thought not. Fuckin' Jessie!'

'I'll call the police,' Daniel said then, feeling that his American alter-ego would say that, at least to save face.

'Call away,' came the reply. 'Your word against mine and anyway, I don't live here – I'll be long gone.'

Taking a cautious look through the gap in the hedge he'd used earlier, Daniel could see the Scot standing near the doors of the building. It was obvious that even though he was chary of being seen, he wasn't going to abandon his position until he was sure the trespasser and her American partner were long gone.

'He's watching,' he said quietly to Chris. 'Come on, let's go. I left my stuff on the hill. Are you OK?'

'I'll live,' she said, wiping her nose on the back of her hand as they started to walk, and regarding the resulting bloody smear dispassionately. 'Thanks to you. Were you following me?'

'Yep. Though I was coming out this way anyway. It seems great minds do think alike.'

'My mind doesn't feel very great at the moment,' she said ruefully. 'Bloody stupid to let myself get caught like that. Where is the little sod, anyway?'

'Behind you.'

Chris turned to look down and Nipper wagged his stump of a tail unrepentantly.

'Bugger!' she said suddenly, grabbing at the camera, which still hung over her shoulder. She stopped, holding it up. A small compartment was open, its hinged flap dangling. 'The bastard took the memory card.'

'What's it got on it? Anything incriminating?'

She frowned. 'Not really. A couple of shots of the view from the top of the hill – but even on full zoom, they didn't show much of the house – and actually, as it happens, a few of the buzzard that really was hanging around.'

'You *are* a birder,' Daniel said as they started to tackle the slope. 'And there was me, impressed with your quick thinking.'

'So if you were close enough to listen to all that, why didn't you come to my rescue?' she demanded.

'You heard him,' Daniel said. 'I'm a Jessie.'

Chris cast him a sideways glance. 'And the real reason?'

'OK. It was obvious he didn't know you and I thought you might just get away with your "innocent rambler looking for her dog" story. But I've met our friend the Scotsman before, and if I'd shown my face he might well have suspected the both of us of being up to no good.'

'You know him? Who is he? I've only seen him from a distance.'

'I've met him. I wouldn't say I know him. But I know enough about him to suspect a whole lot more.'

'Such as?'

They were both breathing hard now as they approached the spot where Daniel had left his backpack. He stopped and turned towards her.

'Such as, he's not been in the country long, and when he did come it wasn't through Heathrow or Gatwick, or any of the conventional channels. *And* he didn't come alone.'

Chris was watching him intently. '*And* . . .? Who do you think came with him?'

'I think he brought Dennie Travers back from the dead. But then you know that, don't you, Ms Haynes? Because Stella King is paying you to prove that very thing.'

# TWELVE

'Who *are* you?' Chris Haynes demanded.

'You know who I am: Daniel Whelan, friend of Tamiko Yoshida.'

'Who? Oh, yes, I remember – the Japanese girl at the fund-raiser. But you know that doesn't answer my question. I saw you with Boo Travers.'

'I saw *you* with Boo Travers,' he countered.

'If you know I'm working for Stella, then you must have realised I only made friends with Boo to try and win her confidence. What's your interest?'

'My only connection is through Tami,' Daniel said, zipping his backpack up and hoisting it onto his shoulders. 'I came to keep an eye on her as a favour to her fiancé, who's a friend of mine. He was worried about a potential stalker, and she needed someone to drive the horsebox to shows because Natalie, who you also met at the fundraiser, has a broken leg. I was at a loose end, I stepped in. Tami knew Boo, but only to say hi to. The trouble started when she called in at Boo's unexpectedly to drop off something she'd borrowed and saw Dennie.'

'She did *what*?' Chris exclaimed, pulling Daniel round to face her. She had a surprisingly strong grip. Taz growled a warning and she let go. 'She saw Dennie Travers? Then why the hell didn't she report it?'

'Because she had no idea that's who it was,' Daniel said. 'She didn't know Boo back when Dennie was around, and the man she saw told her he was her brother. I didn't guess until yesterday, and even then, when I showed Tami a photo, she wasn't certain it was the same guy. He's grown a heavy beard, I gather.'

Chris groaned. 'When I think of all the times I've tried to drop in unexpectedly, with just that aim in mind – but they've got those bloody electric gates.'

'Yeah, I know, but they'd been left open when we got there. Accidentally, I imagine. Just the luck of the draw.'

Daniel turned and glanced back down the hill to the shed. 'He's still there. If we want a look at the Land Rover, we'll have to come back later, but I've a strong suspicion he'll have moved it by then.'

Chris frowned again. 'So, what's so special about that Land Rover? And why does he keep it so far away from the house?'

'I'm pretty sure it's the one he used to drive into Tamiko's car and kill her sister,' Daniel said grimly.

'He killed her *sister*? Why?'

'Because one Japanese girl looks pretty much like another from a distance, and because she was driving Tami's car.'

'God, that's awful! But if Tami didn't recognise Dennie, why on earth did he do it?'

'I think, because he could. Because the opportunity presented itself. Hana just happened to be in the wrong place at the wrong time and paid the price, poor kid. I get the impression this Cal bloke might be something of a loose cannon. The police suspected it was a 4×4, possibly with bull bars, but they've never found it. In fact they didn't find anything to convince them that it was anything more than an unfortunate hit-and-run accident.'

'But you did?'

'Not for sure, but I have a suspicious mind, and when Tamiko saw a photograph of Steven Allen at the fundraiser and pointed out that it wasn't the man she'd seen at Rufford Manor that time, and Boo tried to make us believe it was her *half*-brother Tami had seen, I decided to check it out. I had already met our friend down there, whose name is John McAllum, or Cal to his friends – if he's got any, so I had an inkling something was going on in the Travers camp.' He gave Chris a brief description of his first encounter with the man and what he'd found out on the Internet about his early and inglorious association with the young Dennie Travers.

'So then you checked out the half-brother?'

'Yes. When someone laid an elaborate trap and tried to abduct Tami, the night after she spoke out about Boo's brother, I found I had a burning desire to see whether Boo did indeed have a half-brother. As it turns out, she does. But as they're not on speaking terms, let alone visiting terms, and he is, anyway, about twenty years younger than the man Tami described, I figured we could rule him out. So Boo Travers was covering for someone. That was when I started to wonder whether the dead husband was really so dead, after all. From pictures I've seen, the man Tami saw fits the description pretty well, or at least as well as anyone can with a beard covering half their face.'

'Stella has been convinced he faked his death, all along,' Chris said as they topped the hill and began to descend the narrow track through the bracken on the other side. 'At first I wasn't so sure, even though it did get him out of a sticky spot.'

'What kind of sticky spot? One would have thought that finally getting his divorce and moving in with his lover and family, he would have got what he wanted.'

'Oh, he had,' she said. 'Until an employee with a grudge, loyal to the old guard, so to speak, raised questions in Stella's mind about the legitimacy of some of the deals he'd been doing. That's where I came in. It's wonderful what you can find out when you have a company's computer system at your disposal.'

'So you're not just an IT consultant. Internet security, don't you call it?'

'That's part of it – the official part that's on my website. Stella called me in ostensibly to check the health of the system and advise about possible upgrades. They had had it done before, and I may have led them to believe I was from the same company,' she said with an air of innocence. 'We picked a time when Dennie was away on business for a few days and I was granted access to almost everything; I wandered about the building quite freely, and what I found, with a little judicious digging and double-checking, was that, not content with marrying the boss' granddaughter and being promoted in leaps and bounds to the very top and a partnership, no less, with all the financial perks that entails – and there were many, believe me – our Dennie was channelling a steady stream of extra wealth into his own pockets by way of payments to bogus companies that subsequently went bust, along with a general skimming of the profits.

'I soon realised we had enough to build a good case against him and as I'd stretched my time at TKC about as long as I credibly could, I got out. I wrote her a detailed report and shortly after, Stella turned everything over to the police. I gather the fraud squad were about to pounce when it seems that someone loyal to Dennie got wind of the fact that the shit was about to hit the fan and warned him.'

'Hence the lost at sea scenario.'

'As you say. I gather the trip had already been planned. It was meant to be a celebration of his meeting Boo, twenty-something years ago. Talk about rubbing Stella's nose in it. It beggars belief that so many people would happily go along with the whole thing, when it was so blatantly immoral. I mean they could hardly be unaware when Dennie and Boo's grown-up sons were there.'

'Hey – it was a free booze up! And anyway, I find there's nothing like money for helping people see only what they want to,' Daniel observed. 'So the party cruise was planned and he adapted it for his own ends. Clever. Plenty of witnesses to testify that it was a tragic accident. Strong currents to account for the fact that a body would never be found. Presumably Harrison was in on it. Did Boo know what was going on?'

'I don't know,' Chris admitted. They were walking along the track on the forest floor now, heading for the car park. 'I have to say, I hope not. For in spite of knowing what I know about her and the way she has lived her life, I find I can't help liking her. I shouldn't, but I do. She's just a likeable person.'

'I know what you mean,' Daniel said. 'I suppose that's what kept Dennie living a double life all those years, that and the kids, I suppose. So why did he wait so long to divorce Stella? Was it the terms of the grandfather's will?'

'You *have* been doing your homework,' Chris said. 'I'm impressed.'

Daniel shrugged. 'Guesswork.'

'Yeah, well, according to Stella, her grandfather never made a secret of the fact that on his death, his majority holding of the shares would be split between Dennie and herself. I think he thought it was a way of keeping them together, because without each other, neither of them would have a controlling share. But he reckoned without Dennie's cunning, because having installed Harrison in a position on the board, their combined shares gave them the majority. You have to remember that at that point in time, no one seems to have guessed that Harrison was his son – he's looking a bit more like his father now he's getting older but he was very young when he joined the company. Also, Stella took no interest in the day-to-day running of the company and quite possibly never met him face to face. It was only after old Aubrey King's death that he "came out" and there was a huge amount of smothered resentment amongst his fellow workers.'

'I imagine Stella wasn't too happy, either.'

'She was already reeling from the divorce, To have him parading his "other family" in front of everyone in the company her grandfather built up, was total humiliation.'

'I saw her yesterday,' Daniel told Chris. 'Tami was giving her a massage and I went along. She's incredibly bitter. But did she really never guess that Dennie had another woman? He must have spent so much time away, surely?'

'I don't know whether she knew, deep down, that he had another life but didn't want to admit it, even to herself. I mean, if she'd hired a detective he'd soon have been found out. But I'm pretty sure she didn't know about the kids, and that was the ultimate betrayal, for a woman who couldn't have any.'

'So what happened to the investigation after Dennie disappeared?'

'Nothing. Oh, they looked into the evidence, of course, but Dennie had been careful not to involve Harrison or anyone else in his schemes. The fraud was entirely down to him, and as he was apparently beyond prosecution, the case was closed; the losses written off. According to Stella, he left all his shares to Boo and Harrison. She now holds only slightly more than a quarter. Can you wonder at it that she was bitter?'

'Not at all,' Daniel said. 'So, did you ever find out who warned Dennie that the game was up?'

'No. I suppose even a bastard like that inspires loyalty in *some* people. Someone probably foresaw a handsome reward for such a gem of information.'

'But that argues that someone else must have known about the fraud, because if, as you say, no one but him knew, who could warn him that it was about to be uncovered?'

Chris shrugged. 'I guess we'll probably never know.'

Daniel filed the thought away. He didn't like loose ends but it could wait.

'So, what now?' Chris asked, then. 'The police?'

'Tamiko's husband is police,' Daniel told her. 'I shared my theory with him but he wanted more than supposition. That's, by and large, what I was doing here today, until I saw your car. The thing is – you haven't got enough to take to the police, or I'd imagine you'd have done so – and neither have I. Between us, we have more, but nothing that amounts to proof. I think we need to have irrefutable evidence that they'll act on instantly, or we might just find that our quarry has done a bunk a second time.'

They had reached the cars now, and Chris picked Nipper up to keep him from committing suicide on the busy road. She looked at Daniel through narrowed eyes.

'Are you saying what I think you're saying?'

'I'm saying that money has influence almost everywhere, and that we should consider no one to be above corruption,' he stated blandly.

'That's what I thought you were saying,' she said. 'Bloody hell! Tell me again what you do for a living.'

'At the moment I'm a kind of minder. Lately, I have been a truck driver,' Daniel said. 'Before that I was in the police force and believe me, I have had enough experience of corruption to last me a lifetime.'

Chris looked at him keenly.

'I believe you. I've seen that look before. So, what do you suggest we do now? Have I totally loused things up getting caught by this Cal bloke?'

'No, I don't think so. Your story was believable and thank God, your camera card shouldn't give anything away – unless there was anything else on there from earlier?'

She shook her head.

'No. I always download and then clear it. So, when did this McAllum come on the scene?'

'Only a couple of weeks ago, I think. In fact, I'm almost certain of it.'

'That fits. About three weeks ago, maybe less, Boo invited me over to ride with her as I had done several times before, and then, over lunch, she broke down and poured her heart out about Spencer's illness. It was the first time she had really talked to me about it. I think there'd been bad news at his latest meeting with his consultant and I tell you, at that point I felt so incredibly sorry for her, I was within an inch of chucking the whole thing in, but Stella can be equally as compelling. Anyway, the next time I called, she almost cut me dead. I thought, perhaps she was regretting letting her guard down like that. She's an immensely strong woman.'

'She probably was regretting it, but not for that reason. It's my guess she'd got word her husband was going to try and get back to see Spencer, and she couldn't afford to have anyone close. I drove Tamiko to a show near Barnstaple that weekend – her sister was alive then and we all went. That was where I first met Boo and Harrison.'

'Harrison was at a show? That's odd in itself. Boo says he rode as a child but these days has no interest at all in the horses.'

'Yes, he told me that himself. Watersports are his thing, he said. Helpful if you want to stage a fake drowning.'

'He has a diving instructor's certificate,' Chris confirmed. 'I believe he and Dennie went diving together a time or two, though Dennie's thing was more sailing. I believe they often went to Portishead, and Harrison used to go down to Devon or Cornwall for the surfing. So, for the drowning, are you thinking scuba gear tethered to a weight on the sea floor at a prearranged location?'

'Something like that, with a boat to pick him up somewhere,' Daniel agreed. 'And maybe he came back in much the same way. When we left the show at Barnstaple, Tami commented that Boo's lorry was going the wrong way – turning away from home. I didn't think much of it, she could have been going for petrol or something, but in hindsight, she could also have been picking up Dennie and Cal if they arrived the night before and had been lying low for the day.'

'Why bring Cal with him? It sounds as though he's a bit of a liability.'

'You're right. Without him stirring things up, Dennie could have been and gone without anyone being the wiser, except perhaps you. I assume the plan *is* for him to go back again – it would be madness to think he could stay for very long. But I think Cal is probably a kind of fixer. I imagine he made the arrange-ments. They go way back. They were partners in crime years before Dennie met Stella and started moving up in the world. Maybe Dennie has been staying with him, abroad. Possibly he's been a go-between – we can only guess at how Boo and Dennie have stayed in touch. It's likely he helped him get away initially, I'd say. All I can say for sure is that the night they tried to abduct Tami – or whatever they were trying to do to her – I had quite a turn-up with someone in the dark and ended up banging his head on the road—'

'Ah, that's why you look like you've been scrapping,' she said, interrupting.

'Yeah.' Daniel touched the bruise on his face; it was still tender. 'Anyway, I relieved that person of the contents of his pockets and one of the things he had on him was a receipt for an Indian takeaway from Lynton, in Devon. It was his first mistake. He's been so careful all along, wearing gloves, using unregistered phones and throwing them away; leaving nothing for forensics.

Even so, I didn't make the connection until today, when Cal took off his cap and I saw the cut on his forehead.'

'Yes, I saw that,' she said. 'So given you're pretty sure it *was* him that night and we know about the Land Rover, are you still saying we haven't got enough to go to the police?'

'Ordinarily, I'd chance it, but this time – given the history of the case – I'd like to see if we can't set our rabbits running before we loose the dogs.'

'You want to scare them into making a dash for it? But isn't that a bit risky? What if they go when we're not looking?'

'But we will be looking. That's where you come in,' Daniel told her. 'I suggest you use the bike, it's easier to tuck out of sight and they won't be expecting it.'

'In spite of your best efforts to tell everyone the other night,' she reminded him sardonically. 'But even though I might look like superwoman, even I can't watch them twenty-four seven. I have to sleep sometimes.'

'I don't imagine they'll take off immediately. I think your performance just now was probably convincing enough to put Cal's mind at rest for the time being. Keep a general look out, as you have been and leave it with me. Give me your number and I'll be in touch.'

'OK. But don't let me down, Daniel Whelan. I've been working on this for so long – I don't want him to slip through my hands now, when we're so close.'

'They won't,' Daniel said. 'Trust me. There's a show tomorrow, if Boo's going – and she told Tami she was, when we saw her last – she'll leave early in the horsebox. Around six, I imagine.'

'Spencer likes her to keep riding. He loves the horses, too, and she said he didn't want his illness to stop her competing. He used to go and watch but she says he tires too easily, these days. You don't think Boo will smuggle Dennie out again in the horsebox?'

'She may do, but not tomorrow, I think. If she's going to the show, she'll head for the M4 and turn towards Reading, not the coast. I'll hang back till I hear from you. If she does go to the show, I wouldn't mind having a little chat with her, maybe rattle her cage a little in the most innocent way. If I'm wrong and she heads the other way, we may have to shout for help.'

                              *       *       *

At six fifteen the next morning, when Daniel was on his way to pick the lorry up from Natalie's yard, he got the call from Chris. He could hear the sound of rushing traffic in the background.

'You were right,' she said, speaking loudly to counteract the background noise. 'She's on the M4 heading east. And Daniel – she has someone with her. I couldn't get a good look, but I think it may have been Harrison.'

'That's unexpected. What are they playing at, I wonder?'

'I don't know, but it's possible it's just as simple as him going along to help with the horses. She used to have a girl who helped in the stables but I imagine that would be a bit awkward at the moment. Harrison's not interested in the horses anymore but he *was* brought up with them, so maybe he's been roped in to help. Anyway, I'll go back and keep an eye on the house now, just in case there's any activity there.'

Daniel continued on his journey, and within the hour, he and Tamiko, Inga and Jahan were also on their way to Reading. He could have done without Harrison Allen being at the show. He had hoped for an opportunity for a few words with Boo on her own, but that wasn't going to be easy with her son hanging around.

In fact, he underestimated just how difficult it was going to be, and by lunchtime, Daniel had begun to suspect that Harrison had guessed what he was after and was actively ensuring that he didn't have a chance to speak to her. The only time he wasn't at his mother's side was when she was actually riding, and halfway through the afternoon, in desperation, Daniel asked Tamiko if he could warm Babs up for her.

'You want to ride her, *here*?' she was taken aback.

'Could I? Look I need to talk to Boo, and Harrison is sticking to her like glue. If I could just borrow Babs for five minutes I could get close to her without him breathing down our necks.'

'But what is it you want with her? You can't ask her about her husband.' Daniel hadn't told Jo-Ji and Tamiko the details of his meeting with Chris Haynes. It wasn't that he didn't trust Jo-Ji, but he was afraid that if he knew more, he would feel obliged to take what he had learned to his superiors, and Daniel knew that, whoever he told, the information would find its way to DI Paxton.

'I just need to talk to her about her half-brother,' he said with a grain of truth.

'Well, I suppose it will be OK,' Tamiko said, imperfectly hiding her doubt. 'But be careful, here Babs is not like she is at home; she is more excitable.'

'I'll be careful,' Daniel promised. He altered the length of the stirrups, climbed aboard and trotted away to the practice ring, where Boo was circling at a walk on her grey horse. Cutting in front of another rider with an apology, he brought Babs alongside her.

She turned to look, her face instantly registering shock and unease.

'What are you doing here?' she hissed at him, glancing around as if to locate her son. He was nowhere to be seen. 'You're not competing.'

'I just wanted to talk.'

'What about?'

'Why you've been avoiding me all day for a start.'

'Avoiding you? I hardly know you. Get over yourself! Anyway, I've been busy with the horses.'

'Last time you made a point of talking to me. Today, every time I get near you, Harrison is somehow in the way.'

'When I spoke to you last time, I was being friendly, nothing more,' she said. 'Now please, leave me alone. You're not supposed to even be in here.'

'What are you hiding?' Daniel asked bluntly, and had the satisfaction of seeing tension tighten the muscles in her jaw and neck.

'Nothing,' she said. 'I don't know what you mean.'

'I went to see Ricky Cardew.'

Boo kicked her horse into a trot and then a canter, and Daniel followed suit, feeling Babs snatch at her bit and toss her head with excitement. They circled the practice area once but then, finding Daniel still by her side, Boo cast him a look of daggers and slowed back to a jog.

'Leave me alone or I'll call the steward,' she hissed.

'Ricky says he's never been to your place. He says you're not even on speaking terms.'

'OK. So I lied about him. I was covering for someone else.'

'Who?'

'What business is it of yours?' she demanded angrily.

'If Tamiko was nearly killed because of who she saw, it's very much my business,' he stated.

She reined her horse in, sharply. The unease was plain to see, now.

'That's ridiculous!'

'Is it?'

Other riders grumbled at the stationary horses blocking their path but Boo didn't seem to notice. She looked down at the grey's mane and Daniel could almost hear her brain churning.

'All right, it was my lover. *Was*. We're finished. There's nothing to tell now, and it's certainly got nothing to do with anything that happened to Tami.'

'Then why so upset by it? Why so defensive?'

'Because he was married, OK? And that's all you're getting, so fuck off and leave me alone!'

The collecting ring steward called Boo's number and she rode across to the ring entrance without a backward glance.

Aware that he'd been a lot longer than the five minutes he'd promised Tamiko, Daniel turned Babs and headed back to the lorry, almost riding down Harrison, who was standing by the entrance to the practice ring.

'What were you doing in there? What were you talking about?' he asked suspiciously.

'None of your business,' Daniel replied. He was sure their conversation would be relayed to him as soon as Boo left the ring, but he derived great satisfaction from the words, anyway.

Dropping the mare back at the lorry with Inga, Daniel collected shades and a denim jacket from the living quarters and then turned and headed away once more. Having given the ants' nest a vigorous stir, he wanted to be within earshot when mother and son discussed his interference.

'Daniel . . .!' Inga's voice followed him and he felt guilty ignoring her, as she was no doubt finding it tricky looking after Jahan as well as helping Tamiko with the horses.

He waved his hand. 'Yeah, sorry. Back in a minute.'

He knew where the Rufford Manor lorry was parked, as he had loitered within sight of it several times already that day, hoping to find Boo alone. This time, after buying a can of beer and a baseball cap on the way, he sat on the grass, leaning against the wheel of a neighbouring lorry with the peak of the cap tipped low over his shades and waited for Boo and Harrison to return.

It wasn't difficult to discern what the topic of their conversation had been since she'd left the ring. As they came within earshot, Boo was saying heatedly, 'Well, what was I supposed to do? He was following me around the bloody practise ring!'

'Is that *all* he said?'

'Yes, I told you it was.'

'Do you think he believed you? About the lover, I mean.'

'Yes. No. *I* don't know, do I? He's not stupid. If he went to the trouble of tracking Ricky down, he's not going to take my word for anything now, is he?'

'But why did he do that? I don't understand why he did that in the first place.'

'Because of bloody Cal, that's why.' They had arrived back at the horsebox now and Boo dismounted and ran her stirrups up, while Harrison stood behind her, kicking the turf with the toe of his canvas shoes. 'If that bloody psycho had just left well enough alone, nobody would have asked any questions and we wouldn't be in this mess. I know your father's known him a long time, but someone needs to explain to him that this is England not South America, and you can't just remove people who get in your way and expect to get away with it!'

'For God's sake, Mum!' Harrison hissed, glancing around in panic. 'Not so loud!'

Daniel kept his head down. He was in the shade of the lorry, just on the edge of Harrison's eyeline and hoped he would escape his notice. It appeared he had, for after a few moments' silence, during which Boo removed her horse's saddle, Harrison spoke again.

'So what are we going to do about this Whelan bloke?'

'Nothing!' His mother rounded on him, dropping her voice until Daniel could scarcely hear it. 'Nothing! There's been too much done already. This has to finish now. Your father and that imbecile he brought with him must go back where they came from. It was a crazy idea to come in the first place and if he'd asked me, I would have told him so.'

'He wanted to see Spencer. You can't blame him for that.'

'And that wasn't such a great idea, was it? The whole thing was completely selfish. Spencer thought he was dead, he'd done his grieving, and now he's grieving all over again for a father who chose to abandon him.'

'It was either that or go to prison,' Harrison said. 'He'll come round, given time.'

'Well, he's not going to get time, is he? I want them out. *Now*.'

'All right, all right. Calm down. It might take a day or two to arrange. It's not like catching a bus, is it?'

'I don't want to know the details, I just want it all to be over.'

A phone started trilling in the cab of the lorry and Boo hurried round the side of the vehicle to retrieve it. She passed within feet of Daniel, who kept his head down, hiding his face, with the beer can on the grass beside him, hoping that if she thought about it at all, she would think he was asleep or drunk, or both.

Under his brows, he watched as she opened the door of the cab, stepped up and leaned in to pick up her phone.

'Yes? Oh, hello, Samantha. Is everything OK?'

There was a pause as the unknown Samantha spoke and then Boo asked, with a noticeable tremor in her voice, 'When? When did this happen? Did he say anything?' Another pause, before she said, 'OK. I'll be back as quickly as I can. No, you did right. I'll be as quick as I can. Let me know what the doctor says.'

'What is it?' Harrison had followed his mother.

'It's Spencer.' Now Daniel could hear tears in her voice. 'He's gone unconscious. Samantha says he was complaining of feeling tired and wanted a drink, and when she went back with some water, he was . . .' Her voice cracked. 'Oh, God! I should have been there! I should never have left him.'

'You weren't to know.'

'But he said he was tired this morning.'

'He's often tired. And anyway, he wanted you to come, he said so. It's not your fault.' Harrison sounded shaken, himself. He tried to put his arms round his mother but she shook him off and almost ran round to the back of the lorry, saying, 'Not now! We must hurry. Come on. Quickly, Harry!'

In almost frenzied haste, they loaded the grey horse, threw his saddle in through the groom's door and within minutes the big diesel engine was fired up and with Harrison at the wheel, they were rocking and swaying away across the field towards the exit.

Daniel uncurled from his position and stood up.

'Has Boo gone?' a voice asked. 'They're calling her for second place in the main ring.'

A petite, perfectly made-up blonde girl was watching the departing horsebox with a mystified expression.

'Bad news from home, I think,' Daniel told her.

'Oh, no! Her son? Poor Boo!'

Daniel thought back over all he'd heard and could only agree.

# THIRTEEN

On the way home, Chris contacted him with the news that while there had been no suspicious departures, Rufford Manor had been visited by several cars, among them a paramedic's vehicle.

'Looks like poor Spencer has taken a turn for the worse,' she concluded. 'As you probably know, Boo came back, hotfoot, mid-afternoon.'

'Yes, I was there when she took the call,' Daniel confirmed. 'I heard quite a bit more, too. I'll ring you when I get back.'

'I feel very sorry for poor Boo,' Tamiko said, when Daniel switched off the hands-free. 'To know your child is dying and there is nothing you can do must be a terrible thing. What did she tell you about the half-brother, Ricky?' she asked, remembering Daniel's earlier conversation with Boo.

'Well, she admitted it wasn't Ricky you saw,' Daniel told her. 'But then, she couldn't really do anything else once she knew I'd seen him. She said she lied because she was covering for a lover, but I'm not so sure.' He was very conscious of Inga's presence, and didn't want to say too much.

'She keeps a lover in her stableyard?' Tamiko opened her eyes very wide, and Daniel laughed.

'Well, I don't know. I suppose he could have been waiting for her there because she didn't want her family to see him.'

'Other people have very odd lives,' she observed.

'You should be a copper,' Daniel said. 'Then you'd see just how odd!'

Chris Haynes was quietly jubilant at Daniel's report that their suspicions had been confirmed. He was ringing from the horsebox, which was parked in the lane outside the cottage while Inga helped Tamiko unload her horses.

'Police, yet?' Chris asked.

'We've still only got my word for it,' Daniel said, 'and my word is worth less than nothing in some quarters. I think we should stick to the original plan of waiting till they run for it before we shout for help.'

'I still think that's a bit risky.'

'Very,' Daniel agreed. 'But in my view, less risky than going through official channels. I can see us being taken in for interviews and to make statements as the bureaucratic wheels start slowly turning and they check out our credentials, too. Meanwhile a little bird tweets in Dennie Travers' ear and he packs his red spotted handkerchief and is gone. Anyway, I think, from what Boo was saying to Harrison, they'll be on the move pretty soon, anyway, and when they do, we'll be right behind them, and that's when we'll call the police – when we've flushed him out into the open.'

'You really don't have a very good opinion of your old colleagues, do you?'

'Just one or two in particular,' Daniel said. 'And I do have my reasons.'

'You can tell me about it over a cup of coffee one day,' she told him. 'OK. If you're sure, we'll do it your way, and on your head be it if he sails away into the sunset before we can stop him!'

'Have you anyone who you can trust to help keep an eye on the place?' Daniel asked.

'Yeah, I've got a mate who owes me.'

'They're the best kind.'

'The thing is, Dennie could leave in almost any vehicle. Covered up in the back of a car or Land Rover, for instance. I'd never know.'

'I know, but we know he won't go without Cal, and the thing is, they don't know we're onto them, so Cal's got no reason to hide. When I spoke to Boo, I asked her what she was hiding, but she's hoping she's covered it with this lover story. I said enough to put the wind up her, but not so much that they think I'm actually on to them. After all, if I was, wouldn't I call the police?'

'Yeah. And I'm still not convinced we shouldn't,' Chris put in.

'If it all goes pear-shaped you can say, "I told you so",' Daniel consoled her.

'That's all very well, Daniel, but I'm doing this for Stella, and I don't want to let her down after all this time.'

'And I'm doing it for Tamiko and her sister,' he said soberly. 'Sorry if you thought I was taking it lightly. I'm not. Look, if nothing happens in a day or two, I might have to push a bit harder but I honestly don't think it'll be long.'

When he arrived back at the cottage after returning the horsebox, Inga and Samson to Natalie's yard, he gave Jo-Ji a brief update on the day's events.

'She actually mentioned Dennie Travers by name?' Jo-Ji asked.

'She said "your father" and she was talking to Harrison Allen,' Daniel said. 'In fact, she said "your father and that imbecile he brought with him", which clearly means Cal McAllum. And she mentioned South America.'

Jo-Ji looked thoughtful. 'It looks as though you were right, but it's still only hearsay. I want to help you, but the problem is with Ropey on leave for another two days, I've more or less got to take it to Paxton because if I don't, I'll have some very awkward explaining to do.'

'To be honest, Joey, the more I think about it, the less I think we should say anything until they actually make a move,' Daniel told him. 'If Chris is right and someone tipped Dennie off last time the police had him in their sights, what's to say it won't happen again. It's only been a couple of years – if he had contacts then, he might still do.'

'Whoa!' Jo-Ji said. 'That's pretty major. I suppose there's no prizes for guessing who your prime candidate might be?'

Daniel shrugged. 'He's got previous. I know that, even if no one else will stand up and say so.'

'Hey, I told you before, some of us believed you, but what could we do? No point in throwing our jobs away, too. One sacrificial lamb is enough, otherwise there wouldn't be any good guys left!'

'Yeah, sorry. But basically what I'm saying is that once Dennie makes a run for it and it's not a matter of trying to root him out of hiding, he's going to be far more vulnerable, and I think that's when we should try for him. If we can get him on the move, will you be able to mobilise the troops?'

'I'll do my best, even if we only stop him for dangerous driving.'

'It doesn't matter, does it? He's a witness to his own crime, just by being alive. He himself is all the proof we need. But don't go underestimating McAllum, he's a nasty piece of work.'

'OK, I'll remember that. I ran a check on the name but nothing came up except a very old conviction, but if he's been out of the country, that would be why. Oh, and I ran a check on the registration you gave me – you know, the Land Rover. It's registered to Belinda Travers – I take it that's Boo. Nothing untoward about it. Tax, insurance, MOT all up to date. No crime in owning a Land Rover, even if you do keep it in an odd place.'

'And I'd lay you a tenner they'll have moved it by now, anyway. It would be interesting to let forensics give it the once over,' Daniel said. 'OK, thanks. Right, now I need to take Taz for a run before you go to work.'

On his words, Taz, who had seemed to be fast asleep, flat out on the kitchen floor, leapt up and ran to the door.

'I wasn't talking *to* you, I was talking *about* you,' Daniel remarked, as he followed him and opened the door. Taz dashed out into the garden, tail waving madly.

It was quite a relief to get out into the fields and woods, and have time to think, but even then Daniel couldn't relax. He was very aware of the risk he was taking in giving Dennie and Cal space to run, but he still felt it was the only option. He just had to hope that Chris' surveillance would be thorough enough.

Taz busied himself with the smells and sounds of the countryside, completely untroubled by any doubts or worries, and watching him, Daniel thought, as he often had before, that for all their supposed intelligence, humans hadn't got the knack for happiness that dogs had. There was probably a moral in it somewhere, but his brain was too crowded to decide what it might be.

When he finally got back to the cottage, the heat of the day was fading and the horses were munching contentedly in their stables.

'You leave your phone behind,' Tamiko said as he let himself in through the back door.

'I thought it was quiet,' he joked.

'Well, it has rung three times,' she informed him.

'I'm glad I didn't take it, then,' he said. 'I'd never have stopped talking!'

He picked it up and scrolled through the call list. One was from Fred Bowden, and the other two from Chris Haynes. He called her back immediately, but frustratingly, there was no answer. Then he noticed there was a voice message.

'Daniel. They're on the move!' Chris' voice came through, sharp with excitement. 'At least, I think they are. It's the Land Rover and I can see McAllum and Harrison in the front. I'm going to follow them on the bike. Ring you back when I can.'

Daniel's heart rate rose as the adrenalin started pumping, but for the moment, there was nothing he could do. Without knowing for sure where they were heading, he couldn't even go after them. If he guessed and got it wrong he could end up miles away. It wasn't Chris' fault. Presumably she'd left the message when she saw the Land Rover leave Boo Travers' property and she wouldn't have known which way they were going either at that point.

Her calls had been twenty minutes before, but he could only keep trying to get her or hope she soon rang back. On her motorbike, she probably wouldn't hear her phone until she next stopped, but when would that be?

In the event, it was over half an hour before his phone rang again and he had started to imagine all sorts of disastrous scenarios. He snatched it off the worktop.

'Chris?'

'Daniel, thank God you're there! Yes, this is definitely it. I was pretty sure it was when I first called, but now they've stopped for fuel and Harrison went in to pay and came back with three cups of coffee. Dennie must be in the back, out of sight.'

'Where are you?' Daniel asked urgently.

'Near Bridgwater – the Esso station. Sorry, I couldn't call before this, I didn't want to stop in case I lost them. The disadvantage of being on the bike – can't easily phone with your helmet on. But, you were right, it looks like they're heading back west, so will you call the police now?'

'I will. Great work. Are you on your own?'

'Yes. And I could've done with one of those cups of coffee, myself, I can tell you. Look, they're on the move again. I'd better get after them if you want me to stick with them.'

'Please, but be careful, OK? I'll let Joey know and then come after you myself, just in case. See you in a bit.'

'Let Joey know what?' Jo-Ji came into the kitchen in his uniform trousers and shirt. 'And I hope I didn't hear you making arrangements to go out, 'cos you know I'm off to work in ten minutes . . .'

'Bugger! You'll have to pull a sickie or something. I've got to go. Travers and McAllum are on the road, heading west, and Chris is after them on her own.'

'Oh bugger, indeed!' Joey said heavily. 'And now you want me to organise a pursuit? You do choose your moments, don't you? It's not going to be easy – especially on a Saturday night. I don't have to tell you how thin we're stretched, and me and Bella are supposed to be working the crowd at the big footie match tonight.'

'I'm sorry. I didn't choose the time, Joey.'

'Yeah, I know. OK, give me the details and I'll see what I can do. Where are they now, exactly?'

Daniel gave him the Land Rover's last known location.

'I think they might be heading for North Devon. Remember the takeaway receipt from Lynton? Anyway, you've got the reg number of the Land Rover because you looked it up for me the other day.'

'OK. I'll see if there's anyone down that way that can keep an eye out for them. But you know, of course, that Lynton and Lynmouth are Devon and Cornwall's patch.'

'Only just. If you can get someone on their tails, it won't matter if they cross the boundary, will it?'

'I'll see what I can do,' Jo-Ji repeated. 'It depends if we have anyone out that way. If we have I'll give them the lowdown, if not, we may have to pass it over to North Devon, anyway.'

'Is that it?'

'It may be the best I can do. You know how it works, Dan. They've got a considerable head start. I'll let you know when I get to work.'

'Well, can you get someone to come over to stay with Tami and Jahan? There shouldn't be a threat, now McAllum and Travers are heading out, and I promised Chris I'd go after her.'

'There shouldn't be a threat if you're right about all this, but we still don't know for sure. And besides, there's still Jafari.'

'Then get someone, but Joey, please, be quick. We don't want to lose these guys. Remember what they did to Hana.' He grabbed his car keys, wallet and phone and stuffed them in the pockets of his jeans and leather jacket. 'Look, I have to go. Don't let me down, mate! I'm counting on you.'

With Taz at his heels, he strode out to the car and within moments was off, heading west for the M5. Once he was on the motorway, given a clear run and no speed traps, he felt he should be able to gain some valuable ground on the slower vehicle.

It was mid-evening, and thankfully the traffic wasn't too heavy, even though there were a number of holidaymakers heading for the West Country. Driving the Mercedes fast, with his eyes peeled for police cars or speed cameras, Daniel was able to cover the first part of the journey in good time but after leaving the motorway and heading west, he was forced to slow down, not only by the narrower more winding road, but also by the number of caravans and motor homes he encountered. To be pulled over for a driving offence would be frustrating beyond imagination. A Saturday evening in the summer holidays had to be the worst time to try and hurry anywhere, let alone on a main road into the southwest. The only consolation was that the men in the Land Rover, presumably still unaware that they were being followed, would also be forced to hold a steady pace. He was fairly confident about the Land Rover's destination and thought it likely that their plan would be to wait until nightfall before heading out to sea, so they would see no need to hurry.

After the first half hour of the journey, Taz stopped looking eagerly out of the windows and lay down. The urgency with which Daniel had set off had given him high hopes that action was imminent but this faded as the pace became more normal, and the long-drawn-out groan that accompanied his settling down was his comment on the disappointing turn proceedings had taken.

The meandering A39 followed the coastline fairly faithfully, albeit a mile or two inland. It didn't pass through any large towns and although Daniel would have liked a progress report from Chris, he felt fairly sure the men up ahead wouldn't be diverging from the road until they reached their destination.

What he began to look forward to more with each passing mile was some communication from Jo-Ji. He had tried to call him for an update but got no reply. Were he and Chris on their own or was a unit even now on their tails? He knew that part of the problem would be the area the men were making for. They were heading into the most outlying area of the Avon and Somerset jurisdiction, away from all the major towns. Finding a squad car that could be tasked with watching out for the Land Rover wasn't going to be easy on a Saturday night, when they almost always had plenty to do nearer home.

Daniel was still a good five miles short of Minehead when his mobile rang and with a wary eye on the road, he answered it.

It was Chris. 'Daniel, I'm sorry, I've lost them. I don't know whether they saw me or what, but suddenly they weren't there anymore.'

'Whereabouts are you?'

'I'm not entirely sure. Well, I mean, I'm still on the A39 but I can't give you an exact fix. It was just past Porlock when I realised I couldn't see them anymore, so I gave it some welly but I'm fairly sure they're not ahead of me 'cos there's quite a few caravans and it wouldn't be that easy for them to get past in the Land Rover. I reckon they must have gone down one of the little side roads. I'm really sorry but I don't know what else I could have done. Any closer and they'd have clocked me for sure.'

'OK. Don't worry. We're pretty certain, now, that they'll be heading for Lynton eventually, so you go there and wait. I'll join you as soon as I can. I've got a few caravans to contend with, myself.'

By Daniel's reckoning, Lynton and Lynmouth were between fifteen and twenty miles away from his current position. He desperately needed to speak to Jo-Ji, to find out what the state of affairs was.

Why the silence? He wondered. Had Jo-Ji failed to raise any support? He couldn't imagine that was so. The police couldn't afford to miss an opportunity of making an arrest of this importance. If Dennie Travers' disappearance had made headline news, his reappearance and capture after more than two years would make even more of a stir and having to admit that they'd the chance to do so but missed it, would be hugely embarrassing to their reputation.

The light was beginning to fade now. The sun had sunk beneath the horizon and the sky had an apricot glow, which bronzed the summer fields and touched the occasionally glimpsed sea with silver and gold.

Daniel found Jo-Ji's number on his phone and rang it but it went, frustratingly, to voicemail. He left a request for Jo-Ji to call back, threw the phone down on the seat beside him and continued driving.

He had just passed Minehead when Jo-Ji finally rang back.

'Joey. Tell me what's happening,' Daniel said.

'You're not going to like it. It's bloody chaos here. There's been a massive pile-up on the M4, and half the guys were already out policing the football match. We're stretched pretty thin and I had a job to find anyone that would even listen for ages. Paxton wasn't exactly receptive when he found out where the tip-off had come from.'

'What are you saying? Are we on our own?'

'No, mate. Of course not, but it might not be the cavalry charge you were hoping for.'

'The bastard! Did you have to go to Paxton?'

'There was no one else. Believe me, I would have avoided it if I could.'

'Surely he can't afford to ignore something like this.'

'He did his best,' Jo-Ji said. 'The problem was me not having any hard evidence. If Boo Travers hadn't rung in to report it, as well, I'm not sure—'

'*What* did you say? Boo Travers rang in to report her husband?'

'Apparently. Switchboard took the call, so he couldn't ignore that one. Even so, there was a lot of grumbling about resources. She didn't give any details about where he might be heading, but of course, that's where you came in. Anyway, eventually he gave me the authorisation to get something started and here I am. So whereabouts are you, now?'

'Near Porlock, on the North Devon coast: A39. I still think they're heading for Lynton, but I'm afraid Chris has lost the Land Rover at the moment.'

'Well, look; it would take forever to get someone down there now. The best thing I can do is pass it on to Devon and Cornwall.'

'No chance of a chopper, I suppose. Unless we catch up with them soon, I've a feeling we'll be chasing them to the coast and if they've got a boat waiting . . .'

'OK, I'll give them your number and suggest they put in a call to the NPAS and see if they can get some air support for you but that'll be their call. You'll have to hope they're more enthusiastic than bloody Paxton. Listen Dan, be careful, OK? Don't try and tackle them on your own.'

'I'm not on my own,' Daniel said. 'I've got Taz and Chris.'

'Yeah, but you know what I mean. A dead hero's no good to anyone and you say you reckon this McAllum is the one who killed Hana. If he can do that in cold blood, I imagine he won't hesitate if you get him cornered.'

'I know. I'll be careful.'

As soon as he had finished talking to Jo-Ji, Daniel rang Chris again and gave her the update.

'Oh, for God's sake!' she exclaimed. 'How did we ever win a war? If Dennie had headed straight for the coast he'd have been on his way home by now.'

'I know, but it's not Joey's fault. Tell it to the government. There just aren't enough bodies to go round. Get something like this motorway smash tying up manpower and everything else has to wait. Maybe the local mob'll be able to do more.'

'OK, well, nothing we can do about it, I suppose. Interesting about Boo, though. Who'd have thought it? Anyway, I'm in Lynmouth now. No sign of our friends, yet. I'm going to head on to Lynton and have a look round, it's only up the hill. How far away are you?'

'Reckon I'll be with you in fifteen to twenty minutes. Let me know if they turn up in the meantime.'

'Will do.'

It was, in fact, only a few minutes later that she called back. 'Dan, they're here! I've just seen them going into a fish and chip shop. Lucky timing; a minute later and I'd have been in there myself. I'm famished!'

'Are they all there?'

'Yeah, even Dennie, though I have to admit, with all that fuzz on his face, I wouldn't have recognised him if I hadn't been expecting to see him.'

'Well, if they've taken the time to stop at the chippie, we can assume they didn't clock you after all,' Daniel said. 'Are you on foot? And whereabouts are you, now? Lynton still?'

'Yes, Lynton. Hang on . . . OK, they're coming out and they're heading off somewhere. I'll try and keep them in sight but I'm a bit conspicuous in all this biking gear.'

'Be careful!' Daniel warned. 'Presumably they'll go back to the Land Rover at some point, so you'd be safer watching that.'

'But I'm nosey,' Chris said. 'I want to know what they're up to. I will be careful, though.' She continued to talk, describing the street she was walking down and then said, 'Wait a minute, they've stopped. It looks like some kind of lock-up garage or something. Perhaps they're picking up— Shit! Harrison just turned round and I think he might have seen me.'

'Get out of there!' Daniel said sharply. 'Quickly! Don't take any more chances. Go somewhere there are people and lay low till I get there.'

She didn't reply and he said her name again, urgently.

There was nothing more for a moment or two and then Chris' voice came again, breathless, 'Yeah, I'm here. There's a pub back aways, I'm heading for that. I think they've got—'

The connection was cut and after saying her name a couple of times more, Daniel put both his phone and his foot down. Whether or not they had spotted Chris earlier, it looked like she and Daniel had now definitely lost the advantage of surprise and he wanted to make sure that Chris was all right. Knowing the geography of coastal towns and villages, he knew it was quite possible that she'd just dipped out of signal area, but given the circumstances, it was also worryingly possible that one or more of the men she'd been watching had caught up with her and confiscated her phone. What else they might do at this critical stage didn't bear thinking about.

Driving faster than was legal or even advisable, it didn't take Daniel long to reach Lynmouth, and from there it only took a matter of minutes to drive up the steep hill to Lynton.

There were a scattering of holidaymakers out and about in the town and consequently a number of cars in the car parks. Daniel drove round two or three with a rapidly growing sense of unease, finding neither Boo Travers' Land Rover or Chris' bike, but then, just as he was starting to think they had been and gone, he saw the Land Rover.

Remembering that Cal would recognise his battered Mercedes from seeing it parked outside the cottage, Daniel drove on round and out of the park, finding instead a place on the roadside, where he hoped it would be less conspicuous. Taking a quick look round and seeing no one he knew, he went back on foot to where the Land Rover was parked and checked it out as swiftly and unobtrusively as he could.

He couldn't see the whole of the inside of the vehicle because it had no side windows and the rear ones had been blacked, but in the front there appeared to be nothing of interest, only the detritus of two or three hours spent on the road.

Going round the back, he ran his hands thoughtfully over the spare wheel in its bracket on the rear door before moving on. Stopping by the offside back wheel, he took a quick look round and then crouched beside it, his fingers finding the tyre valve cap. When he straightened up after a moment or two, he found a man and a woman in shorts were observing him with justifiable suspicion. He put a finger to his lips, winked and smiled brightly as he walked away, leaving behind the gentle hiss of escaping air.

In the far corner of the car park there were three motorcycles parked in their own dedicated bay, and it was to these that he went next. Two were sports bikes and of no interest, the third was a BMW, designed for on and off road use. A fairly big machine for a woman to handle off-road, but then Chris Haynes was no shrinking violet. He thought back to the day he'd seen her at Stella King's in Bath and was almost certain this was the bike he'd seen then, but there was one way to be sure. Coming to a decision, Daniel walked briskly back to his own parked car, ignoring the couple who were still watching him. He hoped they wouldn't call the police.

From the back seat he took Taz's harness and a dual-purpose lead. Observing these preparations, Taz, who was already whining in anticipation of finally getting out of the car, started to bark in excitement and Daniel had to have words with him. The last thing he wanted was to draw any further attention. On his own, with care, he might avoid being noticed by Cal McAllum and the two Traverses, but with Taz beside him the chances of that dropped to negligible. However, at the moment, he had a job for the dog to do.

As soon as they approached the motorcycle parking bay, he could see by the German shepherd's reaction that the BMW was indeed Chris' bike. Taz began to snuff the air and his tail waved gently with pleasure as he recognised a friend who he had walked with. Fitting the dog's harness, Daniel thought what a different world it would be if humans had the same powerful scenting ability that dogs had. Once he had clipped the lead to the harness, Taz needed no further command. He loved to track, and tracking a friend was especially pleasurable.

The trail led first to a small corner shop, still open despite the lateness of the hour. The front page of a local paper was displayed on a board outside, its headline catching Daniel's eye. 'Missing Birdwatcher Found Dead on Beach. Andrew Delacourt, the London solicitor reported missing three weeks ago has been found dead . . .' He sighed inwardly. Another tragedy. Another family's life shattered. Taz leaned into his harness and he moved on.

From the corner shop, the dog took him to a cut-through between two buildings that overlooked a fish and chip shop, which was presumably from where Chris had phoned him earlier. He was pulling to carry on down the hill, but Daniel made him wait. From the corner of his eye, he had seen a familiar figure emerging from a side street and heading across the road.

Harrison Allen. Daniel had only just left the car park in time, then. Hopefully the flat tyre would keep him busy for a bit.

Giving the dog his head once more, they continued downhill at a brisk pace, following a street whose landmarks Daniel recognised from Chris' description. Worried that Taz would lead him right to the place where the men had been, he started to shorten the dog's lead, but suddenly Taz checked and veered off to the left as he came across the fresher track she had left when she retraced her steps. On the pavement Taz came face to face with a group of young holidaymakers carrying cans of drink but totally ignored them, head down, intent on his work.

Ahead, there was a pub sign, swinging in the breeze, and Daniel wasn't surprised when the dog led him to the door but here again he checked and turned left, going up a narrow side alley, barely wide enough for a small car.

The alley was poorly lit but looking ahead to where it sloped up to a more populated street, Daniel could see a figure standing in the entrance. Taz was pulling into his harness like a draught horse and when they were twenty or thirty feet away, the person turned and saw them.

'Hey, Daniel!' Chris called, low voiced. 'My God! Am I pleased to see you!'

'Likewise,' he said. 'You had me worried when your phone cut out like that.'

'Bloody reception's useless round here,' she said disgustedly. 'I've spent the last half hour in the pub down there, sat in the corner waiting to see if Harrison appeared. He did come in but it was absolutely heaving in there and I don't think he saw me. Gave me a fright, though, I can tell you. I'm really sorry. I hope I haven't ruined everything. I was so bloody keen to see what they had in that garage, it never occurred to me that one of them might turn round and come back.'

'And what *was* in the garage?'

'Well, I didn't get much of a look but I think it was a load of surfing and canoeing stuff. Boards, oars, wetsuits, that kind of thing.'

'You said Harrison was a keen surfer,' Daniel said. 'Maybe

he stores his gear here. Nice area with loads of good beaches within easy driving distance. Makes sense. And it would explain why they decided on this spot to make landfall when they arrived the other week. If they already had storage here, what could be better?'

'I wonder if they're still there,' Chris said. 'I've only just come out of the pub and I didn't like to go back down there, just in case they were watching for me. Was Taz tracking me? Did he take you down there?'

'No, we didn't get that far because he picked up your scent coming back this way. The Land Rover was still in the car park as of ten minutes ago but I did see Harrison heading that way. Let's go and see if it's still there now.'

'He was probably going to collect it, then, don't you think? And maybe go and pick up the others and any gear they're taking.'

'Well, hopefully I've slowed him up a bit. I wedged a bit of grit into the tyre valve cap. I reckon in a couple of minutes it should have been flat as a pancake.'

'They have a spare on the back,' Chris reminded him. 'Should have done two.'

'I only just got away with one! I had a couple of holidaymakers giving me the evil eye as it was, and besides, I only wanted to slow them down. If I'd wanted to keep them here, I'd have done something a lot more permanent.'

'Well, it doesn't look like it slowed him a lot,' Chris observed. They had reached the car park and the Land Rover was nowhere to be seen.

'OK,' Daniel said. 'Either a super-fast wheel change or he's got a compressor on board.'

'If there's an inflatable boat in that lock-up, he probably has got a compressor,' Chris said, looking depressed. 'Standard kit. So what now? We don't know where they're going, except to the coast.'

'No, we don't,' Daniel agreed, 'but we soon will. I stuck a tracker on the Land Rover and I have the receiver in my car.'

'Aha! Not just a pretty face, are you?'

'I do my best,' Daniel said modestly. 'However, we'd best get after them, if we're going to try and stop 'em, 'cos there's no sign of the cavalry, yet.'

'OK. I'll follow you, then,' Chris said. 'The bike might come in handy if they go off-road.'

The Land Rover was pretty easy to pick up, the GPS device showing it travelling back along the A39, the way Daniel had come just a short time before. To start with, it held a steady pace and with a little judicious overtaking he managed to get a distant sight of it, but soon after that the Land Rover sped up considerably and then turned off the main road into the myriad of tiny, steep banked lanes that lay between that and the coast.

'So you've clocked us, have you?' Daniel murmured, turning into the same lane shortly after. Behind him, Chris turned, too.

In the following ten or fifteen minutes, Daniel was heartily glad he'd deployed the tracking device, as the roads were incredibly narrow, winding and, from time to time, very steep. In many places, grass grew along the middle, and passing places were few and far between, a fact that was brought home to him as he rounded a bend and came radiator to radiator with the towering yellow and green bulk of a John Deere tractor. Thankful that the roads were dry, Daniel applied his brakes in something of a hurry and came to a halt only a couple of feet away from its two blazing headlights. The look on the farm worker's face told him there was no earthly hope of him backing up, so Daniel put the Merc in reverse and, looking over his shoulder to make sure Chris had tucked her bike out of the way, started back the way he'd come.

Chris had found a shallow gateway to pull into, and as he backed past her, she made a movement with her gloved hand, indicating that she would carry on.

Daniel was forced to keep backing, the high banks offering no way of getting off the road, and the occasional gateway being too frustratingly shallow, and after what must have been a quarter of a mile or more, he finally came to an isolated farm cottage, with a driveway just big enough to take the car.

As he pulled in, the tractor driver accelerated past him without so much as a wave of his hand.

'Cheers mate! My pleasure,' Daniel muttered. He put the car into gear and resumed his pursuit once more, hoping against hope that he wouldn't meet any more traffic.

Driving far faster than was sensible, Daniel sped back along the lane, past the place where Chris had pulled in and onward. He assumed that if she hadn't got a sight of the Land Rover before she reached a place where there was a choice of routes, she would wait for him.

The lane he was following was so deeply sunk between its banks, and the hedges so high, it almost felt as if he were driving along an endless tunnel, or within a maze. He imagined from above he would look like one of those unhappy lab rats trying to find its way through a labyrinth.

The light was fading into dusk anyway, but down in the lanes, it already felt like night, and when Daniel rounded a sharp bend and his headlights picked out the motorbike lying against the grassy bank, it was all he could do to avoid hitting it.

'Shit!'

The Mercedes' two nearside wheels mounted the opposite bank and tipped the car at a crazy angle, before he steered back onto the road again, the suspension clonking unhealthily as he did so. As the shock passed, he saw with relief, the leather-clad person of Chris Haynes, sitting on the bank a sensible fifty feet or so further up the road.

He drove until he was level with her, stopped and got out.

'Are you OK. I nearly had a heart attack when I came round the corner!' he told her.

'*You* did? What about me? When I came round the corner they were backing towards me. They must have caught sight of me following. I thought I was a goner. There was nothing I could do except steer up the bank and bail.'

'So are you OK?' She had taken her helmet off and under the spikiness of her short blonde hair, her face looked a little pale and drawn in the indirect glow of the car's headlamps.

'Yeah. I'll live. I was lucky, really. Got thrown clear. Sorry about the bike. I tried to move it but I couldn't. I think I've busted my collarbone. Your mate Cal got out of the Land Rover and started to walk back and for a moment, I thought he was going to finish me, but one of the others called him away. He's a psycho, that one. Oh, and he said, "Tell your boyfriend, to go home. If I catch him following, he'll go over the cliff." Charming, eh?'

'Yeah, charming,' Daniel agreed, lightly. McAllum couldn't

know that he'd chosen the threat that would most chill Daniel's blood. Most risky situations he could face with at least equanimity, sometimes even enjoying the rush of adrenalin generated by a tough physical challenge. However, the prospect of tackling heights induced in him a panic that was entirely irrational, turning his muscles to jelly and then stone.

With an effort, he put the thought out of his mind, looking about him. 'We must be near the coast now, surely. How much further can they go in the Land Rover, I wonder.'

'They went down that track,' Chris said, lifting her good arm awkwardly across her body and pointing.

Daniel looked down the beam of the car's headlights to where the road ahead bent left-handed and disappeared, while branching off to the right was a farm track, overhung with untended hedges.

'I suppose that's why they wanted to take me out, here,' Chris continued. 'A bike might have the advantage across country. Especially a bike like mine. I'm sorry, Dan. I feel so stupid. Bastards!' she swore suddenly, kicking her booted heel violently into the turf and then wincing as the jolt hurt her shoulder.

'Don't. I'd probably have done just the same,' Daniel said.

'Oh, and they had a kayak on the roof, one of those lightweight ones, I'd say. Easy enough for them to carry down to the sea when they can't drive any further. Mind you, with this wind picking up, they might not find that too easy.'

Looking thoughtfully at the track the men had taken, Daniel turned and went back to where the bike lay on its side, braced his foot against the wheel and hauled it upright. It was no light weight and he wasn't surprised that Chris hadn't managed to do it with her injured shoulder, however tough she might be. He looked it over in the poor light and then wheeled it forwards towards the car. The wheels turned without catching on any bent metal, and an idea began to form in his mind. The Mercedes was a good old workhorse but it wasn't an off-road vehicle. If he could get the bike to start, he might be in with a chance of catching up with Dennie and Co.

Sitting astride it, he turned the key and the display lit up. So far, so good. Checking it was in neutral, he pressed the power button and with a roar, the BMW came to life.

'Yay!' Chris shouted. 'Can you ride it?'

'I've done a bit of biking in the past,' Daniel confirmed. 'Do you mind?'

'Course not. Go for it!'

'If I move the car along a bit, you can sit in it and direct the troops, if they ever get here.'

'I can move it. You go, but here – take my helmet.'

Daniel put it on, and with a sketchy salute, turned the bike towards the farm track and cautiously opened the throttle.

# FOURTEEN

I t didn't take Daniel long to get the hang of the unfamiliar motorbike. He'd ridden off-roaders before and although those had been far lighter, the principle was the same, try to relax and let the bike find its own way through the ruts and bumps.

Long, thorny sprays of bramble caught at his clothing as he rode down the farm track and the cool night-wind whistled through the open visor of the helmet he'd borrowed from Chris. He was glad of his leather jacket, even though it wasn't as tough as proper biker's gear, it kept his arms from being lacerated and would afford some protection if he came off. Just behind the bike ran Taz, thoroughly enjoying himself.

Daniel had given Chris Jo-Ji's number and, as he left her, she was trying to reach him to find out what, if any progress, he had made in mobilising the local police force to come to their aid. In the bike's headlight, Daniel could see the stunted trees in the hedge, shivering and swaying in the rapidly strengthening wind, and began to wonder if a helicopter was going to be an option.

The track he was following crested a rise and started to go downhill, becoming ever more uneven, and it took all his limited skill to keep the bike upright. Taz ranged alongside as the BMW slowed and Daniel shouted at him to keep back. His control was too precarious for it to be safe for the dog to run close. Skidding a little on loose stones as he turned a corner, he gritted his teeth as the track dropped ever more steeply and then suddenly his light picked out the Land Rover, parked up ahead.

He rode to a halt some ten feet behind it, warily scanning it for any sign of life, but it appeared to have been abandoned, for the time being, at least.

Knowing it could be a trap, Daniel advanced slowly, his feet walking each side of the bike, but when he drew level and cautiously peered in, there was just enough ambient light for him to see that the cab was empty. They had continued on foot then, and just ahead was the reason why; a five-bar gate with a padlock on it, and beyond, uneven rock-strewn turf with a footpath running through it.

Either they had left their bolt-cutters behind, or they had decided progress over the terrain beyond the gate would be so slow as to be not worth the effort of getting it open. Some of the outcrops of rock were sizeable enough to cause problems even for a Land Rover. For Daniel on the bike, though, there was a pedestrian's gate, narrow, but passable. He walked the bike forward, leaned to open it, rode through and pushed it shut behind him, the habit ingrained from his rural upbringing.

How far ahead were they? The ground was rising again, here, and with care, he rode the bike along the footpath between the rocks, eventually coming out of the shadow of the trees and onto flatter turf. The path was following the hedge line here and he was able to gather speed. There would obviously be no element of surprise with the noise the bike made, but what he lacked in stealth, he made up for in pace. He felt sure he must be close behind them now. He had no plan, as such, except to try to delay or disable them until the police caught up, as surely they must, soon.

Then, looking ahead, he saw for the first time the outlines of two figures against the darkening sky, carrying something bulky. The kayak. He almost had them.

It was only after he had travelled another twenty feet or so that the significance of just *two* figures impacted on his brain, and by then it was already too late.

The third man stepped out from the shadow of the hedge swinging a branch with force at shoulder height and hit Daniel before he had a chance to brake or swerve.

Because of the raised profile of the off-road bike, Daniel took the full force across his arms and chest instead of his neck or head, but it was still sufficient to knock him backwards off the machine. He landed on his back heavily enough to drive the breath out of his lungs, and the bike careered onwards for a few feet without him.

Struggling for air, Daniel saw the sky black out as something moved between him and the moon. The dark shape took on form as his attacker stepped closer, raising the branch above his head with obvious intent. Daniel braced himself to try and roll away at the crucial moment, but in the instant the branch began to drive downwards, there was an angry snarl and a furry torpedo launched through the air, attaching itself to the arm that wielded the branch and throwing the man off balance and crashing to the ground.

'Good boy, Taz! Hold him!' Daniel gasped, but he needn't have bothered. Taz had no intention of letting go anytime soon. He'd been spoiling for action all evening, and this was way too much fun to give up until he absolutely had to.

The man Taz was pinning down wasn't enjoying it half so much, dividing his time between crying out in pain and fear, and using some choice language in his entreaties to Daniel to call the dog off.

Daniel rolled over and climbed to his feet, taking off the helmet and walking shakily over to where the German shepherd was detaining his suspect to the accompaniment of some of his choicest canine vocalisations.

'If I call the dog off, you have to lie still,' Daniel told the man. 'If you move, he'll have you again.'

'All right, I'll lie still! Just get the bloody thing off me!' came the reply, and Daniel was mildly disappointed to discover that it wasn't Cal that the dog had taken down, but Harrison Allen.

'Off, Taz!' he commanded, and the dog reluctantly released his prisoner, backing off a step or two and smacking his chops with an anticipatory relish that said more than words could ever have done.

'Roll over. Face down. Hands behind your back,' Daniel told the man. He unclipped Taz's lead from where he often carried it, across his chest, and tied Allen's wrists firmly. He then rolled him onto his side and tied the laces of his trekking shoes together before using the loose end of the lead to loop through these, pulled his ankles back towards his hands and secured them there. When he'd finished, Harrison Allen looked like nothing so much as a lassoed and hog-tied calf. Taz was circling him hungrily, willing him to make a move but Daniel's efforts had been so thorough that he quite clearly wouldn't be going anywhere until someone released him.

Standing up, Daniel went over to the motorbike, but that, too, wasn't going anywhere for a bit; its headlight smashed and the clutch lever snapped off. So, it was Shanks's pony from now on, but from what he could see of the way ahead through the murky evening light, the loss of the bike wasn't the drawback it might have at first seemed. And at least he knew he wasn't far behind the two remaining men.

It appeared that the narrow path, which was little more than a sheep track, followed the hedge line for a little further then crested the horizon and disappeared. Daniel could hear the sea now as a distant roar, and had an uneasy suspicion that just over the rise, there might be a drop of some considerable magnitude. Even the thought of it reduced his mind to a quite illogical level of fear.

Taking his phone from his pocket, he found he still had a signal, and thinking that this might not be the case once he descended to sea level, he pulled up Chris' number and rang her as he started to walk.

'Dan. Where are you? Are you OK?'

'Relatively speaking, though the bike will need a few repairs, I'm afraid. It was a good job I put the helmet on, thanks for that. Anyway, I'm not far behind them. Any word from the police yet?'

'Yeah, finally. They're sending someone out here. I tried to instil some sense of the urgency of the situation, but I'm not sure whether I succeeded.'

'Well, if they come this way, they'll find Harrison Allen trussed up like a turkey and waiting for them.'

'Oh, well done!'

'Don't congratulate me. If it wasn't for Taz, it would have been me they found, and in a lot worse state. Speak soon.' He put the phone on silent and returned it to his pocket.

As he crested the rise, the wind whipped at his hair and rippled through his clothing, and the noise of the sea on the rocky shore below became much louder. High above, streamers of cloud flew across a clear sky, intermittently hiding the moon from view, and somewhere off to his left came a regular flash that he guessed was the lighthouse at Foreland Point.

By the light of the moon, Daniel could see that the path dipped sharply and swung along the line of the cliff with steps cut into it, crudely paved in places with pieces of rock. To all appearances, an easy enough way to make the descent; easy enough, that was, except for a sufferer of acrophobia.

To add to Daniel's unease, someone had hammered two pieces of metal piping into the ground and added a crossbar of wood, on which hung a notice. He didn't really need to read it to guess what it said, but in the dim light he used his phone to illuminate the lettering and read it, anyway.

DANGER! CLIFF EROSION. PATH UNSAFE.

It seemed an odd place to choose to descend to sea level, as Daniel knew from studying the map that there were many places where the shore could be reached with the minimum of climbing, but it was quite possible that Daniel and Chris' pursuit had panicked the men into changing their planned route or even taking a wrong turn. Whatever the case, it seemed that they had gone down this path, and if he were not to lose them, he would have to tackle it as well.

Taz had already run down the first few steps and now came back to stand in front of him, waiting for Daniel to make a move, his tail waving gently and his teeth gleaming in the moonlight.

'It's all right for you,' Daniel muttered, and the dog ran round him and came to heel, watching him eagerly.

The steps and path were about eighteen inches wide at the top, and he wondered whether the warning notice was just an obligatory one to dissuade the unwary public or whether it signified a greater, specific risk. Either way, he told himself, if he didn't attempt the path, he'd not only be letting Chris and Stella down, but also Hana and Tamiko, to say nothing of letting the obnoxious Cal get the better of him.

Hardly aware of having reached the decision, he found himself stepping down the first flight of crudely cut steps, eyes firmly fixed on his feet and not on the vast, beckoning nothingness to the side. Although the poor light couldn't be said to constitute ideal cliff-walking conditions, it did mean that the full visual horror of the situation was largely hidden from Daniel.

On the fourth step, he was buffeted by Taz impatiently pushing past him and swore, grabbing at the rock beside him. The wind seemed to be getting stronger, whistling around the cliff face and rocking him back on his heels. Way below – he didn't care to speculate how far – he could see, even though he tried not to look, the pale frothing lines of the surf, endlessly crashing on the shore. The cliff below him wasn't completely vertical but it might as well have been because the slope was such that none but an idiot would attempt it without a rope. Any careless footfall might land on loose rocks or stones and start a slide it would be impossible to check. The path was the only option.

On down the steps Daniel went, counting each one to focus his mind; to keep it from dwelling on the yawning emptiness beside him. He'd reached twenty-three when the steps turned inwards, following the contours of a giant fissure in the rock and enfolding him in a deceptive feeling of security.

It was sadly temporary. All too soon, the path wound outwards again and appeared to narrow as it rounded the corresponding outcrop on the other side. At this point, there were no helpfully placed slabs to accentuate the path, just a gently shelving rocky surface, scattered with loose stones, which had an uncomfortable tendency to roll underfoot. Several times, Daniel's foot slipped and he froze, feeling the familiar waves of cold panic rising like a tide and threatening to engulf him.

All at once the sight of a light bobbing ahead of and below him claimed his attention and he paused to get a better look. In his absorbing battle with his own wayward mental processes, Daniel had almost forgotten the reason he was putting himself through the ordeal. The bearers of the light had to be Cal and Dennie Travers. By the look of it, they had gained ground on him, impressive considering they were apparently carrying a canoe of some kind, which must have been catching the wind.

He sensed Taz's excitement levels rising and had a sharp word with him. The last thing he wanted was the dog racing off down the cliff path and tackling the two men on his own.

Standing still made him aware of the tremors that afflicted his muscles and, setting his jaw, he quickened his pace, forcing himself to conquer the heart-pounding fear. He had to hurry. Bad enough to have to make the descent; he didn't want to have gone through the nightmare for nothing.

The dog, perhaps sensing his renewed purpose, forged ahead and then at his command stopped dead, getting in his way.

'Taz! Keep going, but go steady, OK? Steady!' Daniel told him. In the semi-darkness he couldn't tell how far away the two men were, somewhere between twenty and fifty yards, perhaps, but with the combined roar of wind and surf, there was little danger they would hear his voice.

Suddenly, he stumbled as the path became steps once more, and grabbed at the rock beside him. Coarse, desiccated grass came away in his hand with a shower of loose gritty soil and he swayed outwards, his head rushing with an awful spinning sensation. Stubbing the toe of his walking boot on a rock at the side of the path he pitched forward and felt himself falling, all his fears coalescing in that one moment of sheer panic.

Totally off-balance, Daniel missed the path and landed on his side on the slope below it. Immediately he began to slide out of control on the loose stones until one hand found and held a jutting rock, arresting his fall. In breathless terror, he wriggled until he lay face down on the incline and scrabbled with his toes until one of them found a tenuous purchase. For a moment it was all he could do just to remain in that position, his heart thumping so hard he felt it was in real danger of shaking him loose from his precarious situation. All thoughts of the pursuit were forgotten, now it was all about survival.

Tipping his head backwards he looked up and tried to see how far he'd fallen. Not far, it seemed, the rocky ledge the path ran on was only inches above the hand from which practically all his bodyweight was suspended, but it might as well have been ten times as far for all the hope he had of getting back up. He could feel the rough stone pressing against the skin of his torso, his jacket and shirt rucked up by the friction of his unplanned descent. Frantically he ran his free hand over the rock surface, trying to find something – anything – to cling to. For the moment he was supported but the fingers of his right hand were already tiring, and he knew that if he started to slide again, he might well not be so lucky.

Even though the task seemed unachievable, Daniel knew he had no option but to try and climb. No one was going to come and help. He had only minutes at the most before the strength in his hand gave out; he could feel it shaking now, the burning ache in his wrist spreading up his arm. Gingerly, he tried taking a little more weight on his toehold in an attempt to ease the burden on his fingers, but as soon as he did so, the stone under his foot gave way and went bouncing away down the cliff along with a shower of smaller stones.

The sudden added strain on his hand was almost his undoing. He cried out and scrabbled for something solid with his free hand, his face scraping the stones. Again, fortune favoured him as his fingers curled into a wiry tussock of some plant that miraculously stayed firmly rooted.

The wind whistled across the slope, cooling the sweat on his body and face, yet at the same time his left hand felt warm, almost hot. Raising his eyes again, he saw the dark outline of Taz looking down at him and heard his characteristic whine as he tried to understand the strange state of affairs.

Daniel felt a glimmer of hope. 'Taz, pull!' he said urgently. 'Pull!'

The dog looked round, backed up and then came forward again, whining more loudly. Although it was too dark to see his face, Daniel could sense the shepherd's bewilderment. The command was normally accompanied by the offer of a rope or tug toy to grasp in his jaws, here there was nothing.

'Taz. Hold it! Pull! Come on, lad, pull!' Daniel repeated, lamenting the loss of Taz's lead, which he had left wrapped round Harrison Allen's worthless hands and feet. The truth was, however, that even if it had still been wearing it across his chest, it was difficult to see how he'd have managed to get at it in his present position.

'Taz! Pull! Hold it! Pull!' He put more authority into his voice, sounding almost displeased, and, still whining, Taz came forward and started to scratch at the ground at the edge of the path, showering Daniel with grit, sand and stones.

'No, Taz! Stop it! Pull, lad! Come on. You can do it! Hold it!'

Finally, when Daniel had almost given up hope, Taz went down on his elbows and reached towards him, mouthing the sleeve of his leather jacket.

'Good boy!' Daniel said by way of encouragement, and Taz let go of the sleeve, stood up and barked.

'No, Taz! Hold it! Pull!'

This time the dog took a firm hold of Daniel's jacket and started to pull.

Glad he had zipped the jacket against the cooling wind when he got on the bike, Daniel curled his fingers round the cuff to stop the sleeve being pulled off his arm. Lifting his knee he dug his toe in higher up the slope, using the massive pulling power of the dog to fund his upward movement.

Aware that in doing so he was effectively trusting his life to Taz's sense of duty and the strength of his jaws, he let go of his only definite handhold and reached higher, keeping up his breathless commands to the dog to pull.

However, Taz seemed to understand what he was doing now, and continued to tug vigorously as Daniel scrambled over the rocky edge and onto the path once more. Indeed, he dragged him two or three feet up the incline before Daniel found enough breath to tell him to stop.

His sleeve was released and the next moment Taz was all over him, whining in delight and licking his face, pleased beyond measure that he had worked out what Daniel had wanted. Whether he had an understanding of just what peril his master had been in, Daniel neither knew nor cared. Once again, his canine partner had saved his skin, and he was almost overwhelmed by the powerful mixture of relief, gratitude and love he felt.

A gust of wind buffeted him as he calmed the dog and sat up, and he recalled the purpose of his presence on the cliff path.

How long had his life-and-death drama taken? While happening it had seemed endless but had, in reality, probably played itself out in just a few minutes. If he hurried, he might still be in time to at least hinder Dennie Travers' getaway.

*If he hurried.* Even the thought of standing up again filled him with horror, but it had to be done and, facing away from the drop, it was. Taz fawned around him, glad to have order restored, supremely indifferent to the danger.

'Careful, you crazy animal, you'll send me over the edge again!' Daniel chided him. 'Come on. Take it steady. Let's go and catch some bad guys.'

Only by concentrating on each individual step, did Daniel accomplish the rest of the descent. He started to count under his breath once more, and when the wind blew the scudding clouds free of the moon on pace sixty-eight he realised that he was within fifteen or twenty feet of the beach, and the worst of his immediate fears dissipated.

The moonlight illuminated a long stretch of gritty sand, littered with rocks and boulders that had fallen from above over the years and centuries gone by. For a moment, Daniel thought the shoreline was empty and his nightmare descent had been for nothing, but then he saw a small light, stationary, quite some way further up the beach.

Wondering why the men had travelled so far along the shore without putting out to sea, he risked a look down at the surf and saw the reason. The jagged rocks that made the beach so difficult to negotiate extended out into the shallows, making the water froth and sending spray high enough for Daniel to taste it on his lips. Any attempt to launch a craft into those seas would be foolhardy in the extreme. It reinforced Daniel's suspicion that the discovery that they were being followed had panicked Harrison into heading for an unfamiliar stretch of coast.

Even though the path became more uneven and rocky, descending to shore level was a piece of cake after what Daniel had just been through. Rough terrain held no fears now the added element of altitude was removed.

Keeping his eyes on the distant torchlight, he didn't think it had moved much, if at all, since he had first seen it. Did that mean the men were preparing to take to the sea?

As he reached the shore, clouds hid the moon once more and Daniel began to hurry as much as he was able in the poor light over the scattered rocks and boulders. Wet with spray and seaweed, they were extremely slippery and some had sharp edges as he found to his cost when he put out a hand to steady himself. It would be very easy to do real damage on these rocks and if he slashed his leg to the bone, he had a strong suspicion it would be no use looking to Cal for first aid.

Worried about Taz's paws, he glanced across at the dog but he seemed to be coping well, a shadow leaping lightly from boulder to boulder with a surefooted ease that Daniel envied.

After pausing to bind a handkerchief roughly around his hand, he continued. Gradually, the rocks became more scattered and the areas in between big enough to allow him to avoid them altogether. He glanced ahead. He could still see the torchlight, maybe twenty yards distant, held fairly still and pointing slightly downwards.

Something they were doing required a steady light. Daniel could only see the indistinct outlines of the two men and while one appeared to be sitting back against a boulder the other was crouched, concentrating on something by his feet.

While Daniel was still wondering what that could be, something caused the crouching man to look up and in the next moment the beam of the torch swung upwards and caught Daniel full in the face. It wasn't an especially powerful beam but enough to make him hesitate, throwing up a hand to shield his eyes. Beside him, Taz growled.

'With me!' Daniel commanded, just loud enough for the dog to hear, and as he continued to walk forward, Taz kept obediently to heel, but he was watchful and bristling at Daniel's side.

'Well. Mr Whelan. I'm glad it's you,' the Scotsman said, raising his voice to be heard over the combined sound of the wind and surf. 'Now I get a chance to settle my account with you.'

'It was a fair fight,' Daniel replied, squinting against the light. 'You had your chance, which is more than you can say for poor Hana.'

He sensed rather than saw the lift of McAllum's shoulders.

'Collateral damage. It happens.'

'She had a three-year-old son, you bastard!' Daniel was surprised at the force of the anger that shook him. 'She was just a girl!'

'No one was ever supposed to get hurt.' That was the other man; presumably the elusive Dennie Travers. His voice held remorse.

'You should have thought of that before you brought this psycho back with you!' Daniel told him. 'Without him blundering around, you'd probably never have been caught.'

'He's not caught, now,' the Scotsman pointed out. 'Just out there, there's a boat waiting for us. Ten minutes at the most and we'll be on our way home.'

'You're not going anywhere,' Daniel stated, moving closer.

'And you're going to stop us, are you?' the Scotsman enquired. 'You and who, exactly?'

Daniel kept moving. The light was still high and it was plain that Cal hadn't spotted the dog, yet. Now just feet away, he could see what they had been doing. Travers was sitting with one leg raised and the Scotsman had been trying to fashion a kind of splint around his lower leg. It looked as though the treacherous rocks had claimed a victim, after all. Beyond the two men, a kayak was wedged between two rocks to prevent the wind blowing it along the beach.

'Me, my partner here, and the police. They're not far behind me. You don't think I'd have been stupid enough to come alone, do you?'

'Where's Harrison? Where's my son?' Travers asked, apparently just realising the full significance of Daniel being there.

'Back along,' Daniel said. 'The dog took care of him, no trouble.'

The torchlight dipped for a moment to locate Taz and, right on cue, he produced his most theatrical growl.

'He's got that bloody dog!' Travers said unnecessarily, his voice rising on a note of panic. He struggled to his feet and picked up an oar to defend himself.

'Well, it's nice that you'll have company,' Cal observed, ignoring his companion. 'Because we'll be long gone.'

Daniel laughed derisively.

'And how far do you think you're going to get on a night like this in that thing?' he asked, pointing at the kayak. 'That sea's getting pretty rough and it doesn't look as though Dennie's going to be doing much paddling. Always supposing you can even get him into the kayak with that leg.'

As if to illustrate his point, a tremendous gust of wind lifted the canoe, tumbling it onto its side, and the Scotsman turned involuntarily to look at it.

Daniel seized the moment to make his move.

Not knowing exactly how incapacitated he was, he pointed at Dennie, shouted, 'Hold him!' at the dog, and launched himself across the intervening space at McAllum while his attention was on the kayak.

Perhaps belatedly aware of his vulnerability, McAllum turned back just before Daniel reached him and his chopping blow missed its intended target and landed on the Scotsman's shoulder, instead.

Cal caught Daniel's arm and twisted it, pulling him off balance and throwing him high to land sprawling on the gritty sand. His knee impacted on one of the many small rocks as he landed, sending a stunning pain up into his thighbone, and as he rolled to avoid the Scot's follow-up kick, he hoped the damage wouldn't prove to be disabling.

Coming out of the roll and up onto his good knee, he discovered to his relief that although it was painful, the other one was still capable of supporting his weight. He just had time to note that Taz was carrying out his orders, albeit somewhat more noisily than was strictly necessary, before McAllum aimed another kick, this time at Daniel's head.

Swaying to the side, Daniel caught the Scotsman's foot and lifted it sharply, tipping him backwards to land heavily on the sand. He climbed to his feet, breathing heavily and waited for Cal to make his next move. Remembering the impressive size of his muscles, he wasn't keen to be drawn into a wrestling match.

Cal wasn't long on the ground. Rolling back and over one shoulder, he surged up and forwards, arms spread, clearly trying to bring Daniel down, but Daniel was ready for him, bringing his knee up into the man's face.

McAllum was tough, he had to give him that. He grunted as his nose took the brunt of the impact, but his arms still encircled Daniel's waist and his momentum carried them both onward. They landed together, with the Scotsman on top, on the stones at the edge of the surf.

Sitting back, Cal swung a vicious right at Daniel that drove his head backwards and made his vision dip out for a moment, but in the next moment an incoming wave broke over them both, shocking Daniel back to his full senses and causing him to choke and splutter as the salty water got into his mouth.

It seemed the wave gave the Scotsman an idea, for instead of punching Daniel a second time, he leaned forward and pressed down on his shoulders, pinning him to the ground, so that the next rush of water also broke over him. Although Daniel managed to get a breath in between, the third wave was far bigger and washed sand and grit across his face, keeping him submerged for what seemed an age.

He reached upwards to try and lock his hands onto McAllum's windpipe, but with the downward pressure on his shoulders, he couldn't quite make it.

The tide was coming in fast, and he knew if he didn't break Cal's hold soon, he never would. He tried to shout for Taz but another smaller wave filled his mouth with water and he spat it out, coughing and choking once more. He could see the Scotsman leaning over him, teeth clenched and lips pulled back in an almost demonic grin, and beyond him, the glow of the moon, cool and uncaring.

Half a breath and then the water covered him again, rushing, frothing and deadly. With an immense effort of willpower, Daniel forced himself to go limp, his arms falling away, and as the wave drained, soughing, back down the beach, he let his head roll with it, hoping Cal would think the job done.

Another smaller wave hissed in, washing against and over his head and body, and he held his breath, keeping his eyes shut; his lungs constricting with the lack of air. He thought it wasn't working – that he would have to give in and gasp for breath, and then he felt it.

At first, just an infinitesimal slackening of pressure, and then a slight shift in balance as McAllum leaned forward to look at Daniel more closely. It wasn't much but it might be the only chance he got.

With all the strength he could muster, Daniel reached up for Cal's head, pulled it down and then, digging his heels into the sand, he bucked his body upward, throwing the Scotsman off over his head.

He rolled away as the surf came in again, fuller and stronger this time, swamping the both of them, and by the time it rushed back out, sucking the sand and grit with it, Daniel was on his feet once more, coughing and gasping, but alive.

Cal was also on his feet, his baseball cap gone and his face twisted with venom. In his hand he held a rock the size of a grapefruit.

Away to his left, Daniel could hear the dog still barking, while in his head he was hearing Jo-Ji's calm voice at a long-ago training session. 'If your opponent arms himself with something, no matter what it is, think of it as a victory. You have him worried, and what's more, you now have a good idea what his next move will be.'

Daniel reckoned Cal would either rush him and try to use the rock as a club or throw it first and charge in behind it. He waited, breathing deeply and trying to give the impression that he was nearly spent. It wasn't hard.

Cal chose the second.

Prepared, Daniel dodged and was ready for him. This time, he sidestepped neatly and clubbed the Scot with a clenched fist to the side of his head, dropping him into the incoming tide. Trying to follow up his momentary advantage, Daniel jumped on him and pulled one arm behind his back, forcing his wrist to somewhere in the region of his shoulder blades and his face into the sand.

This time when the next wave crashed in, it was Cal who was set spluttering and coughing. Daniel gritted his teeth and held him while one more wave washed over him, but he was at a disadvantage. While Cal held life cheap, Daniel wasn't a killer, and even though the Scotsman had demonstrated that he would have drowned Daniel with absolutely no compunction, now the tables were turned, he found he couldn't do the same.

Still keeping a firm grip on Cal's wrist, Daniel stood up and pulled the Scotsman upright. Both of them were soaked and covered in gritty sand, and Daniel's wet clothing quickly chilled in the gusting wind despite the relative warmth of the summer night.

Above, the moon sailed in a large expanse of cloudless sky and he could see that Taz had his man under control. Grabbing one of the kayak's oars with which to defend himself had quite patently not worked as Travers now lay back against the rocks with the oar at his feet, while Taz stood over him, his muzzle just inches from the man's face. Daniel could only imagine what grisly promises the dog was uttering between barks.

Marching his own captive out of the surf, Daniel would have

liked a wall or something solid to reinforce the arm lock he had in place, but there was nothing. He tried to secure Cal's other arm by looping his own free hand under the man's armpit but he wasn't quite quick enough and the man was incredibly strong.

Erupting into action Cal stabbed his free elbow backwards into Daniel's ribs, and with the space he gained, twisted his body round the opposite way and followed up with the heel of his palm to the side of Daniel's jaw.

Because he was close, it was more of a shove than an actual blow, and although Daniel staggered back, he was ready when the Scot came after him. Half-turning, he brought his knee up and lashed out in a martial arts style side-kick of which even Jo-Ji would have been proud.

The result was all he could have hoped for. McAllum was stopped in his tracks, doubled over in pain as the wind was forced from his lungs, and Daniel followed it with a clubbing blow that dropped him on the spot.

High above the beach two moving pinpoints of light had appeared, in the general direction of the cliff path, and Daniel's spirits rose.

'Stay down!' he advised, hovering over Cal as he struggled to get to his feet, ready if necessary to deal out more of the same. 'Give it up, man. The police are here. It's over.'

The Scotsman shook his head but whether as a negative response or to clear it, Daniel couldn't tell. After a moment, he sat back, as though giving up, but before Daniel could readjust to this new development, Cal rolled back over one shoulder and came up into a big cat crouch, his eyes on Daniel's face and his right hand dropping to his ankle. As he came upright, moonlight gleamed on smooth metal.

He had a knife.

# FIFTEEN

'Meet my friend,' Cal invited, smiling. He turned the blade from side to side to make sure the moonlight caught the four deadly inches of honed steel. It looked wickedly sharp, and nothing about the Scotsman suggested that he didn't know exactly how to use it.

'Meet mine,' Daniel countered. 'Taz! To me! Get him!'

The smile left the Scotsman's lips as he turned to face the new threat but even as he did so, the dog was in the air and the next moment McAllum was on the ground, muscles and all. He wasn't Dennie, though, to be paralysed by fear, and Daniel had to move quickly to prevent him from transferring the lethal blade to his other hand with what would have been tragic consequences for Taz.

Twisting the knife out of his grasp, Daniel tossed it into the rocks at the foot of the cliff, but he wasn't prepared to gamble on him not having another one hidden on him somewhere. Excited by the less frequently used 'Get him!' command, Taz was tugging hard, his jaws clamped round Cal's forearm, pulling him, inches at a time, over the stony shore, while the Scot tried to twist onto his knees and scramble after him to ease the pressure.

Daniel circled dog and man, and as soon as Cal accomplished the turn, pushed him flat and dropped onto him. Immediately, he had the satisfaction of hearing the Scot cry out as Taz tried unsuccessfully to drag him further with Daniel's additional weight applied through a knee to his back.

'OK. Good lad,' Daniel told the dog, grabbing the man's free arm. 'I've got him now. Off.'

He had to repeat the command before the excited German shepherd reluctantly obeyed him. He backed off, but didn't move far, watching their captive with hungry intensity, willing him to make a move.

This time, however, Daniel had Cal safely under control and

he wasn't about to make the mistake of trying to move him again when help was on the way. The two lights were still there on the cliff, slowly but surely descending and coming closer, and somewhere, above the crashing of the surf and the blustery wind, Daniel became aware of a deep throbbing that was almost more of a vibration than a sound.

Another light shone out, closer to hand, and with a shock Daniel realised he'd almost forgotten Dennie Travers. While he and Taz had been busy with the Scotsman, the fugitive had managed to get to his feet and was trying to pull the kayak down the beach. In this he was hampered by his leg injury, which was clearly severe. He had reached the edge of the incoming tide by the time Daniel saw him and was struggling to hang onto the kayak as the surf lifted it.

Taz growled a warning and stepped forward.

'Give it up, man! How far do you think you're going to get?' Daniel shouted. 'There's a chopper on its way, can't you hear it? You've got no chance.'

'You're lying! They wouldn't bring a helicopter out in this wind!'

'Not a police one, no. But the RAF would fly. That sounds like a Sea King to me.' Daniel had no idea what kind of helicopter it was, but he knew it must be one of the bigger ones and now wasn't the time to worry about absolute honesty. 'You'll never make your pick up,' he added. 'The guy'll see that coming and run.'

Travers paused, looking up at the sky and listening, just as the wind dropped for a second or two and the sound of the approaching helicopter was unmistakable. In that instant, he finally appeared to give up. His shoulders drooped, and he let go of the kayak and hobbled painfully back up the beach to above the waterline where he sat down abruptly, as if all his muscles had let him down at once.

'Watch him,' Daniel told the dog, even though it was hardly necessary. The fight had gone out of Dennie Travers, as clearly as if someone had flipped an off switch.

Taz transferred his full attention to Dennie, and with a sigh, Daniel relaxed and waited for deliverance.

*        *        *

In the event, it was two policemen, on foot, who reached him about five minutes later, approaching with torches, batons and a good deal of caution.

'Sergeant Rollins and PC Rayworth, Devon and Cornwall police,' one of them announced. 'Can you identify yourself, please?'

'It's OK, I'm the good guy,' Daniel said with weary amusement. 'Well, depending who you talk to, that is.'

'Daniel Whelan?'

'That's right. Allow me to introduce Dennie Travers, back from the dead, and currently in the custody of my dog, Taz. And this worthless bastard I'm kneeling on is John "Cal" McAllum, late of somewhere abroad. You can arrest him for murder, aggravated assault, possession of an offensive weapon, vehicle theft – take your pick really. He killed the sister of a friend of mine and probably would have killed me, too, if it hadn't been for Taz. I really could have done with you about ten minutes ago.'

At his first words, one of the policemen had started towards Travers but he faltered in his purpose as Taz showed him a full set of gleaming white teeth.

'Er . . .?'

'Oh, sorry. I gave him a job to do. Taz! Off, man! All finished.'

With a disappointed glance at the policeman, Taz obediently left his post and returned to Daniel.

'It's dark. If he'd seen your uniform, he wouldn't have done that,' Daniel told him.

The second policeman approached to within a foot or two of Daniel and pointed at McAllum. 'Is he OK?'

'Unfortunately, yes. A bit the worse for wear, but nothing to speak of.'

'Right, well, I'll take over now, sir.'

Daniel didn't move a muscle.

'Actually Sergeant—'

'Constable. Rayworth.'

'Well, constable, if you don't mind me suggesting it, I think I'd like to see cuffs on this one before I move. He's a bit lively and I've had enough grief for one night.'

The policeman shone his torch in Daniel's face, causing him

to screw up his eyes, but apparently what he saw there decided him to take the words seriously.

'Fair enough,' he said, producing a set of handcuffs.

'Any thoughts on how you're going to get these two back to civilisation? Because Travers is in no fit state to climb back up that path,' Daniel said, once Rayworth had relieved him of his captive and read him his rights. He stretched his own stiff and bruised joints and muscles. 'Unless that chopper we heard a moment ago is here on your say-so.'

'No. There's been a mayday from a yacht in distress along the coast,' the policeman told him. 'That one was from Chivenor. Ours can't fly in this wind. I'll have to call it in and see what they suggest.'

'I presume you found the other guy on your way here. Name of Harrison Allen. Dennie Travers' son.'

'We did. Well trussed up and complaining of a sore arm. You and your dog have certainly been busy tonight. Three detained suspects, two with puncture wounds. You'll put us out of a job! Did you train him yourself?'

'Yeah. He's an ex-police dog.'

'Ah. I thought so,' Rayworth said, in the satisfied tone of one proved right in an assumption. 'So you are – were . . .?'

'Bristol Met,' Daniel told him. 'Ten years. I left last year. Don't ask.'

It took the best part of half an hour and several calls back to Control, but eventually the Sea King, whose original call-out had proven to be unnecessary, was re-routed to the beach to pick up the five men and dog.

Daniel had not much cared whether they were taken off by sea or air, just as long as he wasn't asked to climb the cliff path again, a sentiment apparently shared by Rayworth, with whom he was rapidly developing a sense of camaraderie.

The knife was retrieved, with Taz's help, from among the rocks, and bagged as evidence, and Dennie Travers' injured ankle was stabilised with an emergency splint by the medic winched down from the helicopter.

The throbbing beat of the rotors was immensely loud as, one by one, the policemen and their suspects were winched up to the dark bulk of the aircraft above, and finally, Daniel and Taz were strapped into their respective harnesses and lifted away from the beach. It was a mystery to Daniel that in spite of his fear of heights, he had never minded flying, and even dangling between a helicopter and the ground held no horrors for him. Taz, gung-ho in this as in all things, seemed to positively relish the experience, which had been included in his training at the dog unit.

The Sea King flew them to Barnstaple Hospital, touching down with exquisite lightness on the helipad to offload its human cargo, before lifting up and away into the night, another mission safely executed.

Inside the hospital, in due course, Daniel was reunited with Chris, who was awaiting an X-ray of her shoulder.

'Ouch!' she exclaimed, glancing at him as he handed her a coffee and sat down beside her. 'You've been in the wars again.'

'You should see the other guy,' he said.

'I think I just did,' she said. 'Unless I'm much mistaken, the walking dead has just been wheeled past in a wheelchair, with a police escort.'

'Ah, yes, but I can't take any credit for that. He slipped on the rocks on the beach.'

'And our friend, Cal?'

'Being checked over by a doctor, then he'll be hauled off to the nick, and it couldn't happen to a nicer guy. I haven't seen Harrison.'

'Came in with me – well, not the same ambulance, thank God! But at the same time.'

'All safely gathered in,' Daniel said, with a sigh. 'God, I'm tired!'

'I should think so. By the way, where's the hero of the hour?'

'On the back seat of one of the squad cars out there – covering it with hairs, if I know him. Apparently someone has been dispatched to fetch my car. I'm impressed. There's a lot more available manpower here on a Saturday night than there ever was in the Met.' Daniel took a sip of the hot latte and shook his head. 'Taz. That daft mutt saved my skin tonight, and not just once. And what can I give him in return? A beef knuckle bone and a bloody tuggy toy! Crazy.'

His phone rang and, surprised it still functioned at all after being immersed in sea water, he fished it out of his jacket pocket, and looked at the display. It was Fred Bowden.

'Hi mate,' he said. 'What am I up to? Oh, not much, really, at the moment. I expect I'll be back soon.'

It was three days later when Daniel drove up to the electric gates of Rufford Manor and gave his name. They opened smoothly and he drove on down the drive to the house, parking the shabby Merc between a massive 4×4 and a sporty hatchback.

The house was built of Bath stone in the Georgian style; rectangular, with tall, square-paned windows. Pink and white roses rambled over the façade breaking up the symmetry, and their spent petals littered the gravel like confetti.

The impressive front door opened as Daniel got out of the car and Boo Travers stood there in jeans and a white cotton tunic, flip-flops on her feet. She looked fresh and attractive and just a little unsure of herself, something Daniel had never seen in her before.

'Thanks for coming, Daniel,' she said, standing back to invite him into the cool interior.

She led the way to the back of the house where an enormous, well-appointed kitchen opened onto an equally massive conservatory containing a dining table and chairs. At the table sat a good-looking young man with very short sandy hair and blue eyes. He wore a T-shirt and the muscles on his upper arms proclaimed the athlete.

'My son, Spencer,' Boo said. 'Spencer, this is Daniel. Would you like coffee, Daniel? I'm just making some.'

'Thank you. Milk, no sugar,' Daniel said, taking a seat opposite her son. He would be in his early twenties, he guessed, and the only clue as to the parlous state of his health were the dark rings under his eyes and the pallor, so marked after the warm and sunny spell they had been experiencing.

Boo retreated into the kitchen and Daniel wondered why Spencer was there. She had made no mention of him when she'd called to request this meeting. It was difficult to know how to open a conversation with the lad. Small talk never seemed so small as when the person you were addressing was terminally ill.

'Did you play rugby?' he asked after a moment. 'You look to
have the build for it.'

'Yeah, for my school and then at university,' Spencer said.
His accent suggested that he'd been to a 'good' school. 'Not
for a while now, of course, but you never know . . . Someday,
maybe.'

'Never say never,' Daniel agreed. 'The docs don't know
everything.'

'You know, you're the first person that's done that,' Spencer
stated. 'Got right to the heart of it, I mean. People usually
either drown me in depressing sympathy or pussyfoot around
the issue, trying so hard not to mention it that it becomes almost
funny.'

'He's wicked!' Boo said, bringing three mugs of coffee to
the table and sitting next to her son. 'He watches people
digging themselves deeper and deeper and doesn't lift a finger
to help them.'

'Well, I've got to get some amusement out of this bloody
disease!' he protested. 'It's not good for much.'

'That's for sure,' Boo agreed. She looked at Daniel. 'I expect
you're wondering why I asked you to come.'

He shrugged.

'I guess you'll tell me when you're ready.'

'The police were here, yesterday,' she said. 'I suppose you know
I told them about Dennie, the night he tried to get away . . .'

'Yes. Joey – Tami's partner – told me.'

She looked down at her mug for a moment, seemingly lost in
thought.

'He told me to. Dennie did.' She looked up and directly at
Daniel. 'When he knew for sure that you were onto him, he told
me to ring them. Once it got out, he knew there'd be trouble
whether he got away or not and he said if *I* reported him they'd
go easy on me. And they have, relatively. That and Spencer, of
course.'

'Something else it's good for,' Spencer quipped, adding in a
more sober tone, 'it was the right thing to do, Ma. He dropped
you right in it, coming back here, and with that bloody psychopath
in tow, as well!'

'I know. How's Tamiko?' Boo asked then. 'I can't tell you

how sorry I am for what happened. I just couldn't believe it when we found out what Cal had done. Dennie was devastated, too. Nothing like that was ever meant to happen. He came back when he heard about Spence. He just wanted to see him.'

'He shouldn't have bothered,' her son said flatly. 'I preferred it when I thought he was dead. At least then I still respected him.'

'Spence, don't!' Boo pleaded. 'He's still your father.'

'I don't know how you can take his side after all he's put you through. It makes me so angry!'

'I love him,' she stated simply. 'I always will. But that doesn't mean that I approve of what he's done.'

'Tami's still grieving,' Daniel told her, in answer to her question. However badly Boo had been used, he wasn't going to lie to make it easier for her. 'She's lost her little sister, but she has Hana's little boy to look after, and that has helped her cope. Looking after Jahan is all she can do for her sister, now.'

'Is his father not around?'

'He is but he's a waste of space and thankfully, it looks like he'll be denied custody. He has a history of abusive behaviour and the kid's terrified of him.' He didn't add that Tami and Jo-Ji had decided to try for adoption; that was their business and none of hers.

'I'm so sorry,' Boo said again. 'Thank God they caught McAllum. He's totally out of control.'

'Tell me truthfully,' Daniel said. 'Did you know Dennie was going to fake his own death that night on the boat?'

Boo looked him straight in the eye and shook her head. 'No, I didn't. He said he thought my reaction would be more natural if I didn't know. Harrison knew, but then they've always been as thick as thieves.'

'A rather apt simile,' Spencer observed, 'Judging by what we've learned since about his reason for going.'

'I don't expect you to believe me, but if I had known, I'd have tried to stop him,' Boo told Daniel. 'It was a crazy idea! He planned for me to join him once the girls had gone to uni. He'd set up a bogus company out there that Harry was busily paying money into, so that we'd have something to live on. But it was never going to work because, for a start, I wouldn't have gone. Once I discovered what he'd run from, I wanted him to face the

music. After all, it was only fraud. He could have done his time
and then we'd have been free of it all. All this –' she waved a
hand at her surroundings – 'isn't important to me. All I ever
really wanted was the chance for us to have a normal life but to
him it represented success. He loved giving me things . . .' She
paused, looking wistful. 'But, whatever his faults, he'd never
actually hurt anyone before all this started with Cal.'

'I don't think Stella would agree with you.' Daniel couldn't
let it go.

Boo looked shame-faced. 'Do you know, I convinced myself
that she must be cold and unfeeling. Dennie would say that she
only cared for her clothes and her smart friends; that she was
practically frigid, and I believed him because it was easier than
the alternative. Easier than admitting that everything about the
life I was leading was wrong.'

'*She* loved him, too,' Daniel told her. 'And what she wanted
more than anything was a family. In her eyes, you had everything
she had ever wanted.'

Boo looked down at her hands, cupped around her mug, and
Daniel saw tears glistening in her eyes.

'I think that's enough, now,' Spencer said quietly but firmly.
'Ma's no angel, but she's been a victim in this too.'

Daniel nodded, liking the young man better for his stance.

'You're right. I'll say no more.'

His mother extended a hand sideways and grasped her son's,
before looking back at Daniel.

'However wrong it was, I can't regret what Dennie and I
had, because it brought me my children. But for what happened
these past few weeks, I'm truly sorry, and I'd undo it all if I
could. Cal ran wild like some character in one of those awful
American films, and he swept Dennie and Harrison along
with him. I just want Tami to know that. I don't expect her
to forgive me.'

Daniel sighed. 'I think she knows it wasn't your fault. I
wouldn't hope for friendship, if I was you, but I don't think she'll
cut you dead. She's a girl in a million is Tami.'

He drained his mug and stood up.

'If there's nothing else, I should probably be going. I've got
to go to the police station again this afternoon.' The prospect of

finding himself amongst his ex-colleagues again was not one he relished.

'No. I just wanted you to know there's no hard feelings,' she said. 'And to try and explain.'

'OK.' Daniel nodded briefly then looked at Spencer. 'Keep on keeping on, mate,' he said. 'Prove the buggers wrong!'

'There's a new treatment,' Boo said as she stood up. 'A kind of immunotherapy. Spence has booked into a clinic in Japan. We're going next month. We had to try.'

'I wish you all the best,' Daniel told him. 'Let me know when you're playing rugby again and I'll come and watch.'

Spencer smiled, nodded and waved a hand as Daniel turned to leave, and he reflected that Boo was right, and however immoral the years of deceit had been, something very good had come of it.

'Thank you for coming, and for listening,' Boo said as she and Daniel reached the front door.

'I'll pass on your message to Tami.'

Daniel turned as he stepped out into the sunshine, once more.

'I don't know whether you're interested, or not, but I'll tell you anyway. Your half-brother, Ricky, has just been offered a job by my boss in Devon.' What Fred had actually said was 'Well, I could do with someone to cover for you, 'cos you're never bloody here!'

'What do you do in Devon?'

'I drive a truck delivering animal feed. He's going to pay for Ricky to get his HGV license in return for signing a fixed term contract and meanwhile, Ricky can pick up his law studies again in his spare time. Ricky's a nice guy. I don't know what your quarrel was with him, but he seems to think it was because he was the result of your father's extra-marital fling.' He paused, looking at Boo through eyes narrowed against the sunlight. 'Double standards, if I may say so.'

He walked away to his car and opened the door.

'It was mostly Steven,' Boo called after him. 'It sounds silly but I think he was a little jealous of Ricky. Of how close he was to Dad, when Dad got older. I think he thought Ricky was trying to cut us out.'

'He wasn't.'

'No. Look, maybe I'll call him. Do you have his number?'

'How about I give him yours,' Daniel said, getting into the car and shutting the door.

In the back, the dog stood up, stretched and yawned, his tail waving a welcome.

'Taz, my lad,' Daniel said, turning to look at him, 'take my advice and stick to tuggy toys, eh?'